Last Kiss GOODBYE

A FATED LOVE PSYCHIC SUSPENSE ROMANCE

FATE'S GIFT DUOLOGY BOOK TWO

AWARD-WINNING AND INTERNATIONAL BEST-SELLING AUTHOR

MELANIE A. SMITH

Published by
WICKED DREAMS PUBLISHING
info@wickeddreamspublishing.com
Boise, ID USA

Cover photo by Jean Wolford Photography
Cover design, editing, and formatting by Wicked Dreams Publishing

eBook ISBN: 978-1-968481-04-9
Paperback ISBN: 978-1-968481-05-6
Hardback ISBN: 978-1-968481-06-3

For those who listen.

"The soul has been given its own ears to hear things that the mind does not understand." – Rumi

CONTENTS

CONTENT WARNING

Last Kiss Goodbye is a psychic suspense romance novel that includes elements that might not be suitable for some readers, including the use of profanity, open-door sex scenes, and other potentially sensitive topics. Visit https://melaniea smithauthor.com/lkgcw.html for a full list (warning: may include spoilers).

PROLOGUE
MATT

Two years ago

"You sure you don't mind sitting in on this?" Dani asks, sliding a manila folder across the conference table toward me. "I know it's not exactly in your wheelhouse."

I flip open the folder, scanning the resume inside. Network Operations Technician. Definitely not my area, but I get why she's asking. We've been short-staffed in that department — and several others — for months, and many of us are pulling double duty as needed.

This position is for third shift — the night shift — which apparently has been difficult to fill. As a social media company, keeping things running in the middle of the night is important, given our near-constant traffic, so I'm determined to do what I can. Even if it is first thing Monday morning, and I'm still waiting for my coffee to kick in.

"Happy to help," I tell her. I keep my voice casual, even

though my pulse kicks up a notch. High stakes for the company aside, this is also the third interview panel she's asked me to join this month. So this may mean something more than helping pick up the slack. I haven't exactly been shy about my desire to join the management ranks, and I'm more than a little pumped that they're clearly receptive to that and are giving me opportunities to prove myself.

Dani leans back in her chair, studying me with her sharp, dark brown eyes. "You know, you're good at this. Reading people. Asking the right questions."

I fight to keep the smirk off my face. It sure helps when you can read someone's past and tell if they're lying with a simple touch. Though that's something I'll never clue my employers — or anyone else — in on. Just play it cool, Roberts.

"Coming from HR's best and brightest, I'll take that as a compliment," I reply with an easygoing smile. "But I'm just trying to contribute where I can."

"It's more than that." She taps her pen against the table. "Your superiors are impressed. You've got management potential, Matt. You're leadership material. And these interview panels? Consider them practice for when you're running your own team."

And there it is. Proof that I was right. I mean, I knew I was. I usually am. But it's nice to have it confirmed.

My chest swells with exhilaration, but I just nod thoughtfully. "I appreciate the vote of confidence."

"Don't let it go to your head," she says with a smirk that tells me my poker face isn't as ironclad as I thought it was. I let a bit of the grin I've been fighting slip out, and she chuckles, then glances at her watch. "Anyway. He should be here any minute. Carmen's bringing him up."

Right on cue, Carmen pokes her head through the door. "I have Ezra Martin when you're ready."

"Send him in," Dani says, straightening her papers.

A guy in his mid-to-late twenties walks in — pressed navy slacks, starched white button-front shirt, no tie or jacket. Short brown hair that looks like it was barely contained with a comb. Standard, slightly awkward tech bro trying to look professional.

"It's a pleasure to meet you, Mr. Martin," Dani says, standing to shake his hand. "I'm Daniela Rodriguez. We spoke on the phone." He nods eagerly, and she smiles warmly in response. "This is Matthew Roberts," she gestures to me. "He'll be part of your interview panel."

"Pleasure, Ms. Rodriguez," he says quietly, turning to me and extending his hand. I resign myself, knowing that if I want that management position, shaking hands is going to be part of the gig. It doesn't always trigger a vision, I try to reassure myself.

Dani takes a seat. "Did you have a pleasant weekend?"

My hand meets Ezra's, and I miss whatever response he gives as a vision slams into me like a freight train.

Blood. So much blood. Blond hair soaked in it. Bright red on pale gold. A woman's flushed face, eyes wide with terror, mouth open in a silent scream. The flash of a knife. The light fading from her eyes. Her body going limp. Dragging her across a concrete floor. I try to pull out as I experience it all more intimately than I ever have before. I can practically feel Ezra's heightened mania as if it's my own. His focus keeps me locked on the feel of her body dragging behind us — him — and my stomach lurches.

Then, as if a switch has flipped, I'm bombarded by a cascade of images. Memories he flips through as he relishes his kill. And all the others. *Oh god, others.* Of the long, heavily forested bridge off the freeway that he buries them all under. And the itch that's already crept under his skin, so much faster this time. He'll need another soon. Very soon.

It's only Ezra pulling his hand away and taking a seat that saves me from the continued horror of his sick pleasure in what he's done. I feel like I might vomit.

Scratch that, I'm *definitely* going to vomit.

I fight hard to hold it back.

"You okay?" Dani asks, and I realize I've been standing there, frozen, for too long.

I inhale a shaky breath, knowing I have to pull it together. I can't let on that anything is amiss. I can't answer the question I see in Dani's eyes.

"Yeah, sorry." I force a smile, resisting the urge to wipe my palm on my pants. It wouldn't wipe away what I Saw anyway. "Probably need another cup of coffee." I retake my seat at the table, trying to focus on the paper in front of me. Anything but looking this monster in the eye. Anything but letting on that I know what he's capable of. The sheet blurs in and out despite my efforts.

Dani chuckles. "Don't we all?"

Ezra laughs too, the sound grating against the torrent of

memories I just pulled that are still tearing through my mind. That I can never unsee. That I already know will haunt me until my dying day.

I fold my trembling hands in my lap, totally clueless as to how I'm going to get through this.

"So, Ezra," Dani begins, oblivious to my internal crisis, "tell us a bit about yourself."

My blood runs cold as he launches into a brief history of his education in IT, summarizing the few jobs he's had, and adding some bullshit about enjoying pickleball and hiking in his spare time, painting the picture of a normal, desirable job candidate.

But all I can see is what he did — violently murder a woman, plan to dispose of her, think of his next kill.

Next kill. The words reverberate through me on a loop that works at my resolve never to expose my secret.

But some things … some things are more important.

Right now, for example, pretending I'm not onto him. Because if he suspects I know anything about that side of him … I try to push that out of my head. All of it, actually.

It barely works. I sit through the interview on autopilot, asking generic questions when prompted, taking barely legible notes I'll never need. Every time he smiles, all I see is the expression on that woman's face. Every gesture of his hands makes me think of them dragging another body.

The interview lasts forty-five minutes. The longest forty-five minutes of my life.

When it's finally over and Carmen returns to escort him out, Dani turns to me. "What did you think?"

"I …" I clear my throat, still in real danger of throwing up what little is in my stomach. "I'm not feeling so good," I admit. "I think I may be coming down with something."

Dani frowns. "Yeah, honestly, you looked a little sick the whole time. Probably the stomach flu. It's been going around. You should get home," she says, rubbing my back empathetically.

I nod meekly, and not just because I'm playing along. I feel like I'm going to be sick at any moment. "Thanks, Dani."

I don't wait for her response. I head straight to the bathroom, where I promptly expel the contents of my stomach. Once it stops, I splash some cold water on my face, but my reflection speaks to how little difference that makes. My dark brown hair is plastered to my sweaty, clammy forehead. My normally brown eyes have dark rings around them, and the whites are laced with red. My skin is pale.

I close my eyes, but all I see is blood.

I take a few deep breaths. It does little to calm me. Jesus Christ. A serial killer just sat in our conference room talking about troubleshooting and mainframes. Like he hasn't killed more women than I care to count. Like he isn't planning to kill more.

I dry heave again into the sink, settling my forehead on the cold stainless steel faucet.

And I know I can't keep this to myself.

For a moment, I contemplate calling my sister, CJ, before I do anything else … but then I realize there's nothing she could say that will change what I must do. And that I can still protect her from this in every way. My twin may have the fitting opposite gift of mine in being able to see the future, but I already know what he's planning. CJ doesn't need to bear this burden too. And the police don't need to know that either of us have abilities that people would kill to get their hands on.

But this guy … he doesn't need that kind of motivation. No, he's happy to kill just for the thrill of it.

And I can't let him do it again.

I know what I need to do.

The fluorescent lights in the police station are making my headache even worse. Or maybe it's the vomiting. Or the weight of what I'm about to do — something I swore to myself I never would.

But here I am. I've been sitting in this uncomfortable plastic chair for twenty minutes, waiting to speak to a detective, replaying my story in my head, making sure I don't slip up. Because I can't exactly tell them how it really went down. That's how I'm justifying all the creative truth — aka lying — that I'm about to do, anyway.

"Mr. Roberts?" The detective appears — mid-forties, disheveled dark hair, tired hazel eyes, coffee stain on his rumpled light blue tie. "I'm Detective Worthington. You said you had information about a crime?"

I nod and follow him to a small interview room that smells like burnt coffee and desperation.

"Before I say anything," I start, gripping the edge of the table, "I need to know that my identity will be protected. I don't want this person knowing I'm the one who came forward."

Worthington's eyebrows rise slightly. "Are you in danger?"

"I could be. If he finds out."

"We can keep your name out of any reports," he assures me. "You'd be listed as a confidential informant." He pauses, giving me a scrutinizing glance. "Why don't you tell me what we're dealing with here."

I take a deep breath. Despite his reassurances, they took my name when I got here, so I know even if the killer never catches wind of this, I'm still potentially exposing myself to trouble. But I have no choice, really, if I want to be able to look at myself in the mirror for the rest of my life, so here goes nothing.

"I was part of a hiring interview today for my company. After the interview, when everyone else had left the room, the candidate ... well, he confessed something to me."

Worthington pulls out a notebook. "What did he confess?"

"Murder." The detective's head snaps up. Clearly he wasn't expecting that.

The word hangs heavy between us.

"Murder," he repeats, disbelief lacing his tone. "How exactly did he confess to that?"

"He said he killed a woman. Stabbed her to death. And that he buried her under the Russian River Bridge off 101."

Detective Worthington's pen stops moving. "And he just ... came out and told you that? With no prompting?" I nod solemnly. Understandably, he looks skeptical. "Did he say why he was telling you?"

I shake my head. "I have no idea. We'd never met before today." I shake my head again, unable to look up. Feeling like if I do, I may vomit again. "He … didn't seem all there."

I dare a glance up to see how he takes that to find his thick brows bunched together. "Did he say anything else?"

This is the tricky part. The part where I have to fully make something up. So I weave together what I Saw with imagined dialogue, careful to make it sound like a confession rather than a vision.

"He said he'd done it before. More than once. And …" I swallow hard. "He said he was going to do it again. Soon."

Detective Worthington leans forward, his pen tapping nearly frantically on the pad. "Did he give you a timeline?"

"Not exactly. But the way he sounded … his anticipation —" I shake my head, pinching my eyes closed, my head pounding with images. "This isn't going to stop. He's going to keep doing it."

"Did he give you anything else? Names? Accomplices? Where under the bridge?"

I shake my head. "Just that the bodies were buried there. He said …" I reach into the memories reluctantly, "… he seemed confident that the police would never find them all."

An ominous, lengthy silence falls between us as he leans back in his chair. As I try to breathe through the discomfort of having this sick bastard's memories in my mind.

"Why do *you* think he told you this?" he finally asks.

"I don't know." I run my hands through my hair, agitated.

"Maybe he just needed to tell someone. Or maybe he thought I wouldn't believe him? Or wouldn't turn him in? I don't know. Maybe he just wants to be caught." I shake my head, knowing it was none of those things. That he had no intention of stopping. No desire to be caught. At least, not that tainted the thoughts in his memories. "In case it wasn't obvious, it freaked me out pretty bad. And as afraid as I am of him … I can't … I can't just let him hurt someone else."

"If he told you, aren't you worried he'll know it was you who turned him in?"

Shit. He's got a point there. I take a deep breath.

"Like I said, he didn't seem all there. Maybe … maybe he won't even remember telling me." I flinch internally, knowing I must sound crazy. Oh god … or guilty. I hope I'm not implicating myself here. Fuck. I huff out a frustrated breath. "I just couldn't *not* say anything. You know?" I ask, desperately meeting the detective's gaze.

I still see suspicion there. But also tentative interest.

He continues to study me for a long moment. "What's this person's name?"

"Ezra Martin. White male, late twenties maybe, just under six feet. Brown hair, blue eyes." I slide a piece of paper across the table. "I wrote down what I could remember. Physical description, background information from his résumé."

"Can we contact your company for his information?"

"That's fine, as long as you don't have to mention that I was involved," I reiterate, taking the paper back and adding Dani's information at the bottom.

"We'll be discreet," Worthington promises, accepting the

paper back. "Is there anything else you haven't mentioned? Any details that might help us?"

I close my eyes, letting myself see it all again. The faces of those women. The carefully practiced routines. His immediate thought of doing it again.

"Just ... please hurry. I really think he's going to do it again soon."

Detective Worthington slides a business card across the table. "This is my direct line. If you remember anything else, or if he contacts you, call me immediately."

I pocket the card and stand on shaky legs, though I'm relieved he seems receptive. "So you'll look into it?"

"We take every report seriously," he promises. He gives me one last assessing look. "Thank you for having the courage to come in today."

"Of course," I manage. "I just ... I couldn't live with myself if I didn't say something."

He nods, extending his hand for a parting shake.

And I flinch. "I ..." I flail for a moment before remembering CJ's practiced response to this. One I always thought was a bit too careful. But one I'm now going to use religiously. "I'm sorry, I don't shake hands."

Those dark brows snap together again, but he retracts his hand with a nod. "I'll walk you out."

I follow him and, minutes later, step into the afternoon sun feeling like I've aged a decade. I get into my car and just ... sit there.

When the shaking stops and I feel like I'm able to breathe again, I check my phone to find a text from CJ.

Where'd you go?

My fingers hover over the screen as I formulate a response. Since we work together *and* live together, it will be hard to hide this from her. But I'm not ready to tell her just yet. And if I play this right, maybe I'll never have to.

I threw up at work so I went home. Sorry I didn't stop by to let you know. Already feeling better now that I'm laying down but I'll stay in my room and keep my germs to myself until it passes.

I toss the phone down on the passenger seat and start the drive back to our townhouse. I may have lied about already being home, but that's one I can turn into truth quickly.

Unlike all the others I just told. But as this morning's vision continues to haunt me, I can't bring myself to regret them or the decision to share what I Saw. I can only trust that they believed me. That Detective Worthington will, as he promised, follow up on this. And that it will be in time to save whoever Ezra Martin plans to kill next.

But I did what I could, even if it meant risking exposure.

Even if they didn't believe me.

Even if it means becoming a target myself.

Those women deserve justice. But more importantly, the one he's planning to kill next, whoever she is … she deserves to live.

I just hope I've given her that chance.

CHAPTER ONE

MATT

"God, Matt, you look like shit," CJ says bluntly as I walk through the door to the new apartment she got with the chef.

I ignore her comment, looking around at her new place. It's not half bad. The living room is bigger than our townhouse's was, even, and much more done to CJ's tastes with pale purple accent pillows and everything. It even smells better than our place did.

"You guys sure didn't waste any time," I reply, hoping the diversion works.

She puts herself in front of me and folds her arms. "Oh, nuh uh, you're not getting off the hook that easy. We have exactly twenty minutes until the housewarming party starts, and I know you didn't show up early just to give me shit about moving in with my boyfriend too fast."

I roll my eyes and push past her, taking a seat on the new, beige linen couch. The one I'd already bought them for their housewarming gift. "I meant unpacking. The boyfriend … well, kind of hard to give you shit about that. Fate and all."

She smirks and sinks down next to me. "I'm not a retrocog, Matt, so you're just going to have to tell me."

Damn. She's obviously not going to give up. My eyes dart around the small apartment.

"Drew's in the shower," she assures me. "Now come on. You're starting to freak me out."

I heave a sigh, wishing there was somehow a way to reverse my ability so I could show her what happened without talking about it.

"I went to add Alyssa to my renter's insurance yesterday and the system asked if I wanted to amend her current policy," I start.

She quirks an eyebrow. "So? I'm sure she has a place in L.A., right? Isn't she based there?"

"Oh, that's not what surprised me," I reply in agreement. "It was the fact that it showed two names on the policy."

CJ's brows now pull together. "So, what, she has a roommate she didn't tell you about? That's weird, but it's not …" She trails off as understanding dawns on her face. "It was a guy, wasn't it?"

My lips pull down into a frown and I nod. "Not just any guy." I pause for effect. "It was Nash Murphy."

She gasps and her eyes go comically wide. "No."

I grimace, knowing CJ already had the guy pegged as a creep, having pulled it off of her accidentally after the director's dinner where, as an invitee due to being a hot influencer of the moment, he hit on her only to end up taking the hostess home when she rejected him. And now we *both* know he's a huge creep.

"Yep. So when she got in late last night, I asked her about it. And I read her while I did. A total invasion, I know, but considering the circumstances I'm not sorry. I don't know how I missed it, Cee, but it was bad." I sigh heavily.

She reaches out and squeezes my shoulder. "Sometimes we choose not to see things that go against what we think we want," she says, sorrow lacing her tone. And I know she's been exactly where I am. "I'm so sorry, Matt."

I shake my head. "Thanks, but save the pity. I'm not quite done." I clear my throat in preparation. Because as much as I can usually turn this shit off, it's really gotten to me. "They'd been dating since before the director's dinner where we all met. They made a plan to seduce us both in some sort of ploy to get more social media exposure for themselves."

CJ scoffs. "How? It's not like we can affect their numbers."

"I know that, but obviously they didn't. Though I think Alyssa was starting to realize that, and she honestly seemed relieved not to have to pretend anymore."

I look away, blinking hard. I can't fucking cry. Especially not in front of my sister.

CJ squeezes my shoulder again. "Hey, it's okay to be upset. I'm here. Let it out."

I look back at her. I want to admit how much I wanted it to work with Alyssa. But deep down I knew we weren't a good match, even without the deception. We had nothing in common. She was a model and fashion influencer who cared more about a picture-perfect image, and I'm a marketing director for a major social media company who'd rather be researching digital trends and coordinating company strategies.

But then, I knew I wasn't with her for the right reasons. Hell, even the sex was only just okay, so I can't say I stayed for that. If I'm being honest with myself, it was thrilling to be with someone who is wanted by most of the men in the country, and probably a lot of women too. It felt like winning.

But I can't say that out loud. I feel like a complete asshole for even thinking it. For having lived it these past few months. Unfortunately, I caved to the ego boost, and I'll always regret it.

"Thanks. If I need to, I will," I respond in a murmur.

But I won't need to. Time to put all of my focus back where it matters. On work. Women are a distraction that's just not worth it.

CHAPTER TWO

ANNA

By the time I make it to Drew and CJ's housewarming party, I'm afraid I might have missed it. I shift the giant philodendron I'm holding to one arm so I can knock on the door.

It opens after a minute to a stoic-faced Drew. "Trouble at the restaurant?" he asks.

I nod and sigh. "Yeah, Scott made me stick around because Becky was late again. But hey, happy housewarming." I shove the pot toward him with a grin. "Feel free to tell me to fuck off if I totally missed the party."

"Well, actually you did," he admits, taking the houseplant and stepping back. "But I was just about to make dinner. Why don't you come on in. I bet you're pretty hungry."

I walk into the apartment and start taking off my jacket. "Starving," I admit. "I missed …" I trail off when my eyes land on CJ and her brother sitting on the couch. I blush hard, not realizing anyone but CJ and Drew was here.

CJ beams when she sees me. "We thought you weren't going to make it." She springs up from the couch and pulls me into a hug.

I squeeze her back with a laugh. "It was touch and go for a bit there, but here I am."

CJ steps back and gestures toward her brother. "You remember my brother, Matt."

I nod and step forward. How could I forget him? Tall, good looking, utterly charming … and hanging all over that model at the dinner CJ coordinated that's the reason we all met. Not that I think he even noticed me, one of the invisible lowly serving staff.

"Yes, but I don't think we ever got to talk face-to-face that night," I tell her.

Matt looks puzzled. "I think I'd remember meeting …"

"Anna," CJ supplies.

"Anna," he repeats, his eyes fixed on mine. "I'm sorry my memory seems to be failing me at the moment."

I push my lips together, trying not to laugh. "It's okay. You were ah … a little distracted at the time," I say, hoping my voice isn't as teasing as I think it is. "It was the dinner event you had last October." He still looks confused, so I add, "I'm a server at Drew's restaurant."

Understanding dawns on his face, and a little smidge of embarrassment.

"Well, it's not exactly my restaurant," Drew objects.

"I knew what she meant," Matt murmurs, looking at me curiously.

"Great. Well. I'll be making dinner," Drew says shortly, heading out of the room.

CJ's eyes dart between Matt and me. "And I need to help him with … the food," she adds lamely. "Be back."

Matt shoots her a dirty look as she passes. She gives him a sublime smile in return. I chuckle a little at the wordless sibling spat. It's something I definitely have experience with, being one of four sisters.

Once she's gone, his gaze turns back to me. He gestures to the couch behind him. "Have a seat. Lord knows what they're really up to. Might as well get comfortable."

I snort as I accept his offer, sinking into the comfy couch, still a respectable distance away, not sure exactly what to think of this guy yet beyond his being totally hot.

"Oh, I know exactly what they're up to," I affirm. "Or I have theories, anyway."

He arches an eyebrow. "Do I want to hear them?"

I grin. "Probably not. So, did I miss anything good at the housewarming party? Was there a raffle?" I sit up straight suddenly. "God, I didn't miss cheesecake, did I?"

Matt chuckles. "No, no cheesecake. Or raffle. Just a bunch of people I didn't know ooh-ing and aah-ing over a thousand square feet of real estate."

He says it jokingly, but something about him is … sad?

"Is it hard for you? I know you and CJ are really close. Twins and all."

"Wow, I think you're the first person to ask me that," he responds.

I shrug. "You just seem upset."

His eyes narrow. "Why would you think that?"

"Dunno. I just get feelings from people sometimes. My mom used to say I'm like a sponge for emotions," I explain. "It's probably just body language or something."

"Hm. Bet that comes in handy as a server."

And it shouldn't, but something about the way he says it irritates me. "It's a good job. Pays well. Even comes with some benefits," I reply defensively.

"I wasn't criticizing," he protests.

"Weren't you?" I challenge. "In any case, it's fine. I get it. Most people don't think of being a server as a particularly respectable job. But I work hard. And even though it's not my endgame, it's given me a lot of respect for people who can do this their whole lives. Because, you know, someone has to."

"So, what is your endgame then?"

I lean forward slightly and look up into his coffee-colored eyes. "Wouldn't you like to know."

He leans forward in return. "That's why I asked."

We stare at each other for a moment, and I swear I feel my skin tingle. A sly grin spreads across my face, and I sit back up.

"Honestly, I'm not exactly sure. My degree is in psychology. That could go a lot of ways. I could be a social worker. I could be a counselor. I could work in human resources. I haven't decided yet."

"Beautiful *and* smart. Well. You really do have a lot of options, don't you?"

I try not to blush at the compliment. Because I'm sure this guy is used to having an effect on women. Hell, he was with one of the hottest models in the country. I'm sure he's used to having whatever he wants.

"I do. But you still haven't told me why you're upset."

He laughs and shakes his head. "You're just as bad as CJ. There's no distracting you, is there?"

"Not used to being challenged by a woman who's not your sister?" I parry back.

His expression goes blank, and my stomach twists. Shit. I went too far. Why do I always go too far?

"Unfortunately, quite the opposite, actually," he murmurs.

And I feel it. The sadness. It seeps out of him with the distinct aura of a broken heart.

I reach out and put my hand on his knee with a contrite expression. "I'm sorry, Matt. For whatever she did to you. Everybody deserves to be loved and respected. It's hard when you think you had that and find out you didn't."

"How did you —"

"Dinner's ready," CJ calls, popping back around the corner.

Matt and I both look up at her, and I quickly withdraw my hand from his knee.

"Or I could go back in the kitchen and make it take a few more minutes?" she asks with a knowing smile.

Matt shifts uncomfortably next to me, so I rise, sparing him the discomfort of continuing our conversation. "Nope. I'm starving. And if Drew's cooking, I'm eating. Let's do this."

CHAPTER THREE

CJ

It's Sunday family dinner time, and I'm primed to check in with Matt about Anna. He very purposely dodged me after dinner last night, ducking out during dessert so we couldn't talk privately afterward. I'm sure it was because he knew I was itching to find out exactly what I walked in on.

"Goodness, baby girl, you are antsy today," Aunt Meg comments as she slices the roast for dinner. "Finding it difficult to be away from Drew for an entire afternoon?" She gives me a teasing smile.

I stick my tongue out at her. "No," I snipe back. "We do both have lives, you know. And since he got yesterday off for the housewarming party, he had to work today. That's not unusual."

She smirks as she spreads the vegetables from the pan around the meat. "So, what is it?"

I tap my foot against the stool I'm sitting on. "I really shouldn't —" I stop mid-sentence as I hear voices coming from the living room. Matt and Uncle Chuck. Matt has arrived. I shoot off the barstool. "Be back."

I can practically feel Aunt Meg's bewildered look as I dart out of the kitchen, but I don't really care. Matt looks up, and when he sees me, he sighs heavily.

Uncle Chuck looks between us. "I'm going to go help in the kitchen," he says uneasily. "You kids behave, okay?"

I pull a face at him as he walks by, at which he chuckles.

"Hey," I greet Matt, sinking onto the couch next to him. "I wanted to talk to you last night, but you bolted."

Matt narrows his eyes at me. "And you didn't take that as a hint that I'm not in the mood to talk?"

"You can't avoid me, dude. I'm your sister. So spill. What did I walk in on when you and Anna were talking yesterday?"

"I don't know what you're talking about," he says, his expression unreadable. Even for me. But I'm not fooled.

I cross my arms and level a look at him. Anna is a tiny blonde with big golden-brown doe eyes. In other words, she's exactly Matt's type, physically anyway. So I know he's full of crap.

"Don't make me read you," I threaten.

He sticks out a hand. "Read away if you must. I've got nothing to hide. We were talking. That's it."

I look down at his hand and back up at him. "Fine. Have it your way. But it didn't seem like just talking."

"So what, now you can See things in present time?" He smirks.

"You know, the first time I hung out with Anna, I thought

about setting you two up. Though that was before I knew about you and Alyssa."

The smirk drops off Matt's face. "Can you please not say her name?"

"Don't you want to know why I didn't set you and Anna up?"

"No, but you're probably going to tell me anyway."

"Damn right I am. You're selfish, Matt. Did you even like Al — the model?"

He stares at me for a solid minute, his face still a mask. "Not really."

"Exactly," I reply, already knowing he didn't. "You don't let anyone in. And Anna is good people. I didn't want to see her hurt."

"Are you telling me to stay away from your friend?"

I snort. "No. I know better, because you wouldn't listen even if I did. I'm simply saying if I saw what I think I saw, take the lesson you just learned and try not to make the same boneheaded mistake."

"Wow, thanks for supporting me during this difficult time in my life, Sis. Really awesome having you in my corner," he says sarcastically, rolling his eyes.

"I'm looking out for your happiness just as much as hers, you know," I assure him.

Matt's face falls, and he looks beyond tired. He scrubs his hand over his eyes. "Okay fine, all-seeing one," he grumbles. "Where did I go wrong this time?"

I yank on his arm so he has to look at me. "You didn't listen to your own inner voice, dumbass. I know you just dated her because it made you feel good about yourself. Because of what other people think."

Matt cringes. "God, hearing it out loud is even worse." He buries his face in his hands again. "I'm a horrible person."

I lean back on the couch with a sigh. "You're not a horrible person. You're actually one of the best people I know. You just need to not be afraid to let someone see that."

He drops his hands in his lap but continues to stare at them. "Maybe I don't know how."

I smile. "Maybe you should practice."

He looks up and shoots me a glare. "With Anna?"

I roll my eyes. "You could do worse."

He shakes his head. "I should probably just take a break from dating. It's too soon. And work is busy right now. Plus, Valentine's Day is coming up. You should never start dating someone right before Valentine's Day." He looks toward the kitchen like he's waiting for Uncle Chuck to save him from this discussion.

"That was three excuses," I point out with a raised brow of suspicion. "Are you scared of Anna?" I try to sound like I'm teasing, but his expression says I hit a little too close to home.

And now I know what I guessed happened between them was probably dead-on. It was just a glance. Just a notion. But it seemed like a connection. And knowing my brother, that's enough to scare him off.

Fake he can do. Realness? That requires being vulnerable.

I reach out and wrap my hand over his, intending to

reassure him. But a vision hits in a few brief flashes. Just moments. It doesn't even pull me in. But it's enough.

Matt and Anna … are going to get married.

Soon.

I gasp and let go, sitting up straight in alarm.

"What?" he asks suspiciously. "What did you See?"

I shake my head. "You don't want to know."

His eyebrows scrunch together. "Well, aren't you all kinds of helpful today," he grumbles.

I press my lips together. I want to tell him, but I know I shouldn't. This path is one he has to find on his own. So I simply shrug, resolving to say anything but the one word that's resonating through me right now. The one word I know he both believes in wholly and runs from with every ounce of his strength.

Fate.

At the same time … that's huge. Can I really keep something like that from him?

Spook him or prepare him … it's a tough choice. But it still feels like this isn't the time. So I drop it, and we return to our normal Sunday dinner ritual. And I vow I *will* tell him … when it will actually help. He's gone through enough lately, and he's clearly not in the headspace for this. But maybe there's something I can do to help with that.

CHAPTER FOUR

ANNA

"Anna, honey, can you come zip me up?" Mom calls from the hotel bathroom.

I set down my mascara and head over to help her with the back of her navy dress. She's already got her hair up in an elegant twist, every golden strand perfectly in place. Meanwhile, I'm still trying to wrangle my blond waves into something that doesn't scream, "I woke up five minutes ago."

"There you go," I say, securing the tiny hook at the top. "You look beautiful, Mom."

She turns and cups my cheek, her brown eyes — the same dark honey shade as mine — crinkling at the corners. "So do you, sweetheart. That color is perfect on you."

I glance down at the ruffled dusty rose wrap dress I'm wearing. Cousin Melissa's wedding colors are "blush and bashful," which basically means every woman in attendance will look like a walking peony. At least this one has pockets.

"Thanks. Though at this rate, I'm going to need a whole

new closet just for wedding outfits," I joke, smoothing down the skirt. "What is this, the fourth one in the last year?"

"Fifth," Mom corrects, spritzing herself with her favorite Chanel No. 5 perfume. "Your cousin Tony's was in December, remember?"

Right. Tony's New Year's Eve wedding. Because apparently my extended family has decided that every month is wedding season.

"And we've still got Rachel's in May, Jeff's in July, and I heard through the grapevine that Christina's boyfriend is ring shopping." Mom ticks them off on her fingers like she's keeping an official tally. Which, knowing her, she probably is.

"Great," I mutter, slipping on my nude heels. "Maybe I should just buy stock in David's Bridal."

We make our way down to the hotel ballroom, joining the sea of relatives already milling around with champagne flutes. The Martella family doesn't do anything small — there must be two hundred people here, and that's just for the ceremony.

"Anna! Teresa!" My Aunt Gina swoops in, air-kissing us both. "Don't you both look gorgeous? Anna, I swear you get prettier every time I see you."

"Thanks, Aunt Gina," I reply, accepting the obligatory cheek pinch that follows.

"Such a shame you came alone though," she continues, because of course she does. "A beautiful girl like you should have a date. When I was your age, I was already married with two kids!"

I force a smile. "Different times, Aunt Gina."

"Nonsense. Love is love, no matter the decade." She pats

my arm before bustling off to terrorize another unmarried cousin.

The ceremony is beautiful — Melissa looks radiant, Antonio tears up at the altar, and his grandmother shouts "Bellissima!" at least three times during the vows. Standard Martella wedding fare.

But it's during the reception, somewhere between the chicken piccata and the cutting of the cake, that Mom strikes.

"You know," she says, swirling her wine glass thoughtfully, "it really is wonderful seeing all your cousins so happy."

Here we go.

"Mm-hmm," I respond noncommittally, taking a large bite of wedding cake. Vanilla with hazelnut buttercream. Good choice. Unlike whatever's going to come out of my mother's mouth next.

"Finding their person, starting their lives together ..." She sighs wistfully. "When do you think it'll be your turn, sweetheart?"

I nearly choke on the buttercream, even though I expected it. "Mom, I'm twenty-three. I've got plenty of time."

"That's what your cousin Lisa said, and now she's thirty-two and freezing her eggs."

"Mom!"

"What? I'm just saying, you're not getting any younger. And you don't even date anymore." She reaches across the table to touch my hand. "It's been almost two years, Anna. Don't you think it's time to move on?"

The music from the DJ feels suddenly too loud, the room

too warm. I pull my hand back, folding it with the other in my lap.

"You know why I don't date anymore," I murmur, my voice barely audible over someone's enthusiastic rendition of "That's Amore" on the dance floor.

Mom's expression shifts from prodding to pitying in an instant. That look — the one that says she knows what I went through, but doesn't know how to fix it — is almost worse than the pressure. It's the look my therapist gives me, too. It grates on my nerves coming from either of them. Just another reminder of how broken I was. And still am.

"Oh, honey," she starts, but I'm already pushing back from the table.

"I'm going to get some air," I announce, grabbing my clutch. "Save me a dance for the Tarantella?"

I don't wait for her response, weaving through tables of relatives until I reach the blessed quiet of the hotel lobby. My hands are shaking slightly as I pull out my phone, needing something — anything — to distract me from the memories threatening to surface.

I scroll through my contacts until I land on CJ's name. She's become the closest thing I have to an actual friend outside of my family. Someone who doesn't look at me with pity or treat me like I'm fragile.

Hey! Random question, but do you want to hang out sometime this week? Coffee maybe?

Three dots appear almost immediately.

Absolutely! Tomorrow afternoon work? There's this great place in the Mission I've been wanting to try.

Perfect. Thanks, I needed this :)

Everything okay?

Yeah, just family stuff. Tell you tomorrow?

Of course. 11 am at Sightglass Coffee? I'll send you the address.

See you then!

I slip my phone back into my clutch, already feeling lighter. One coffee date with a friend who doesn't know my entire history, who won't judge me or look at me like I'm broken. That's what I need right now.

———

The aroma of freshly ground coffee beans hits me the second I walk into Sightglass, and I spot CJ at a corner table, her dark hair pulled up in a messy bun, completely absorbed in whatever she's reading on her phone.

"Hey," I say, sliding into the seat across from her. "Thanks for meeting me."

"Are you kidding? I love hanging out with you." She grins, tucking her phone away. "Plus, Drew's been in a mood. Something about a vendor shorting them on deliveries yesterday. I'm glad to get a break from Chef Grumpypants."

I laugh. "Yeah, that about sums him up."

CJ smirks and flags down a server. "What's your poison?"

"Cappuccino, please," I tell him, then turn back to CJ. "So, um, thanks again. For meeting me. Yesterday was ..."

"Family wedding?" she guesses, and I must look surprised because she adds, "You mentioned family stuff, and I know you went to like … a bunch of weddings last year. So I just figured it was yet another one. Plus, you have that slightly shell-shocked look people get after spending too much time with extended relatives."

"Oh man, you're *good*. Yep. Fifth wedding in the past year," I confirm. "With at least three more on the calendar. I swear, my cousins are having some sort of wedding competition or something."

CJ snorts into her latte. "And let me guess — lots of questions about when it's your turn?"

"God, it's like you're reading my mind!" I laugh, so relieved that she gets it. "My mom literally compared me to my cousin, who's freezing her eggs."

"Ouch."

"Yeah." I fidget with my napkin. "She means well, she just ... worries. Because I don't really date."

CJ tilts her head, studying me with those perceptive dark eyes, but she doesn't push. Doesn't ask the obvious question. I appreciate that more than she knows.

"Well," she says finally, "if you ever want to shut them up, I'm surrounded by attractive, available guys at work. I actually have someone in mind I'd thought about setting you up with before."

I laugh despite myself. "That's very sweet, but you really don't have to do that."

"They're totally trustworthy," she adds. "Scout's honor. And cute, if that matters."

I pause, ready to reject her offer. But then again ... "How cute?"

She grins. "I mean, I guess you'll have to be the judge of that. But I'm pretty confident you'll be into him. He's smart and just an all-around good guy. And even if you don't hit it off, it's just one date, right? If it's terrible, you never have to see him again, and I won't set you up ever again." She holds up her hand. "I promise."

Deep down, I'm still terrified to get back into the dating pool, despite all the counseling I've been through. But on top of my desire to just be *normal* again for once, the memory of Mom's pitying look, of Aunt Gina's comments, of being the only person under thirty at that entire wedding without a plus-one ... they're stronger motivators than my own wishy-washy longing to overcome my fears. Because frankly, I don't think I can handle another wedding solo.

"All right," I agree. "But you're going to be the one I call if I need a fake excuse to leave."

CJ lights up. "Oh my god! I'd love that!"

I scrunch my face up and laugh. She's so weird, and I totally dig it.

She shakes her head. "Sorry ... I just ... I always wanted a friend I was close enough with to bail each other out of bad dates and stuff like that." She dips her head to take a sip of coffee, but I don't miss the blush on her cheeks.

"Awww, CJ, that's so sweet," I say, reaching over and squeezing her hand. "You're totally that friend. Actually, family aside, you're my closest friend."

CJ looks up, still blushing, but squeezes me back.

"You're mine too," she admits.

I give her a reassuring look as I withdraw my hand. "Then

it's settled. The date goes south, I text, you call with an emergency. And if he turns out to be a serial killer or something, I'm blaming you." I shift, trying to hide my anxiety.

"Deal," CJ says, already pulling out her phone. "How's Thursday? I can have him meet you someplace public. Ooh! There's a great cocktail bar Drew took me to the other night. It has fabulous views of the city. And it's busy but not so packed as to be overwhelming. It'd be the perfect place to meet and just have a drink."

"That works for me," I agree. "How fancy is it?"

She shrugs. "It's San Francisco. You know how it is. Everywhere you go, anything goes. You could wear anything from jeans to formal wear, and nobody would bat an eye either way. So just wear whatever makes you comfortable."

"Good point," I agree with a nod, already half-regretting this decision. Even the superficial issue of deciding what to wear already has me anxious. Not to mention all the other issues I've got with this. But CJ looks so pleased, and maybe ... maybe it *is* time to at least try. If nothing else, to prove to myself that I can do this.

"You're doing a good thing," CJ says, reaching across the table to squeeze my hand briefly. "And if it helps, he's the kind of guy who would walk you to your car and wait until you're safely inside before leaving. Total gentleman."

"That does help, actually," I admit.

"And if it doesn't work out ... well, maybe it'll get your mom off your back for a while."

I snort. CJ really knows how to sell the idea. "That's worth it right there."

She laughs. "All right, I'll set it up with him and text you the deets."

I nod and we move on, spending the rest of our coffee date talking about safer topics including Drew's restaurant drama — since I've got a shift with him tonight, it's good to know exactly what I'm walking into — CJ's latest project at work, the new yoga studio that opened up near my apartment. Normal friend stuff. The kind of conversation where no one looks at me with pity or asks probing questions about my past.

As we're leaving, CJ turns to me. "Hey, Anna? For what it's worth, I think you're brave. Whatever your reasons for not dating ... taking this step is huge."

I blink back the sudden moisture in my eyes. "Thanks. That means a lot."

"And if nothing else, will you text me after? I want all the details. Unless it turns out to be terrible, in which case text me during and I'll call with that fake emergency." She rests her hand on my forearm reassuringly.

"You're a good friend, CJ," I tell her, leaning in for a hug.

"Right back at you," she says, hugging me in return. "Now go forth and prepare for a totally no-pressure date with a nice, cute guy that hopefully, at least, will reassure you that there are some good ones out there."

I smile as we part ways, feeling lighter than I have in months. I'm going to meet a guy for a drink. That's barely even a date. More of an introduction, really. I can do that.

What's the worst that could happen?

I swallow hard as I head to the restaurant. Because I know what the worst is. I've lived it. And even though I know the odds of history repeating itself are practically nil … it's not the kind of thing you forget. Ever.

And yet, I know that I'm going to have to let it go enough to do this. Because I need to start living my life again. All of it.

After all, I'm not a robot. Watching everyone around me pair off makes me remember the good parts of dating. And I want that, deep down, under the fear.

So, having drinks with someone that has CJ's stamp of approval seems like a pretty good place to start.

I hope.

CHAPTER FIVE

ANNA

It didn't take me as long as I'd expected to choose an outfit. Checking out the bar online, the swanky, modern space located on the top floor of a hotel in Union Square immediately evoked the vibe of my favorite eggshell, strapless, figure-hugging dress. Because of its color, I'm not able to wear it often, given that most of my needs for dresses are for weddings. And anything white adjacent is a big no-no.

The dress also gives me confidence I desperately need, and my blond waves are blown out and perfectly styled for once. I look like a million bucks, if I do say so myself. Which is probably the average yearly income of people that frequent places like this.

As if I wasn't already nervous while I ride the elevator up, that thought kicks it up about fourteen notches. But CJ has great intuition, so I'm dying to know what it was about this guy that made her want to set us up. Cue all the self-doubt. Sigh.

When I get off the elevator, I do my best to look confident. I walk in, poised and ready. Until I realize I'm not sure how I'm going to recognize the guy. She didn't send me a picture; she just said he was cute. And that he'd find me. That's how much I trust CJ … or thought I did. As I stand here, getting nervous, I'm definitely questioning that trust.

Instead of panicking, I decide to focus on scanning the room. The place is definitely just as swanky as it looked online, and I can glimpse the stunning views CJ boasted of. It is also pretty packed, which is not surprising considering it's just after work on a Thursday evening. Something about the anticipation of Friday makes restaurants and bars busier than you'd expect on Thursdays. But even with the sizeable crowd going about their conversations, I feel someone staring at me just before my eyes meet theirs like magnets being drawn together.

Matt. Sitting at a table just on the other side of the bar by the windows. He looks confused, and suddenly I am too. I'm not meeting Matt, am I? If I were, why would he look so bewildered while waving me over? And why wouldn't CJ have told me she'd intended to set me up with her brother?

Either way, I refuse to be shaken by this turn of events. In fact, it'd be a relief that it's someone I already kind of know. So I square my shoulders and cross the space, stopping just short of his table.

"Anna, I thought that was you," he says, rising to greet me. "What are you doing here?"

"Hey, Matt, it's nice to see you," I greet him. "I'm actually meeting someone here. CJ set me up with one of her coworkers."

Matt cocks an eyebrow. "Well, I don't see anyone we work with here," he replies, looking around the room.

Well, that settles it. CJ definitely set me up with her brother but apparently didn't want either of us to know that's what was going on.

"What are you doing here?" I ask, testing my theory.

His eyes stop wandering to meet mine. They are as intense as the waves of emotion coming off of him. Confusion. And curiosity, perhaps? It's a little disconcerting as I've never gotten such immediate, powerful impressions from someone before as I do from him.

"I meet my mentor here on the first Thursday of every month," he explains. "But he's late. That's not really like him."

I laugh as the pieces click together. "Who's in charge of scheduling that meeting?" I ask on a hunch.

Matt's face scrunches up. "CJ," he replies slowly. And then I can see the moment he realizes it too. "She didn't."

"Oh, I'm pretty sure she did," I assure him as I watch him go from confused to irritated. "Look, we can just go our separate ways and pretend like your sister didn't totally try to set us up without our permission. It's cool." But in a sense, I'm relieved. Because CJ is right, her brother is cute. More than cute. Devastatingly handsome, really. But he's also someone I've met before, and someone I know I can trust, given that he's my best friend's brother. I hope he doesn't take me up on the offer.

Matt looks at me for a minute. And I look back. I can practically feel the tension between us. And I'm surprised that it's the good kind. While I knew I found him attractive, the last time we met he was wallowing in his own misery. I didn't think he noticed me much more than the first time we'd met, clearly still hung up on whatever went down with the model. But not quite two weeks later, I see little of that pain in his heated gaze. A gaze that is affecting me more than it should, as I feel the flush creeping into my cheeks.

"No," he finally says. "No, actually … Anna, would you like to join me for a drink?"

I grin widely, completely unable to play it cool. I was so nervous before, but it's like all that has evaporated, and I'm a bit giddy because of it.

"I'd love to." I'm surprised to find I actually mean it. This night has taken a sharp turn from my expectations. In a good way.

He pulls out a chair for me, and I take a seat, then he takes his across from me. "Well, since I guess this is supposed to be a date, I can tell you now that you look absolutely stunning," he says, his eyes dropping to my dress.

"Thank you. You look as handsome as you always do," I reply, eyeing his navy suit. Then I blush hard, realizing I just admitted that I always think he looks handsome.

I look back up when I hear him chuckle.

"Why's that funny?" I ask.

"It's not, you're just cute when you blush," he admits, resting his chin in his hand and leaning in.

And that makes me blush again. "You think I'm cute?" I ask in a teasing tone.

He leans forward. "Actually, I think you're gorgeous."

My breath catches in my throat despite myself. "And you're a charmer," I reply matter-of-factly.

His eyes stay locked on mine, not allowing me to brush off his compliment. We simply stare at each other, the energy crackling between us speaking for itself. I'd forgotten what this felt like. And how exciting it can be.

Finally, he leans back. "No," he replies slowly. "I'm just used to going after what I want."

I arch an eyebrow. "Oh, really?" It's all I can do not to give him a ration of shit for having seen him do exactly that before. So clearly this isn't a rare occurrence for him, even if it is for me.

"Yes. Even though I promised myself I'd be more careful now. You just …" He trails off, his eyes scanning my face.

I shift in my chair, the tension still hanging between us suddenly making me antsy. "What?" I prompt.

"Something about you makes me want to forget the rules. All of them."

This time my chest tightens. I have rules too, and if I'm honest with myself, he's making me feel the same way right now.

I pull a shuddering breath through my lips, finally remembering what I'd purposed to forget. "Matt, I —"

"Be honest. That day after the housewarming party. I've never been read like that by anyone before. You seemed unnerved by it too. Am I wrong?"

My eyes widen at the abrupt change in subject. "No," I say softly. "You're not wrong."

He studies my face again like he's trying to solve a puzzle. "I think we should get out of here. Go somewhere where we can get to know each other better."

"Get to know each other better," I parrot. "And that means …"

He leans forward. "It means whatever you want it to mean, Anna." His husky tone sends shivers up my spine as a smirk settles on his lips. Funny how with the wrong guy the implied proposition would be beyond sleazy. Because let's be real; he almost certainly means sex.

But on Matt's lips? The offer is more appealing than it should be.

Thankfully, while he affects me, I have to laugh at what my nonna would call his sfrontatezza. Because a) that's not going to happen. And b) I was exactly right about where his mind is at right now. It's slightly comforting knowing that in this respect, he's just like most other guys.

"You mean go somewhere and have sex."

He chuckles. "I wouldn't be opposed to that," he admits.

I shake my head. "That sure explains a lot." I pause, internally tensing at the implication that this attitude is linked to his failed relationship. Even if there's truth in that, it wasn't a kind thing to say. Still … "There are other ways to get to know someone, you know."

"Are there?" he asks, a teasing note in his voice. "Because it seems like the most enjoyable way."

The way he's smiling, the glint in his dark eyes, I have to

admit to myself that it's tempting. He's tempting. But it's for exactly that reason that I shouldn't. That I can't. And all the other reasons, too.

I roll my eyes. "If you really think there's something here, I'm game to actually get to know you," I tell him. "But I'm going to need to take this slowly." I resist reminding him he was recently upset over a breakup, and maybe he should reconsider the speed of his hookups accordingly.

But as his eyes sweep over me again, all thought skitters from my overanxious brain. And I can't help feeling like he sees everything I'm not saying. Like *he's* reading me now. The heat he makes rise in my cheeks. The way I'm already fantasizing about him undressing me, because even if I'm not going to jump into bed with him, that doesn't mean I'm not thinking about it. And if he didn't before, as the thoughts pass through my head, I know they're showing up on my face for him to see. I've never had a good poker face.

"I respect that. But you should know I really don't come on strong unless I feel like there might be something there. I swear I'm not one of those guys that just says nice things to get in your pants."

Despite being tempted to think he is exactly that kind of guy, I hear the honesty in his words. Not a red flag, I admit to myself, but definitely a yellow one. It both intrigues me and makes me uneasy.

"I appreciate that. But that's … not exactly my issue," I say nervously.

He tilts his head. "Is it okay to ask what is?"

I chew nervously on my bottom lip. "It's … unusual."

And it's not something I've ever told anyone. It's not something I'm sure I want to tell him, at least not yet.

He huffs a laugh. "I'm good with unusual," he replies drily. "You're not going to scare me off."

"It's not that. I shouldn't have even said anything. I just … can we just get to know each other? I like you. At least, what I know about you so far," I admit.

"And you think I'm handsome," he teases.

I blush hard. "I do. And … hopefully we'll get there. But there's a lot I'd like to know about you first."

Matt nods slowly. "I'm sorry. I'd never ask you to do or say anything you weren't ready for," he assures me. "I hope you know that."

I take a deep breath, some of the tension in my shoulders lessening. "Thank you," I murmur, purposing to focus on the here and now. On getting to know this gorgeous man. If I just focus on that, I think I can do this. Baby steps.

Matt reaches across the table and places his hand on mine, rubbing his thumb over my knuckles. I get lost in his warm brown eyes as he gazes at me across the table.

"Of course," he replies. "What would you like to know about me, Anna?"

His swirling thumb sends tingles up my arm, making it hard to think, so I retract my hand. "What are you going to do to CJ for canceling your meeting?" I ask, trying to lighten the moment.

Matt leans back and laughs. "Thank her?" he responds. "I can always reschedule that meeting. But I am curious about what she told you to get you to show up to meet someone who you clearly knew nothing about, besides that he worked with my sister."

I scrunch my nose. "Well, actually, I was kind of the one that started it …"

I tell Matt about my family. About all the weddings, and the crap my mother, aunt, and every other female over forty in my family gives me about being single. Perhaps because of our earlier conversation, he doesn't push on *why* I'm single, merely listening and sympathizing with how annoying it must be. I explain how I basically invited the setup given the pressure, so I didn't ask too many questions, simply trusting CJ. But that I was relieved to see it was him.

And then we move on to all the things *normal* people talk about on dates. We both order drinks we barely touch because the conversation flows so well. Since we talked about my job and background at the housewarming party, he tells me about his job as a social media marketing director. Then he asks about my hobbies. You know, besides going to all the weddings. Even though I joke that's practically a second job in itself.

I ask about what it's like being a twin. Working with your twin. He reminds me he also lived with CJ until recently, though he seems guarded about their relationship. Not in a worrying way, more in a … protective way? I definitely get a protector vibe from him.

We move on to likes and dislikes. Movies. Books. Hobbies. My list is pretty short. Shopping and reading. Though very different books from Matt. I'm all about fiction of every genre, where he prefers books on leadership and management. Practical, though he seems to live and breathe his job.

But nothing about his vibe is ever off. Even if he's forward, he's honest, and, like CJ said, seems to be an all-around good guy. And I get such potent feelings from him, so I know I'm not mistaken. He's assertive, though, so perhaps it's just his natural confidence projecting his emotions so strongly. It makes me more comfortable with him, especially when he walks me to my car and doesn't even push to kiss me. He does ask me if he can see me again, which I agree to. And as I drive away, I'm happy with that decision.

I can tell despite his forthrightness about his desires, Matt respects my need to take this slow. I feel good about seeing him again, and that gives me hope. I've learned to trust my read of people over the years, especially since what happened to me. Because I ignored my reservations then.

And it almost got me killed.

CHAPTER SIX

MATT

"Smells good in here," CJ announces as she walks through the door of what used to be our shared townhouse. "What are you making?"

I don't bother looking up from the stove where I'm stirring the contents of the pan. "Mushroom risotto. And before you ask, yes, there's enough for you."

"I wasn't going to ask," she says, hopping onto one of the bar stools at the kitchen island. "I was going to assume."

I snort. I'd intended to invite her for dinner anyway, since I know Drew usually works Friday nights, but I was in meetings all day and, even though she's my assistant, we barely spoke, and all about work stuff. And I've been itching to talk to her about *non*-work stuff.

"Of course you were." I grab the white wine and add another splash to the pan. "Speaking of assumptions, we need to talk about last night." I give her a pointed look.

CJ tries for an innocent expression that doesn't quite land. "What about last night?"

I huff out an unamused laugh. "Oh, I don't know. Maybe the part where you canceled my mentor meeting and set me up on a blind date without telling me?" I turn to face her, wooden spoon still in hand. "With your friend Anna."

"Technically, I set her up on a blind date. You just happened to be there." She's fighting a smile, the little shit.

"CJ." I use my best big-brother no-bullshit tone.

"Matt." She puts her hands on her hips and raises an eyebrow.

I shake my head and turn back to the risotto. "You know, if you wanted to set us up, you could have just asked."

"Would you have said yes?"

I consider that for a moment. "Probably not," I admit. Given the events of the last few months, I hadn't even considered getting back into the dating pool so soon.

"Exactly. And Anna would have overthought it and talked herself out of it. This way, you both got to meet naturally, with no pressure."

"Naturally?" I scoff. "There was nothing natural about realizing my baby sister had played us."

"Younger by fifty-seven seconds is hardly 'baby sister' territory," she reminds me. "And besides, it worked out, didn't it? Anna said you two had a good time."

I plate the risotto and slide a portion in front of her before taking the stool beside her. "So you two have talked about it already?" I try to say it calmly, despite dying to know what Anna has said to her.

"We texted a little," CJ admits, taking a bite. "Oh my god, this is amazing. Where did you learn to make risotto?"

"YouTube Culinary Academy. Don't change the subject."

She grins. "Fine. She said you were a perfect gentleman, well mostly, anyway, and that she had a nice time. But that's all you're getting. I want to hear what you thought."

I take a bite, buying myself time. What do I tell her? That I haven't been able to stop thinking about Anna all last night and today? That there's something about her that pulls at me in a way I can't explain? That I already feel like I know way more about her than I ever knew about Alyssa? And how much that freaks me out?

"She's cool," I finally say nonchalantly. "Different from what I expected."

"Different how?" CJ asks with a note of suspicion.

"I don't know. She's just ..." I set down my fork. I contemplate not admitting this, but it's CJ. "Honestly? I tried to read her, Cee. During the date. Not on purpose at first. But I got nothing. Absolutely nothing."

CJ's eyebrows rise. "Nothing at all?"

I nod. "It was like hitting a wall. And then later, she mentioned having an 'unusual' issue about dating but wouldn't tell me what." I run a hand through my hair. "I don't like not knowing what I'm dealing with."

"Maybe she was just really present in the moment," CJ suggests. "Remember how Drew was when we first met? I couldn't read him easily either because he was so focused on the now."

I shake my head, knowing that guys are way simpler

than girls when it comes to that sort of thing. And that's not what this seemed like. "I get that, but this felt different. More like she was actively blocking me somehow." I push my risotto around, not sure how to put the feeling of resistance I encountered into words. "What if she's hiding something?"

CJ sets down her fork angrily. "Matt. Listen to yourself."

"What?" I look up at her mid-bite, confused.

"You're more concerned about not being able to invade her privacy than you are about actually getting to know her." Her voice has that edge it gets when she's about to lecture me. "Did it occur to you that maybe it's not fair to use your ability to get information she's not ready to share?"

"I wasn't trying to —"

"Weren't you? You just said you tried to read her during the date," CJ interjects into my forming protest.

I open my mouth to object, then close it. She's not wrong. "Fine. I did. But only because I didn't want to get burned again," I admit. Until Alyssa's betrayal, I'd always made it a policy not to try to read dates or girlfriends until and unless they gave me a reason to. But since Alyssa … it's hard to want to take that chance.

CJ's features soften, and she puts a hand on my shoulder. "I know. But Anna's my friend. She's a good person who's obviously been through some stuff — stuff she didn't even tell me about, by the way, and that I didn't push her on either. And if you're going to date her, you need to respect her boundaries too."

"Then why set us up if you're so worried about me

mistreating your friend?" The words come out sharper than I intend.

CJ gives me a tolerant look. "Because I think you could be good together. You're both smart, both have a wicked sense of humor when you let your guard down. And honestly? You've been moping around since the Alyssa thing. I thought you could use some cheering up."

"I haven't been moping." It even sounds like the lie it is to *my* ears.

CJ rolls her eyes. "You reorganized your entire spice cabinet by expiration date, Matt. That's moping."

I can't help but laugh. "It needed to be done."

CJ smirks. "Sure it did." She reaches over and squeezes my arm. "Look, maybe it was too soon. Maybe you're not ready to date someone new without comparing them to ... previous bitches who stomped all over your heart for social media clout. But that's not Anna. She's obviously been hurt before too and is just cautious. Given what you've both told me about how the date went, she has good reason to be when you're coming on that strong that fast."

"I wasn't *that* bad."

CJ gives me a look.

"Okay, fine. I might have suggested we leave together after talking for all of five minutes."

"Matt!" CJ slaps me on the arm. So, obviously Anna hadn't shared that tidbit.

I shrug. "What? She's gorgeous, and we have chemistry. Sue me." But even as I say it, I know CJ has a point. "You're right, though. I'm being an ass."

"You're being yourself, which sometimes means being an ass," she corrects with a raised eyebrow. "But you're capable of being better. Anna deserves that."

I nod slowly. "I like her, Cee. More than I expected to. Once she said she wanted to take things slow, I respected that. I didn't push."

"That's good. That's growth."

"But this thing with not being able to read her ..." I shake my head, not sure how to get past how badly I got burned in my last relationship.

"Let it go," CJ says firmly, as if it's that easy. "Let her tell you whatever it is she's hiding when *she's* ready. Get to know her the way normal people do — by talking, by spending time together, by building trust."

"Normal people," I mutter sarcastically. "Right. Because that's totally us. We're the epitome of normal."

CJ snorts. "You know what I mean. Promise me you won't try to read her on purpose. That you'll give her the space to open up on her own terms."

I meet her eyes. She's in full protective mode, but she's also right. I've been so focused on what I can't see that I've been ignoring what was right in front of me — a smart, beautiful woman who actually seems to like me ... so far, anyway.

"I promise," I agree. "No reading her on purpose. I'll let her tell me things when she's ready." I blow out a breath. That's easier said than done, but I can already see that Anna is different. That we're different together. If I want her to open up to me, trust me, I'm going to have to be trustworthy.

"Good." CJ nods as if hearing my unspoken thoughts and picks up her fork again. "Now tell me more about this date. Anna was light on the details."

I tell her about the rest of the evening — how easily conversation flowed, how Anna called me out on my bullshit with humor instead of judgment, how she looked in that dress. CJ listens with a knowing smile.

"You really do like her," she says when I finish.

"Yeah," I admit. "I really do."

"Then don't screw it up by being an inconsiderate asshole."

"Thanks for the pep talk, Sis," I say drily.

"Anytime." She grins sublimely and polishes off the last of her risotto. "For what it's worth, I think she likes you too. She wouldn't have agreed to a second date if she didn't."

I lift a shoulder. I know she does. That doesn't mean it all doesn't scare the shit out of me. "We'll see," I say, but somehow I'm still smiling, thinking of Anna. "I'm taking her out next Friday. Somewhere public, very nice and totally appropriate, with no suggestion of leaving together after five minutes."

"Look at you, learning and growing," she teases.

"Shut up and help me clean the kitchen."

"What, no dessert?" she pushes.

I snort. "There's ice cream in the freezer. Boy, Drew has spoiled the hell out of you." I bump my shoulder against hers to let her know I'm teasing. I'm glad he's taking such good care of her. I'd have worried about her complete lack of cooking skills had she moved in with anyone else.

As we fall into the familiar rhythm of washing and drying dishes, I find myself looking forward to Friday. Maybe CJ's right. Maybe I need to stop trying to see into Anna's past and focus on the possibilities of the future instead.

Even if not knowing is driving me absolutely crazy.

CHAPTER SEVEN

ANNA

"Pass the garlic bread," Dad calls from the head of the table, and three hands reach for the basket at once.

"I got it first," Francesca protests, batting away Lucia's hand.

"Age before beauty," Lucia counters, snatching the basket.

"Then I should get it," Sophia chimes in from beside me, her husband Tony laughing at the familiar sisterly chaos.

This is Friday night dinner at the Martella house — loud, unruly, and absolutely mandatory unless you're literally dying. Even then, Mom would probably bring you soup and set you up on the couch so you wouldn't miss it.

I pass the salad to Tony, who's clearly learned after three years of marriage to Sophia to just stay out of the garlic bread wars. Across from him, Johnny — Lucia's husband of eighteen months — is deep in conversation with Dad about the 49ers' chances this season.

"Anna, you're not eating," Mom observes, because of course she notices everything. "Are you feeling okay?"

"I'm fine, Mom. Just pacing myself." I take a bite of her lasagna to prove my point. "It's delicious, as always."

"Of course it is, it's your nonna's recipe," she says, but she's smiling. "Marcus, would you like more?"

Marcus, who's been dating Francesca for almost two years, knows exactly how to play this game. "Yes, please, Mrs. M. Best lasagna in the city."

"Such a nice boy," Mom says, not at all subtle as she loads up his plate. "Francesca is lucky to have you."

Francesca rolls her eyes, but she's smiling, her hand linked with Marcus's on top of the table. There's something about them tonight — an energy I can't quite place. Marcus seems more nervous than usual and keeps darting glances at Francesca. My money's on Francesca being pregnant.

"So," Sophia says, turning to me with that older sister look that means trouble. "Any exciting plans for the weekend?"

"Just work tomorrow night." I spear another piece of lasagna. "The restaurant's been crazy busy."

"All work and no play," Lucia tsks. "You need to get out more."

I'm about to respond when Marcus suddenly stands up, his chair scraping against the floor. The entire table goes silent.

"Actually," he says, his voice shaking slightly, "before we go any further with dinner, there's something I'd like to say."

Oh my god. I realize suddenly by Francesca's shift in

energy that I was all wrong. My stomach lurches. He's *not* about to —

Marcus drops to one knee beside Francesca's chair, pulling out a small velvet box.

Damn. He is.

"Francesca Marie Martella," Marcus begins, and Mom and Francesca both immediately start crying while Sophia and Lucia cover their mouths with a hand, tears in their eyes. "These past two years have been the happiest of my life. You make me laugh every day, you challenge me to be better, and you've shown me what a real partnership looks like."

Francesca has both hands over her mouth, tears absolutely streaming down her face.

"I love your ambition, your kindness, and yes, even your inability to load a dishwasher properly." That gets a watery laugh from everyone. "I want to spend the rest of my life debating the right way to fold fitted sheets with you. Will you marry me?"

I roll my eyes even though I know it's exactly what my super OCD sister wants to hear from her future husband.

Thankfully nobody is paying attention to me anyway.

"Yes!" Francesca practically shouts as he opens the box. "Yes, of course, yes!"

The room erupts. Mom is sobbing, Dad is clapping Marcus on the back, and my sisters are group-jump-hugging Francesca while she tries to put on the ring with shaking hands. I join the fray, genuinely happy for her even as a small part of me mentally calculates the damage to my bank account and closet space.

"Let me see, let me see!" Sophia demands, grabbing Francesca's hand. The ring is perfect for my girliest sister — an oval pink diamond in a rose gold setting that catches the light beautifully.

"I'm thinking next fall. Maybe October?" Francesca says, already in planning mode. Marcus nods agreeably. "Anna, you'll be my maid of honor, right?"

Since we're closest in age, we've spent the most time together. Though we're the least alike. But she's my sister.

"Of course," I say, hugging her again. Because what else am I going to say? No, I'm tired of weddings and tulle and overpriced bridesmaid dresses that I'll never wear again?

"This calls for champagne!" Dad announces, disappearing into the kitchen.

Twenty minutes later, after multiple toasts and Mom calling at least three relatives to share the news, we finally settle back down to dinner. But the interrogation I've been dodging is apparently just beginning.

"So," Sophia says, fixing me with that look again. "Speaking of relationships ..."

"Subtle," I mutter into my champagne.

"Are you seeing anyone?" she continues, undeterred. "Because Tony has this friend from work —"

"Oh my god, did Mom put you up to this?" I look between Sophia and Mom, who suddenly seems very interested in her lasagna. "She did, didn't she?"

"We're just concerned," Mom says, not even trying to deny it. "You're twenty-three, Anna. You haven't dated anyone in almost two years."

"Some of us are focused on our careers," I say, even though waiting tables isn't exactly a career, for me anyway. And isn't exactly why I haven't dated.

"You can focus on your career and still date," Lucia points out. "I met Johnny while I was in law school."

"And I met Tony during tax season," Sophia adds. "Busiest time of the year for an accountant."

I look at Francesca for support, but she's too busy admiring her ring to help me out. Traitor.

"Look," I say, setting down my fork. "If it will get you all off my back — yes, I actually went on a date last night."

The table goes silent. Even Dad looks up from his plate.

"You did?" Mom's voice rises about an octave. "With who? How did you meet? What does he do?"

"Breathe, Teresa," Dad says mildly, but he's looking at me with interest too.

"His name is Matt," I say, figuring I might as well give them something. "He works at a social media company. We met through a mutual friend."

"Is he Italian?" This from Nonna, who's been suspiciously quiet until now.

"I ... don't actually know," I admit. Nor do I care, even though I know they do ... well, most of them do. As long as I get married before twenty-five, Mom won't care either. "His last name is Roberts, so probably not?"

Nonna makes a dismissive sound but doesn't comment further.

"How did it go?" Francesca asks, finally tuning back in. "Are you seeing him again?"

"It went well. And yes, we have another date next Friday." I take a sip of champagne, hoping that's enough to satisfy them.

"Friday night?" Mom says. Sophia exchanges a look with Lucia, probably expecting a rebuke for my potentially missing family dinner. "That's a good sign. Friday night is serious date night." I breathe a sigh of relief. Apparently, death *or* a date will pass as an excuse to miss it.

"It's just dinner," I protest.

"But you like him?" Mom presses. "He's a good boy? Respectful?"

I think about Matt suggesting we leave together after five minutes and have to hide a grin. Respectful might not be the first word I'd use, but he did back off when I said no.

"Yes, Mom. He was a perfect gentleman." *Mostly anyway*, but I keep that thought to myself. "And his sister is one of my closest friends, so I know I can trust him."

"That's good," Dad says, nodding approvingly. "You meet the family, you know what kind of people they are."

"It's not like that," I start, but Mom's already off and running.

"You should bring him to dinner here instead," she says. "We'd love to meet him."

"Mom, we've had one date."

"So? Your father met the family on our second date."

"Different generation," I remind her, the familiar refrain.

"A good man is a good man, no matter the generation," she counters.

"Can we just —" I gesture around the table. "Can we

focus on Francesca's engagement for five minutes before planning my hypothetical future?"

"She's right," Francesca says, coming to my rescue. "This is my night. Everyone pay attention to me and my gorgeous ring."

The conversation shifts back to wedding planning, and I breathe a sigh of relief. But I catch Mom watching me throughout the rest of dinner with that look — the one that says she's already planning my wedding in her head, too.

"For what it's worth," Sophia leans over to whisper while Mom grills Marcus about his family's availability for an engagement party, "I'm glad you're putting yourself out there again. After ... you know. It's good to see."

I nod, not trusting myself to speak. Because she's right — this is a big step for me. Even if only my mother and Sophia know the full story of why I stopped dating, the rest know something happened. Something that changed me.

"Thanks," I finally manage. "He seems like a good guy."

"Good," she says firmly. "You deserve that."

As I watch Francesca beam at Marcus, her ring catching the light every time she moves her hand, I let myself imagine what it would be like. To be that sure about someone. To trust them that completely.

It's been a long time since I've let myself even consider the possibility.

But maybe — just maybe — I'm ready to try.

"Anna," Nonna calls from her end of the table. "This Matt. He makes good money?"

"Nonna!"

"What? It's an important question. You can't live on love alone. Besides, you want a big wedding, yes?"

I shake my head laughing. "Sure, Nonna," I say placatingly, even though I've had enough of big weddings to last me a lifetime. "And don't worry. He's in management, and he seems to do well."

She nods approvingly. "Good. You bring him soon. I'll make my special sauce. We'll see if he's worthy."

I groan, but I'm smiling. This is my family — overwhelming, intrusive, and absolutely convinced that their primary job is to see me married off before I hit twenty-five.

But they love me. And after everything I've been through, even if they don't all know the details, they just want to see me happy.

As we clear the table and Mom brings out her homemade tiramisu — because of course there's dessert — I'm actually looking forward to next Friday. To seeing where this thing with Matt might go.

But despite my family already on board, I'm still not ready to add yet another wedding to my calendar. Especially not my own. I've got a long way to go before I get there.

CHAPTER EIGHT

MATT

Friday night, the maître d' leads us through the dimly lit restaurant, past tables draped in white linen and couples leaning close over candlelight. I chose this place specifically because it's Michelin-starred and impossible to get reservations — the kind of restaurant that's supposed to impress. But watching Anna nervously take a seat and immediately start contemplating the multiple forks at her place setting, I'm second-guessing myself.

"The wine list, sir," the sommelier says, presenting a leather-bound tome that probably weighs more than my laptop.

"Just water for me, thanks," Anna says quickly, and I hand the wine list back unopened.

"Make that two waters. Sparkling."

When he's gone, Anna relaxes slightly. "Sorry. I just ... wine makes me sleepy, and I want to actually remember this date."

"No apology necessary." I study her across the table. She's wearing a black dress that's elegant but understated, her blond hair pulled back in a way that shows off her neck. She looks beautiful, but also uncomfortable. "You know, we can go somewhere else."

"No, this is nice. Really." She gestures around the restaurant. "Very ... fancy."

The way she says 'fancy' tells me everything I need to know. A server brings our waters and takes our order, then Anna and I talk about our weeks while we wait for our food.

Our appetizers arrive quickly — some artistic arrangement of microgreens and foam that costs more than most entrées — and Anna stares at it like it might bite her.

"I think it's beet," I offer. "With ... goat cheese mousse? Maybe?"

She carefully eats it, and I follow her lead.

"It's good. All three bites of it," she says with a smirk.

I can't help but laugh. "Not exactly filling, is it?"

"I've served bigger portions as amuse-bouchées at our restaurant." She sets down her fork. "Can I be honest?"

"Please."

"This is beautiful. The ambiance, the service, the tiny food that costs a fortune." She meets my eyes. "But it's not really me."

"Thank god," I say, probably too enthusiastically. "It's not really me either."

"Then why —"

"Because I'm an idiot who thought I needed to impress you?" I lean back in my chair. "Look, I know you're not supposed to talk about these things, but … my last relationship was all about appearances. Going to the right places, being seen with the right people. I guess I defaulted to that."

Anna tilts her head, studying me. "You don't need to impress me, Matt. I already said yes to the date."

"So what would you have chosen? If you were planning this?" I ask, curious.

She grins. "Honestly? Probably burgers and fries somewhere casual. Maybe eaten outside if it's nice enough. I'm a simple girl with simple tastes."

"Then that's what we'll do next time," I decide. "You plan it. Show me what you actually like."

"Next time," she repeats. "Someone's confident."

"Hopeful," I correct. "There's a difference." She gives me a small, encouraging smile that makes my heart beat harder. I return the look, knowing I must come off like a sap. But for her? I'm okay with that.

Our entrées arrive — portions slightly larger but still artistically plated within an inch of their lives. Anna cuts into her chicken, which is decorated with what appear to be flowers.

"Are these edible?" she whispers, pointing at the purple petals.

"I think everything's edible at these prices." I reach over and pluck one from her plate, then pop it in my mouth. "Tastes … flowery."

She laughs, and the sound does something to my chest. "You're *really* not a fancy restaurant guy either, are you?"

"Not even close. Most nights I'm cooking for myself at home. Nothing elaborate — pasta, stir-fry, whatever's in the fridge."

"You cook?" She sounds genuinely surprised. "That's impressive."

"YouTube Culinary School strikes again. Plus, if I let CJ cook, we'd have lived on burnt ramen and undercooked hot dogs. So it was either learn to cook or survive on takeout." I pause. "What about you? Coming from a big Italian family, you must have some secret recipes."

Anna's laugh is self-deprecating. "You'd think, right? But no, I'm hopeless in the kitchen. My mom tried to teach all of us, but I'm the only one who never got the hang of it. I can make exactly three things: cereal, cake — the only lesson from my mother that stuck — and reservations."

"Then it's a good thing you've got me," I say without thinking, then immediately want to take it back. Too much, too soon.

But Anna just smiles. "My family would love you. A man who can cook? You'd never escape their dinner table."

"Do I get to meet this family?" I ask, trying to sound casual.

"Oh, they're dying to meet you," she says. "My mom's already planning the menu. But I figure I should give you a while longer before I subject you to that circus."

"That bad?"

"Four daughters, two sons-in-law, one soon-to-be son-in-law, and my parents who believe their main purpose in life is to see us all married off." She shakes her head. "Plus my nonna, who will definitely interrogate you about your income and your intentions."

"Sounds intimidating."

"They are. But in the best way." Her expression softens. "I want to make sure you like me enough first. Before my family scares you away."

"I already like you enough," I tell her, meaning it.

"Good." She pushes her half-eaten entrée away. "So, Sunday? For our casual date?"

"Sunday it is. Your plans, your rules."

"My rules," she repeats, something flickering in her eyes. "I like the sound of that."

———

Sunday afternoon arrives crisp and clear — one of those perfect San Francisco days where the fog burns off early and the temperature actually climbs above sixty-five. Anna texts me an address in the Inner Richmond, and I find her waiting outside a hole-in-the-wall burger joint, wearing jeans and a soft buttery yellow sweater that brings out the golden sheen in her brown eyes.

"This is more like it," she says by way of greeting. "Best burgers in the city, and they don't serve twenty-dollar truffle fries."

We order at the counter — double cheeseburgers, regular fries, and milkshakes — and she insists on paying. "My plan, my treat," she says firmly. Sensing it's important to her, I shrug amicably.

"Where to?" I ask when we have our food.

"Golden Gate Park. There's this pond where you can feed the ducks, and the grass is perfect for picnics." I nod, knowing exactly where she means. It's gorgeous. Very romantic … with the right person, anyway.

We find a spot near the water, settling into the soft grass and spreading out napkins as a makeshift blanket for the food. The burgers are exactly as good as promised — juicy, messy, perfect.

"See?" Anna says, gesturing with a fry. "Isn't this better than edible flowers and foam?"

"Infinitely." I watch her lick ketchup off her thumb and have to look away. A man can only take so much temptation. I watch a duck swim lazily across the pond before looking back at her. "Though the company was good both then and now."

"Smooth talker." But she's smiling.

We finish eating and stretch out on the grass, watching families feed the ducks and joggers circle the path. The sun is warm on my face, and I can't remember the last time I felt this relaxed.

"Can I ask you something?" Anna says after a while.

"Shoot."

"What do you see in your future? Like, beyond work?"

I prop myself up on one elbow to look at her. "That's a big question for a second date."

"Third, technically. If you count the accidental setup." She's lying on her back, eyes closed against the sun. "I'm just curious. You seem so focused on your career."

"I am," I admit. "Maybe too focused. I guess I always

figured the rest would fall into place eventually. Marriage, kids, the whole thing."

"Big family or small?"

"I haven't thought that far ahead." I study her profile. "You're one of four, right? How is that?"

"Chaos," she says immediately. "Wonderful, overwhelming chaos. Someone always needs something, there's never enough bathroom time, and privacy is basically a myth. But ..." She opens her eyes, turning to face me. "It's all I know. And it's mostly good. Always having someone to talk to, never being alone on holidays, built-in best friends."

"Sounds nice."

"It is. But it's also hard to imagine getting from where I am to there, you know?" She gestures vaguely. "From barely dating to family dinners to babies and mortgages."

"Step by step, I guess." I reach out to brush a strand of hair from her face, then catch myself. "Sorry. I should ask —"

"It's okay." She catches my hand before I can pull it back. "I don't mind when you touch me, Matt. Though I know I'm sending mixed signals about the physical stuff."

"You're not," I assure her. "You've been clear about wanting to go slow. I respect that."

She gives me an indecipherable look. "Do you ... *want* to kiss me?"

The question catches me off guard. "Anna ..."

"It's not a trick question." She's still holding my hand, her thumb tracing patterns on my palm. "I'm just wondering."

"I've thought about it," I admit. "A lot, actually. But given that you want to take things slow, I figured I should wait."

"Wait for what?"

"For you to kiss me. Or for you to ask me to kiss you." I meet her eyes. "I want you to be in control of the pace here. No pressure, no expectations."

She's quiet for a long moment, and I wonder if I've said the wrong thing. Then her lips pull up at the corners — and she looks a little surprised.

"That might be the nicest thing a guy has ever said to me."

"If basic respect ranks that high ... well, I guess didn't expect such a low bar to clear."

She laughs, releasing my hand to sit up. "Maybe. Or maybe I've just dated some real jerks."

"Their loss." I sit up too, brushing grass off my shirt. "So what else is on the agenda for this casual date?"

"Well, we could walk around the park, hit up the Japanese Tea Garden, or ..." She grins. "There's a bookstore nearby that has an entire section of business and leadership books. I thought you might like that."

"You remembered my boring reading preferences?"

"Not boring. Just ... focused." She stands, offering me a hand up. "Besides, they also have a great fiction section for me."

I let her pull me to my feet, maybe holding on a little longer than necessary. And not just to try reading her. Which I still can't do, anyway. Huh.

And then I kick myself for even trying. I need to stop that. I promised CJ, after all. But also because she's right. It's a dick move.

"Lead the way," I say, squeezing her hand and letting go.

As we walk toward the park exit, though, she firmly twines her fingers with mine and asks, "So what would you do? If you weren't so focused on work?"

I run my thumb over her soft skin, focusing on how good it feels and letting go of the urge to seek answers I have no right to demand. "Travel, maybe. See more than just conference rooms in different cities." I glance at her. "What about you? If you weren't waiting tables?"

She's quiet for a moment. "I always thought about being a therapist. Mine helped me through a lot, and I'd like to do that for other people. But the postgraduate work seemed overwhelming at the time."

"It's not too late," I point out. "You're what, twenty-three? Plenty of time to go back to school."

"Maybe." She sounds unconvinced. "It just feels like such a gigantic leap."

"Most good things are." Well, that was a mouthful. She's quiet, like the simple statement hit her hard too. We reach the bookstore, and I hold the door open for her. "But for what it's worth, I think you'd be great at it. You have this way of reading people, understanding what they need to hear."

She looks up at me, something unreadable in her expression. "You think so?"

"I know so." We share a long look that sends shivers down my arms. How her gaze can strip me so bare is beyond me.

Inside the bookstore, we separate — her to fiction, me to business — but I watch her browse instead of looking at books. She's completely absorbed, pulling titles off shelves and reading back covers, occasionally making small sounds of interest or dismissal.

This is her in her element. Relaxed, unguarded, happy.

"Find anything good?" she asks when we meet back up, each carrying a small stack.

"A few things. You?"

"Two novels and a cookbook, because apparently I'm an optimist." She peers at my stack. "*Leadership in Crisis, The Innovator's Dilemma*, and ... is that a mystery novel?"

"You're a bad influence," I tease her. "I figured I should branch out. So we can talk about books."

Anna's eyes widen a fraction and her mouth pops open. "I'm honored." She heads for the register. "My treat again?"

"Absolutely not. You got lunch."

"But this was my idea —"

"Anna." I step closer, lowering my voice. "Let me buy you books. Please."

She blinks up at me, and for a moment I think she might kiss me right there in the bookstore. I stifle a smile, and she nods. "Okay. Thank you." We stare into each other's eyes for a moment, and a feeling of what I can only describe as "untetheredness" washes over me. Like her golden gaze has ripped me from the ground I stand on, the world around me, and my very own mind.

She breaks her eyes away and turns to head toward the register. I take a deep breath. Whatever just passed between us ... well, it has me shaken.

I'm immediately re-tethered as we head outside, where the sun is setting, painting the sky in shades of orange and pink.

I'm filled with a sense of peace, and I realize … we've spent the entire afternoon together.

It was easy. Fun. I've been more comfortable with her than I remember ever being with any woman, much less one I've only been out with a few times.

"I should probably get home," Anna says reluctantly. "You know, since I work tomorrow."

"I'll drive you," I offer, suddenly desperate for just a little more time with her. She nods and follows me to the car.

The ride is silent at first as she fidgets with her bag of books. "I had a fantastic time today."

"Me too. Thank you for showing me your version of a perfect date."

"Was it?" She sounds genuinely curious. "Perfect, I mean."

I think about it — the casual meal, the effortless conversation, the complete lack of pretense. "Yeah. It really was."

When I pull up to her building, she doesn't immediately get out. "Matt?"

"Yeah?"

"I'm glad CJ set us up. Even if she was sneaky about it."

I smile warmly, my eyes involuntarily snagging on her full mouth. But there will be a time for that. I can feel it. "Me too. Can I walk you to the door?"

To my surprise, she leans across the console and kisses my cheek — quick and light, but it still sends electricity through me. "Thanks, but no need." She looks shyly at me, and I realize she's avoiding the awkward "do I invite him up or not" moment, so I let it go. "Goodnight, Matt."

"'Night, Anna."

I wait until she's inside the building before driving away, my cheek still tingling where her lips touched. It wasn't the kiss I'd been imagining, but somehow it was better. A promise of things to come, when she's ready.

Step by step, like I told her.

I can be patient.

For her, I can definitely be patient.

CHAPTER NINE

ANNA

My phone buzzes while I'm folding napkins during the pre-dinner lull at the restaurant. Matt's name on the screen makes me smile before I even read the message.

So what's the plan for Friday? My turn to pick, right?

I glance around to make sure Drew isn't lurking, then type back quickly.

That was the deal. What did you have in mind?

I was thinking I could cook for you. Fair warning though — it won't be as good as what you're probably used to.

I snort, attracting a look from one of the other servers. Turning away, I type: *Fishing for an invitation to Friday dinner with my family?*

I suddenly realize I may not have told him our family dinners are usually on Friday nights. And he may interpret that as me subtly pointing out that he made me miss last week's, and would do it again this week. So I quickly go to type another message to reassure him I meant nothing by it.

But his response comes through before I can figure out how to say that without sounding lame.

I mean, if you're okay with it, I'd actually love that.

My stomach does a little flip. That's ... unexpected.

You realize that's kind of serious, right? Meeting the family?

This time his response is immediate.

Maybe I'm serious about you.

I stare at the screen, my heart doing that annoying flutter thing it's been doing lately whenever Matt says something like this. Before I can overthink my response, I type back.

Maybe?

Definitely.

I bite my lip to keep from grinning like an idiot. One of the other servers — Becky — nudges me.

"New boyfriend?" she teases.

"Something like that," I admit, then quickly type: *Friday at 7. Don't say I didn't warn you.*

Can't wait. What should I bring?

A hearty appetite and thick skin.

That bad?

You'll see.

———

By Friday evening, I'm a nervous wreck. I've changed outfits three times, finally settling on a simple blue sweetheart A-line dress that Mom bought me last Christmas. Conservative enough for a family dinner, but still nice enough that Matt will notice.

"You're being ridiculous," Sophia says, catching me checking my reflection in the hallway mirror for the tenth time. "It's just dinner."

"It's not just dinner. It's Mom and Dad and Nonna and all of you vultures ready to pick apart everything about him."

"We're not that bad." She pauses. "Okay, we're exactly that bad. But if he can't handle us, better to know now, right?"

She has a point, and it's honestly the only reason I invited Matt to family dinner this early in the relationship.

Oh god. I just thought of this as a relationship — as if I didn't already know that I'm way more into him than I expected to be.

But if anyone can vet a potential partner — read put him through his paces to see exactly how serious he is about sticking around — it's my family.

The doorbell rings before I can answer my sister's probably-rhetorical-anyway question, and my stomach drops.

"I'll get it!" Mom calls out, already rushing to the door in her good apron — the fancier one without stains.

"Mom, wait —"

Too late. She's already throwing open the door.

"You must be Matt!" she exclaims, and I hear the assessment in her voice already. Tall, check. Handsome, check. Well-dressed — and looking deliciously sexy in dark jeans and a navy button-down shirt, I note — check.

"Mrs. Martella, it's a pleasure to meet you." Matt's voice is warm, confident. "Thank you for having me."

"Oh, none of that Mrs. Martella business. Call me Teresa. Come in, come in!"

I hang back as she ushers him inside, watching as he hands her a bottle of wine and a bouquet of tulips.

"These are beautiful," Mom gushes. "Such a gentleman." She gives me a pointed look over her shoulder.

I can almost hear her telling me to lock this one down. I step forward and grin at Matt. "Hi." I give him a slightly self-conscious little wave.

Matt's face lights up when he sees me. "Hi," he breathes. "Wow. You look stunning, Anna."

"She is beautiful, just like her mother," Dad says, appearing from the living room with his hand extended. "Joe Martella."

Matt shakes his hand firmly. "Matt Roberts. Great to meet you, sir."

"Sir, I like that. Marines?"

"No, sir. Just raised right."

Dad nods approvingly, and I can already see him mentally moving Matt into the "acceptable" category. He's by far the easiest family member to impress.

"Come meet everyone else," Mom says, leading us into the dining room where the whole family has assembled like some kind of welcoming committee. Or firing squad, depending on how you look at it.

"Matt, these are my other daughters — Sophia, Lucia, and Francesca. Their husbands, Tony and Johnny, and Francesca's fiancé, Marcus."

Matt handles the introductions smoothly, shaking hands

and remembering names. When we get to Nonna at the head of the table, she eyes him critically.

"You Italian?" she asks without preamble.

"No, ma'am. Irish and German, mostly."

She makes a dismissive sound. "You eat Italian food?"

"Every chance I get."

"Hmm. We'll see." I can't help grinning behind my hand. Nonna is definitely going to be the toughest nut to crack.

I guide Matt to his seat next to mine, leaning close to whisper, "I'm so sorry."

"For what? This is great." He seems genuinely relaxed, which makes one of us.

"Oh, not for anything that's happened yet. For whatever happens next," I reply with a grin. Matt's eyes go a little wide.

Dinner starts with the antipasto, and I watch nervously as Matt samples everything. When he tries Mom's stuffed mushrooms, his eyes actually close.

"These are incredible," he says. "Is that pancetta?"

Mom beams. "You cook?"

"A little. Nothing like this though." He turns to me. "How do you stay so thin eating like this?"

"I don't live at home anymore," I point out. "My cooking is more like ... bowls of Honey Nut Cheerios."

"She's the only one who didn't inherit the cooking gene," Francesca says. "It's tragic, really."

"I have other talents," I defend myself.

"Like what?" Lucia asks innocently.

I kick her under the table and the conversation moves on.

But the interrogation begins in earnest with the pasta course.

"So, Matt," Dad says, twirling his fork expertly against his spoon, "Anna tells us you work in social media management?"

"Yes, sir. I run the marketing division."

"Ah, marketing. Excellent field. Is your company stable?"

"Dad," I warn.

"Very stable," Matt answers anyway. "And growing. We're actually expanding the team this quarter."

"That's wonderful," Mom says. "And you live alone?"

"I do. I have a townhouse in Noe Valley."

Nonna perks up at this. "You own or rent?"

"Nonna!"

"What? These are important things to know."

Matt chuckles. "I bought it two years ago."

The table goes quiet for a moment as everyone digests this information. A twenty-seven-year-old who owns property in San Francisco? I can practically see the wedding bells in Mom's eyes.

"Tell us about your family," Sophia says, clearly trying to give me a break from the financial interrogation.

"Not much to tell. My aunt and uncle raised me, and they live up in Marin. I have a twin sister, CJ — she's actually the one who introduced Anna and me."

"A twin!" Mom exclaims. "How wonderful. Are you close?"

"Very. We actually work at the same company."

"Family is important," Nonna declares, apparently

deciding to give approval. "You take care of your family, you're a good man."

The main course arrives — Mom's famous chicken parmesan — and Matt's appreciation reaches new heights.

"This is honestly the best meal I've had in months," he says. "Maybe years."

"You should come every Friday," Mom says immediately. "We always have room for one more."

"Mom," I protest weakly, but Matt nods.

"I'd love that, if Anna's okay with it."

All eyes turn to me. I take a large sip of wine.

"So," Francesca says with a sly grin, "what are you two doing for Valentine's Day? It's on Sunday, you know."

"We know," I say firmly. "And it's none of your business."

"Anna Marie, don't be rude to your sister," Mom scolds.

"She's being nosy!" I protest.

"I'm being interested," Francesca corrects. "There's a difference."

"We haven't really discussed it," Matt says diplomatically. "But I'm sure we'll figure something out."

Johnny, bless him, chooses this moment to ask Matt about the 49ers' off-season moves, and the conversation shifts to safer territory.

I spend the rest of dinner in a state of mild anxiety, waiting for someone to say something truly embarrassing. It finally happens over dessert.

"Anna used to practice kissing on her pillow," Lucia announces apropos of nothing. "She'd put lipstick on and everything."

"I was twelve!"

"Fourteen," Sophia corrects. "I have pictures."

"I will murder you in your sleep," I hiss.

Matt leans over to stage whisper, "I practiced on my hand. Less laundry."

I burst out laughing despite my mortification.

"See?" Mom says triumphantly. "He's perfect. He makes her laugh."

"Okay, that's it. We're leaving." I stand up, tugging Matt with me. "Thank you for dinner. We're going now."

"But I made cannoli," Mom protests.

"We'll take some to go," I say firmly, already pulling Matt toward the door.

There's a flurry of goodbyes, Mom packing up a portion of dessert, Dad shaking Matt's hand again, and Nonna declaring that he's "acceptable for a non-Italian."

Finally, we escape to Matt's car.

"I am so, so sorry," I say the moment we're alone. "They're insane. All of them. I understand if you never want to see me again."

Matt turns to face me, and he's ... laughing?

"Are you kidding? That was great. Your family is wonderful."

"They interrogated you!"

"It was nothing I couldn't handle, and it was coming from a good place. They care about you." He reaches over to take my hand. "I had a great time, Anna. Your mom's an incredible cook, your dad's hilarious, and your sisters clearly love you even if they show it by embarrassing you. Hell, CJ and I still do that to each other, too."

"You're serious."

"Completely. In fact ..." He starts the car but doesn't drive away yet. "I'd really like to cook for you on Sunday. For Valentine's Day. If you're okay with that."

I study his face in the dim light from the streetlamp. He means it. He survived my entire family and wants to cook me dinner for Valentine's Day.

"At your place?" I ask carefully.

"If you're comfortable with that. Or I could cook and bring it to yours, if you prefer."

The fact that he's offering options, that he's thinking about my comfort level, makes the decision easier.

"Your place is fine," I say. "But I'm bringing dessert from the restaurant. Drew makes this chocolate lava cake that's basically heaven on a plate."

"Well, I can't say no to that." He lifts my hand to his lips, pressing a gentle kiss to my knuckles. "Thank you for tonight. For letting me meet them."

"Thank you for not running screaming into the night."

"It would take a lot more than your family to scare me off, Anna."

The way he says it, quiet and certain, makes me believe him. Maybe I'm not the only one getting serious here.

"Take me home?" I ask softly.

"Of course."

As he drives, I sneak glances at his profile, trying to reconcile this man who charmed my entire family with the smooth-talking player I first pegged him as. Maybe people are more complicated than first — or second — impressions suggest.

Or maybe, just maybe, I'm bringing out a different side of him. The same way he's bringing out a different side of me — one that's learning to trust again, one step at a time.

When he walks me to my door, I turn to face him. "Fair warning: if you come back for Friday dinners, it'll only get worse. They'll start planning our wedding, picking out baby names ..."

"Kind of naïve of you to assume they haven't already started," he says with a grin.

I laugh. "You're probably right. Nonna was definitely mentally measuring you for a tux."

"I look good in a tux," he says huskily.

"I bet you do." I bite into my bottom lip.

He cocks an eyebrow and his mood shifts. And I just know he's about to say something inappropriate.

I hold up a hand. "Don't let that go to your head, though. *Either* head."

Matt laughs. "Okay, okay," he responds, holding up his hands in defeat.

I smile softly. "Take the cannoli," I say, handing him the container.

He raises an eyebrow but takes it. "You sure?"

I wave a hand. "I've had plenty over the years. You'll love it. Trust me."

Matt smirks. "I do," he says, his words and tone contrary to the cocky expression.

I laugh. "I'm really glad you came tonight."

He beams, wide and honest, and butterflies erupt in my already too-full tummy. "Me too," he murmurs, then reaches out and cups my face gently, thumb stroking my cheek. "Can I tell you something?"

I nod, not trusting my voice.

"I was nervous. About tonight. Meeting your family. It's been a long time since I've done the whole 'meet the parents' thing."

"How long?" I ask, curious. And also to avoid admitting … I've never brought anyone home to meet my family.

"Years. Probably since college? I can't even remember." His thumb is still moving in gentle circles. "So this was big for me too."

The admission makes my chest tight. "Matt ..."

"I just wanted you to know. That I'm taking this seriously. That you're not the only one stepping out of their comfort zone here."

I look up into his eyes, mesmerized by the emotions pouring off of him. A mix of desire and vulnerability that leaves me breathless and aching to show him how I feel about that. And yet, I still hesitate.

"I should go," he says roughly, "before I forget about taking things slow."

"Okay." I nod, but contrarily step closer to him. Close enough to see green flecks in his coffee-colored brown eyes. His pupils dilate, and he inhales slowly.

"God, Anna, you smell so good." He closes his eyes. "You're killing me here."

"Sorry," I breathe, forcing myself to step back. "Goodnight, Matt."

"'Night, beautiful. I'll text you about Sunday."

I nod again, tearing my gaze from his. It takes an immense amount of effort. Like he had me hypnotized. Under his spell. Which, I guess I am. But can I trust it?

It's that thought that moves my feet.

Once inside my apartment, I lean against the door and exhale slowly. The most important takeaway of the evening is that my family didn't scare him off. He seemed to truly enjoy himself. And now he wants to cook for me.

I am in serious danger of falling for this man.

How in the hell did this happen in two short weeks?

But as I close my eyes and remember the heat in his, I know it doesn't matter how. I'm standing on the edge … and it's time to let go.

CHAPTER TEN

MATT

I check the beef in the oven for the third time in ten minutes. It's fine. Everything's fine. Except for the fact that I've changed my shirt twice and rearranged the table settings at least four times.

"Get it together, Roberts," I mutter, adjusting the flowers in the center of the table one more time. Clichéd as it is, I couldn't resist the deep red roses I passed while shopping for dinner. I hope she likes them. I make a mental note to find out what her favorite flowers are.

The doorbell rings at exactly seven, and I take a deep breath before answering. Anna stands in my doorway wearing a red dress that hugs her slender frame from chest to hips, showing off her creamy shoulders and long legs. It makes my brain short-circuit for a moment.

"Hi," she says, holding up a white box. "I brought dessert, as promised. Drew's famous chocolate lava cake."

"Hi." I step back to let her in, trying not to stare. "You look incredible."

"Thank you. It smells amazing in here." She follows me to the kitchen, setting the dessert box on the counter. "What are you making?"

"Beef marsala with roasted vegetables and garlic mashed potatoes. Nothing too fancy."

"It sounds perfect." She peers into the dining room, taking in the table settings and flowers. "Matt, this is beautiful."

"I wanted it to be special." I hand her a glass. "Sparkling cider. Since wine makes you sleepy."

She looks touched that I remembered. "Thank you."

"Dinner should be ready in about fifteen minutes. Want a tour while we wait?"

"I'd love that."

I show her around the townhouse — the living room with its exposed brick wall, my home office that's really just a desk crammed with work papers, the small backyard patio. She asks questions about the photos on the walls, mostly of CJ and me at various ages, plus a few of my aunt and uncle.

"Are these your parents?" She points to an older photo on the bookshelf — a young couple holding hands, sitting on the low cliffs of Half Moon Bay State Beach. My chest twinges.

"Yeah. That was taken a few years before CJ and I were born."

"You have your mom's eyes," she observes.

I clear my throat. "They actually passed away when we were kids. Car accident."

"I know, CJ told me a while back." She touches my arm gently. "I'm so sorry, Matt. That must have been so hard."

"It was. We were lucky that we had our aunt and uncle to take us in. They raised us like their own." I cover her hand with mine. "But thank you."

The oven timer saves us from the suddenly heavy moment.

"Dinner's ready," I say, grateful for the distraction.

The meal goes better than I could have hoped. Anna praises everything, which gives me a rush. Not gonna lie, I know I'll never compare to her mother's cooking, but a guy has to up his game to at least try.

We fall into easy conversation about her family dinner aftermath — my glowing review of her mother's cannoli was apparently the clincher that has her and Anna's grandmother already planning our wedding — work stories, and random topics that somehow lead from favorite movies to whether hot dogs are sandwiches. She says yes, but I maintain they're in their own category, and that's like calling cereal soup, which makes her laugh and concede the point.

"I can't believe you actually cooked all this," Anna says, pushing her empty plate away. "That was restaurant quality."

"YouTube Culinary School," I remind her as I stand to clear the plates. "Dessert?"

"Not yet. I'm too full." She follows me to the kitchen, helping put all the dishes in the sink. "Can we just ... sit and talk for a while?"

"Of course."

We settle on the couch, Anna kicking off her heels and

tucking her feet under her. The living room is dim, lit only by a few candles and the city lights through the window.

"Thank you for tonight," she says softly. "This is the nicest Valentine's Day I've had in ... well, a really long time."

"Me too." I'm grateful that my relationship with Alyssa was relatively short-lived and didn't taint any of my Valentine's memories, because this is the first one I've actually had with someone I'm dating. And I want to remember how special this is. How special she is. I shift to face her better. "Anna, can I tell you something?"

She nods, watching me with those golden brown eyes that seem to see right through me.

"I know we're taking things slow, and I respect that. But I need you to know — I'm not playing games here. I won't hurt you." I take her hand, threading our fingers together. "Whatever happened before, whoever made you cautious ... I'm not him."

Her breath catches. "Matt ..."

"You don't have to tell me about it. Not until you're ready. I just wanted you to know that I'm serious about this. About us." I swallow hard, realizing how true it is. How much she's gotten under my skin already. How much I hope that isn't a huge mistake.

She's quiet for a long moment, and I can practically see her weighing something in her mind. Then she shifts closer, her free hand coming up to rest on my chest. Tingles erupt from where her hand rests.

"I believe you," she whispers. Then, even softer: "Kiss me?"

Warmth spreads through me at her request, but I hold back, not wanting our first kiss to be as forceful as my desire for her is right now. Instead, I cup her face gently, giving her time to change her mind. When she doesn't, I lean in slowly, pressing my lips to hers. The kiss is soft, tentative at first, despite the desire I've had building for her. At that thought, I feel her hand fist in my shirt and —

The vision slips through the sensation of our kiss.

Dark. Terror. Running. A face I recognize, but it's choppy, like a badly edited film. Flashes of fear, a date gone wrong.

Then it cuts off abruptly, leaving me disoriented. I must have pulled back, because Anna's looking at me with concern.

"Are you okay?"

"Yeah, I ..." I shake my head, trying to clear it. I wasn't trying to read her ... so that must have been all her. "Sorry. You just ... you take my breath away." I stroke her face, unsure why the vision was so strange. Why she was thinking of something like that ... when I just told her I won't hurt her.

And then it hits me — she was remembering whoever *did*.

Fuck. Someone ... someone she was dating? Literally *hurt* her. The realization hits me like a freight train.

She smiles, apparently buying the excuse, and leans in to kiss me again. I pull myself together so this time I'm ready for it, but the vision still overwhelms me.

Clearer now. A restaurant. Anna across from a man I recognize with stunning clarity — the man from the interview two years ago. Ezra Martin. She's uncomfortable, trying to leave. He's insistent. Flash forward — she's in danger, real danger, running, captured, and then —

I break away, my heart hammering. It can't be. The odds are astronomical. But I'd know that face anywhere. I turned him in after all.

I ... saved her?

His next victim. The one he had started to itch for. It was going to be Anna.

"Matt?" She touches my face. "What's wrong?"

"I ..." How do I even process this? Is it a coincidence that CJ set us up? Or is this fate playing its hand?

My stomach turns because I already know the answer. This is exactly the kind of thing CJ would See. "Anna, your past. The thing that made you stop dating ..."

Her whole body goes rigid. "Why would you bring that up right now?"

I take a deep breath. "I'm not trying to pry, I just —"

"Don't. I ... I can't." She's already standing, reaching for her shoes. "I should go."

Shit. I *knew* she was thinking about it, remembering the person she couldn't trust. While trying to trust me. And I had to say something. I had to push. *Fuck.*

"Anna, wait. Please. I'm sorry, I didn't mean to —"

"This was a mistake." She doesn't look at me as she slips on her heels. "I thought I was ready, but clearly I'm not."

"Anna —"

"Thank you for dinner," she says formally, like we're strangers. "I'll see myself out."

And then she's gone, leaving me standing in my living room with the ghost of her kiss on my lips and the weight of what I now know crushing my chest.

"Shit!" I growl. I sink onto the couch, head in my hands.

The woman I'm falling for is the same woman whose life I saved two years ago. The vision that haunted me for months, that drove me to risk exposure by going to the police — it was all leading to this moment.

CJ knew. She had to have known. That's why she set us up.

But now Anna's gone, and I don't know how to fix this. How do I tell her I know what happened to her? That I'm the reason she's alive? That maybe we were always meant to find each other?

How do I tell her any of that without revealing what I can do?

The candles flicker in the empty room, and I've never felt more alone. I was so wrapped up in the revelation that I pushed too hard, too fast.

And now I might have lost her before we really even began.

I clean everything up, tossing the flowers into the compost bin. The dark petals scatter ominously, and I slam the lid closed. The haphazard pile of crushed roses and errant petals feels like a pretty suitable metaphor for how the evening ended. Something beautiful that I ruined.

I head up to my room, stripping down to my boxers and climbing into bed. I lay there for a long time, staring at the ceiling, cursing my idiocy, until my phone buzzes. For a moment, hope flares — maybe it's Anna. But it's only CJ.

How did tonight go?

I stare at the message for a long moment before typing back.

We need to talk tomorrow.

That bad?

It's complicated.

Call me?

I sigh. I can't. I'm only beginning to really process this. I need to think.

Tomorrow, CJ, please.

It's my inability to talk about it right now that makes me realize how hard I'm falling for Anna. Because I hate that I hurt her. I hate that I scared her. I hate that she's not here, in my arms.

I set the phone aside. The flowers. The dinner. The dessert she brought that's still sitting in the kitchen. All the effort to make tonight perfect, and I ruined it by pushing too hard.

But even worse than that is the knowledge sitting heavy in my chest. Anna was supposed to have died two years ago. But somehow I saved her before I even knew her. And now she's here, in my life, making me feel things I haven't felt in years.

If that's not fate, I don't know what is.

But fate doesn't mean much if she won't let me in. If she can't trust me enough to share her pain. If I can't be worthy of her trust.

I turn off the lamp on the nightstand, letting darkness fill the room. Tomorrow I'll talk to CJ, figure out what she knows. But tonight, I'm alone with the truth and the memory of Anna's terrified face in that vision.

The same face that looked at me with such trust just moments before I ruined everything.

———

I barely sleep, and by seven a.m. I'm knocking on CJ and Drew's apartment door. Drew answers, looking annoyed.

"It's Monday morning," he grumbles. "And early."

"Sorry, man, I need to talk to CJ."

"It couldn't wait until you guys were at work?" he grouses. But he steps aside, not waiting for me to answer as he gestures for me to enter. "She's in the shower. I'll let her know you're here."

I nod and take a seat on the sofa.

A few minutes later, CJ emerges dressed, with wet curls hanging heavily around her concerned face.

"Matt," CJ says, her brows drawn. "What's up? Everything okay?"

I shake my head. "I told you we needed to talk."

She sits down next to me. "The date?" she asks. I nod, and she grimaces. "That bad, huh?"

I take a deep breath. "I need to tell you something. About Anna. About what I Saw."

"Matt —"

"Just listen. Please." I run my hands through my hair. "We kissed last night. And … I had a vision. I swear I wasn't even trying to this time. But … it was choppy, weird, not like anything I've experienced before. But I saw enough."

CJ puts a hand on my knee. "What did you see?"

"The killer I turned in two years ago …" I meet her eyes. "Anna was his next target, CJ. She's the woman I saved."

CJ's face goes carefully neutral, which tells me everything I need to know.

"You knew," I say flatly. "When you set us up, you knew."

"I didn't know that specifically," she says quietly. "I swear, Matt. I didn't know she was connected to that case."

"But you Saw something when we were talking at Sunday dinner. I know that look you got. I let it go because I figured if it had anything to do with me, you'd tell me. But apparently I was wrong."

She sighs, leaning back into the cushions. "I Saw you two … together."

"Together? Like … how?"

She shrugs. "Together. A couple. That's all I'm telling you."

"CJ —"

"No." Her voice is firm. "I've already interfered enough by setting you up. The rest has to happen naturally."

"Naturally?" I laugh bitterly. "There's nothing natural about any of this. The woman I'm falling for is only alive because of a vision I had two years ago. That's not natural, that's —"

"Fate," CJ finishes quietly. "And you've always believed in fate, Matt."

I slump back next to her, resting my head on her shoulder. "She ran. I asked her about it, and she just … shut down completely and left."

"Of course she did." Once again, CJ's voice has that edge

that means I'm about to get lectured. "Matt, what did you think would happen? She's clearly been through trauma, and you had to go there. Even I didn't guess it was that bad."

"I know why she was being cautious now. I understand —"

"Do you? Because from where I'm sitting, it looks like you got information she wasn't ready to share and immediately tried to use it to get more out of her."

"That's not what I was doing."

"Wasn't it?" She leans forward. "You couldn't read her the normal way, so the second you got something, you pounced. Even though you promised me you'd let her open up in her own time."

The truth of it stings. "I just ... when I realized who she was, what she'd been through ... I wanted her to know she could trust me. That she was safe with me."

"By immediately bringing up the thing she's clearly not ready to talk about?" CJ shakes her head. "That's not how trust works, Matt."

"I know. God, I know. I fucked up." I drop my head into my hands. "How do I fix this?"

"That depends. Do you really want to?"

I look up sharply. "Of course I do."

"Then you need to decide what's more important — your need to know everything, to be in control, or actually building something real with Anna."

"It's not about control —"

"Isn't it? You've spent your whole adult life using your ability to stay one step ahead, to protect yourself from getting hurt. But Anna blocks that somehow, and it scares you. Probably because it reminds you of how Alyssa played you."

Ouch. Boy, my sister really knows how to one-two punch you with the truth. And I want to deny it, but she's right. She's always right about this stuff, as much as I hate to admit it.

"So what do I do?" I ask quietly.

"Whatever it takes," CJ says simply. "If she's really the woman who you saved, then maybe that means something. That you're meant to be in each other's lives. Hell, we've *both* Seen it now. But that will not happen if you keep pushing her away by demanding more than she's ready to give."

"I don't even know if she'll talk to me again."

"Then you'd better figure out how to fix that." She covers my hand with hers and gives me a reassuring squeeze. "Matt, I've Seen you two together. That future is possible, but only if you stop trying to control everything."

"What else did you See?" I ask, desperate for something to hold on to.

"Nothing I'm going to tell you, so quit trying to pry it out of me. You can't control what I share either, Matt. But moreover, this is your path to walk." She pauses. "Though I will say this — Anna's worth fighting for. She's honest and loyal and one of the least judgmental people I've ever met. And she needs someone who'll be patient with her, who'll let her heal in her own time."

"I want to be that person," I admit, to myself as much as to my sister.

"Then prove it. With actions, not words."

I nod slowly. "You're right. You're always right."

"I know." She gives me a sad, sisterly look. "For what it's worth, I'm sorry. About Alyssa. About all the other times you've been hurt. But don't let that fear cost you something real."

I sigh heavily. "When did you get so wise?"

"When I stopped running from *my* fate," she says simply. "Now go. Figure out how to fix this."

"Right now?"

CJ huffs a dry laugh. "No, we have to get to work right now, dummy. And maybe you should give Anna a little space to calm down."

I nod, standing to leave, then pause. "CJ? Do you think she'll forgive me?"

"I mean … only Anna can answer that," she replies slowly. "For what it's worth, I think she probably wants to. But you have to give her a reason to."

I nod and head for the door, my mind already racing. Flowers won't fix this. Neither will grand gestures or fancy dinners.

What Anna needs is exactly what I promised her — patience, understanding, and the space to trust me on her own terms.

The question is whether I've already ruined my chance to give her that.

CHAPTER ELEVEN

ANNA

I've been staring at the same page of my book for twenty minutes, the words blurring together as my mind replays last night over and over. The beautiful roses. The perfect dinner. The candlelight. The way Matt looked at me like I was the only person in the world.

And then how I ruined it all by running away like a scared rabbit.

"Shit," I mutter, tossing the book aside and flopping back on my bed.

The thing is, I know I overreacted. Matt wasn't even crossing any lines — he just mentioned my past, acknowledged that something had happened. It was considerate, actually. Letting me know he understood.

But the timing ...

I sit up, frowning. Why did he bring it up right then? Right after our kiss, when I'd been remembering —

No. That's crazy. There's no way he could have known

what I was thinking about. It was just unfortunate timing. A coincidence.

My phone buzzes on the nightstand, and my heart jumps when I see Matt's name.

I'm so sorry about last night. I shouldn't have pushed for information you weren't ready to share. I don't know what I was thinking. I promised you we'd go at your pace, and I broke that promise. I understand if you don't want to see me anymore, but I hope you'll give me another chance.

I read it three times, my chest tight with conflicting emotions. Part of me wants to protect myself, to stay safe behind the walls I've built. But the bigger part — the part that's been waking up since I met Matt — knows I can't keep running forever.

I type back before I can second-guess myself.

I may have overreacted. You weren't really pushing, It's just complicated.

His response is immediate.

You didn't overreact. You have every right to your boundaries. I should have respected them better.

God, why does he have to be so understanding? It would be easier if he was a jerk.

I don't want to stop seeing you.

Are you sure? Because I meant what I said — we go at your pace. Whatever that looks like.

I take a deep breath, thinking about his kiss, about how right it felt before my past came crashing in.

I'm sure. I just had trouble staying in the moment. Letting go of my issues while we were ... you know.

I understand.

Maybe we just need more practice?

There's a pause before his next text, and I can almost see him trying to figure out how to respond.

Practice sounds good. But are you really sure? I don't want you to feel pressured.

I'm sure. I need to get past this, Matt. I WANT to get past this. With you.

Okay. How about dinner tomorrow? Something casual. No pressure.

I'd like that.

We make plans for takeout and a movie at his place, and I set my phone down feeling lighter than I have all day. Maybe I can do this. Maybe I'm finally ready to let someone in.

———

Tuesday night, we barely make it through the first action scene of the movie before we're kissing on his couch. It's easier this time — I stay present, focused on the feel of his lips, the way his hand tangles in my hair. When memories try to intrude, I push them away, anchoring myself to this moment, this man who's being so patient with me.

"You okay?" he murmurs against my lips when I shift closer.

"More than okay," I assure him, and I mean it.

We spend the rest of the movie like teenagers, making out during all the dialogue and only coming up for air during action sequences. It feels good. Normal. Like maybe I'm finally breaking free from the shadow that's followed me for two years. Kissing Matt makes me feel alive. Desired. And so turned on it physically hurts.

Thursday is even better. Matt takes me to a ping-pong social club, which sounds weird but turns out to be ridiculously fun. We're both so much worse than our opponents, and end up laughing so hard we can barely hit the ball. Other couples rotate through to play against us, and we lose spectacularly every time, even though Matt's not half bad. Probably because I'm utterly hopeless.

"I think we need more practice at this too," Matt says after our fifth straight loss.

"Practice sounds good," I agree, then blush when I realize what I might have implied, since we're basically repeating what we'd said about kissing. Which we've been practicing *plenty*.

His eyes darken, but he just grins. "Good thing I'm a patient teacher."

When he drops me off, we make out in his car like teenagers again. I'm the one who deepens the kiss this time, my hands fisting in his shirt as I pull him closer. The center console is digging into my ribs, but I don't care.

"Anna," he breathes when we finally break apart. "You're killing me here."

"Good," I say, surprising myself with my boldness. "It's only fair, considering what you do to me."

He groans and kisses me again, and I lose track of time until someone walks by and we remember we're parked on a public street.

"Friday?" he asks. "Your family dinner?"

"If you're brave enough to face them again."

He smirks. "Delicious food and a delicious woman?" He runs his nose down the column of my throat, causing me to shudder. "Always," he murmurs against my skin.

It takes a while longer to disentangle myself for the last time. And even longer to fall asleep that night, since I can't stop imagining his mouth on other parts of me.

———

Friday dinner is even more chaotic than last week. Francesca spends half the meal discussing wedding plans while Nonna grills Matt about his family's medical history. When I chastise her, she simply says, "You need to know these things before you have babies!" I facepalm hard at how many leaps and bounds ahead of where we are that is, but Matt handles it with grace. He handles it *all* with grace, even when Lucia "accidentally" mentions my high school boyfriend who turned out to be gay.

"At least you helped him find himself," Matt offers, which makes everyone laugh.

"See?" Mom says. "He gets it. Anna paves the way for everyone else's happiness. Now it's her turn." She winks at Matt, and I want to crawl under the table, but he just reaches over and squeezes my hand reassuringly. And surprisingly, it works.

When dinner ends and he drives me home, I find myself not wanting the night to end. Wanting to be closer to him. I realize that his expert handling of my family is a huge turn-on.

"Do you ..." I take a breath. "Do you want to come up? For a drink ... or something?"

Matt studies my face carefully. "Are you sure?"

I smile faintly at the question that he seems to ask so frequently. The very question that tells me I can trust him. I *do* trust him.

"Yes." And I am. I'm tired of being afraid, tired of letting the past control my present. "I'm sure."

My apartment is small even if it's cozy, and suddenly I'm nervous having him in my space. His isn't that much bigger, but it's so much more ... well, grown up than mine.

"Make yourself comfortable," I offer.

"That won't be hard. I already feel at home," he assures me.

I blush and turn away. "What would you like to drink?" I head toward the kitchen, twisting my fingers together nervously.

"Anna." He catches my hand before I can get far. "You're nervous." He squeezes my hand, pulling me back toward him. His eyes search mine. "We don't have to do anything you're not ready for," he reminds me.

The sincerity in his tone unravels the anxiety inside me. He really is too good to be true.

"Thank you," I say, letting him pull me into his embrace. I reach up and kiss him softly. "And I know. That's why I trust you."

He cocks an eyebrow. "You do?"

I nod slowly. "I do."

His pupils dilate, and he leans in. "That means … a lot," he murmurs before capturing my lips with his.

And this kiss … it's different. In the best way. It's heat and urgency and raw passion. My whole body responds, curling against his as his hands run down my back and under my shirt. His hands on my bare skin send a jolt through me, and I gasp into his mouth.

He pulls away abruptly with a stunned look on his face. "You felt that?"

"Yes. And I want to feel so much more," I respond, looking daringly into his eyes as I pull him toward my overstuffed fuchsia couch.

The backs of my knees hit the edge of the cushions and I pull him down with me. Our lips meet again, fervently, as Matt's hand slides up my bare thigh and little jolts shoot up my leg, mini episodes of the same feeling as before, this time accompanied by an emotion emanating from Matt that I can't place. It's heady. But it's more than desire. More than the fire in my blood. More than the connection between us.

The idea dances away as Matt leans me back into the cushions, settling over me, a leg between my thighs. I arch into him, my breasts pressing against his chest. His mouth dips to my neck, and the jolts zing from where he touches straight to my core.

God, I forgot how good this feels.

And when his hand slides under my shirt again, I don't tense up. I squeeze his hips with my legs in encouragement. As he flicks open the clasp of my bra, I sigh in anticipation.

As his fingers work under the cups and find my nipples, I cry out with pleasure.

Pleasure — how I missed it. This. Him. As if *he's* what I'd been missing all this time.

"You're unbelievable," he whispers.

My eyes open — when they closed, I don't know — to find him staring down at me with dark eyes, his tongue darting over his lips.

"Can I?" he asks, tugging at the hem of my shirt.

I grin and lift my torso so he can remove it. He takes my bra with it, too, and the cool air hits my heated skin, causing my nipples to pucker and ache with need.

Matt sucks in a breath and leans in. His tongue flicks out, teasing one of the hard peaks. I bite my lip and whimper at the sensation. He blows a cool breath over my breast and then dives on it, sucking hard and sharp.

"Oh my god," I breathe as the pleasant pain makes me writhe under him.

And when he does it to the other, I almost lose it, my hands threading into his thick, dark hair.

"You like that?" he asks in a low voice as he slides a hand over my skirt.

I nod, both in answer and encouragement, tilting my hips up. Now that he's reminded me I can feel this way, I want more.

"Say it, Anna," he goads me.

I whimper again at his husky tone. "Yes, I like it. I want more, Matt. Now."

He grins and lets his hand slip under my skirt, over the

inside of my thigh, his thumb tracing the silky fabric between my legs.

"Don't be such a tease," I groan. "Touch me."

He kisses me gently. "Anything for you." He slips a finger into the damp curls under the fabric, and my hips buck upward. And suddenly he's pulled back. I almost cry in frustration until I realize he's removing my panties.

I freeze, unsure of his intentions. Because as much as I want to explore each other, I'm not ready for sex yet.

He stops and holds up his hands, my panties straddling my thighs. "I just want to go down on you," he clarifies. "If that's okay." He says it softly, pleadingly, like he needs it as much as I do.

I let out a relieved laugh. "That is so much more than *okay*," I assure him. And now that I know what he plans to do, I wiggle out of my skirt *and* panties, flinging them onto the coffee table.

"Good," he murmurs, getting an eyeful of me. "Because holy fucking shit, Anna, you are beyond gorgeous." His hands skim up my ankles, over my knees, then cup under them, parting my legs. "And I'm going to enjoy the hell out of this."

He dips between my legs, his mouth meeting my dripping sex with an enthusiasm that catches me off guard. His tongue sweeps from top to bottom and then back up, swirling around my clit in a way that instantly has heat searing through my veins, the beginnings of an orgasm already tightening my core.

"Matt ... oh ... I —" I grasp for words as he absolutely goes to town. All coherent thought skitters out of my mind as he uses his tongue, then fingers, then both, all while watching my reactions.

His dark eyes on me as he adjusts his swirling, licking, and thrusting is a level of intimacy I'm not sure I even knew existed.

He reaches up as his fingers work inside me and pinches each of my nipples in turn. Along with the earnest look on his face, it's too much. I throw my head back and come hard.

As I descend, his strokes soften, his other hand gently grazing down my stomach and hip. He withdraws and slides over me, his mouth capturing mine gently. I can taste myself on him, and it sends a shiver through me. I wrap myself around him … only to realize he isn't missing even a single article of clothing, while I'm completely naked.

And because I can feel his hard length against my core through his clothes, I know it's not that he doesn't want to be.

Somehow, I'm fully at his mercy, and he's made me feel nothing but totally in control and worshipped.

I reach down between us, stroking him over his pants.

"You don't have to do that," he says, though he pushes into my palm and groans against my neck.

"I know." And yet, I do it again.

"Fuck, Anna, that feels so good …" he says. He pulls back and looks at me. "But I think we should stop. I … I don't want to push this too far, too fast."

I bite my lip as tears sting the backs of my eyes. He's right. If I keep at this, we'll end up having sex. And that would be more than I could handle right now. Matt is so much more than I thought he was, but I'm still not ready for that level of trust and intimacy.

"You're right," I concede. "But I *will* pay you back for that. Soon."

He smirks and kisses me gently. "I look forward to it."

He sits up and helps me back upright. I slip my clothes back on and settle against his chest, his arms encircling me.

We talk for a while, continuing the intimacy with laughter over the outrageous things my family said tonight. He tells me stories about his aunt and uncle, and CJ, of course, while they were growing up. And while we didn't get fully physically intimate, I can't imagine being emotionally closer to someone that I am with him tonight.

I can't help but feel like what we've done on this couch, physical and otherwise, is monumental. Every touch, every kiss, every form of intimacy we've shared is a victory over the fear that's held me captive for so long.

"It's getting late. And while I'd love to do this all night, I know you have to work tomorrow," Matt murmurs against my hair.

I nod reluctantly. "I do. But thank you … for everything," I say, looking up into his dark eyes.

Matt grins so wide his eyes crinkle at the corners. It's an expression I haven't seen on him before. But I can feel the unadulterated joy it came from. "I should thank you. This was — and I swear, this is the God's honest truth — one of the best nights of my life, Anna." He shakes his head, chuckling as if he himself can't believe it.

I lean in and smile against his lips as I kiss him. "I believe you," I assure him. "It was for me too." And I realize it's true. Even though there was nothing earth-shattering that happened, somehow it is. We both changed our patterns tonight. We both became vulnerable in ways that were difficult for us. And it feels *good*.

It takes a good deal more kissing before we make it all the way to the door and through our final goodnights.

While I'm getting ready for bed, I catch sight of myself in the mirror. My lips are swollen, my hair's a mess, and I'm grinning like an idiot.

I'm high on Matt. On us. And on the fact that I pushed through my fear.

That's why this night was so special. Because I broke through to the other side of fear, and found everything I didn't know I was looking for.

Matt, yes, perhaps. But more importantly, myself. The adventurous, daring person I used to be before that one night changed my life. And I can feel the healing that's begun. And the hope that's been reborn alongside it.

———

Saturday morning, I practically float out of the door on my walk to work. Lunch prep will already be in full swing, and even though Saturday afternoons have nothing on the Sunday after-church lunch crowd, I know it's going to be nonstop. But nothing can dampen my mood today. I'm humming as I approach the restaurant, replaying last night in my mind.

The walk to the restaurant's employee entrance takes me

through an alley that's usually empty this time of day. But halfway through, my high is abruptly cut off by the strong feeling that someone is watching me. The hair on the back of my neck stands up and goosebumps erupt over my skin, even under the thick raincoat I'm wearing. I glance over my shoulder, sure someone's behind me, but the alley's empty. A cold wind off the bay roars through the narrow space and I realize it was just the weather.

"Get it together, Martella," I mutter, laughing at myself as I push through the restaurant's back door into the familiar chaos of the kitchen.

"Well, well," Drew says, looking up from his prep station. "Someone looks happy today."

I beam widely, my brief paranoia — surely a remnant of the old Anna — falling away as I'm reminded of how happy I actually am.

"It's a beautiful day," I say innocently.

"It's fifty-five, cloudy, and windy as fuck. I'd hardly call that 'beautiful.'" He gives me an appraising smirk. "Your unusually perky positivity wouldn't have anything to do with a certain Roberts twin, would it?"

I try to school my expression but fail miserably, grinning like an idiot again. "Maybe."

Drew laughs, shaking his head. "I know that look. I've had that look. The Roberts twins are clearly dangerous that way."

"CJ's really got you wrapped around her finger, doesn't she?" I tease.

"Completely." He says it without shame, then his

expression shifts back to business. "Now stop mooning and get to work. Becky's a mess today. Table six has been waiting ten minutes for their coffee."

"Yes, chef," I say with a mock salute.

"Smart ass," he mutters, but he's fighting a smirk.

I throw on my apron and grab the coffee pot, then head out to the dining room, still riding high on my good mood. Drew may be happier since he moved in with CJ, but he's still a grump at heart. I guess my happiness hasn't changed my sassiness either. So even if some things are the same, things are changing. *I'm* changing.

And for the first time in a long time, I'm okay with that. I'm okay with all of it — Drew's Jekyll and Hyde act, learning how to date again, letting myself fall for someone … the feeling that maybe my life is finally getting back on track. That I'm finally *letting* my life get back on track, even if it's scary. There's nothing worse than standing in your own way, and I know I've been doing too much of that.

But I've got a good job, great friends, an overbearing but loving family, and a man who makes me feel things I thought I'd never feel again.

I have nothing to be afraid of anymore.

CHAPTER TWELVE

MATT

"You're disgustingly happy," CJ observes from my office doorway on Tuesday morning. "It's weird."

I look up from my computer, unable to suppress my grin. "Can't a guy be in a good mood?"

"Not you. Not like this." She comes in and perches on the edge of my desk. "This is about Anna, isn't it? How are things going?"

"Good. Fantastic, actually." I lean back in my chair, thinking about the past week. Movie night turned make-out session. Ping -pong and laughter. Friday dinner with her family. And then Friday night …

"Okay, now you're being gross. Stop thinking whatever you're thinking."

"I wasn't —"

"You were. That's your sex face."

"I don't have a sex face."

"You absolutely have a sex face, and it has scarred me

since we were eighteen." She shudders dramatically. "But seriously, I'm happy for you. Both of you."

"Thanks." I mean it. After our talk last week, I've been trying to follow CJ's advice — letting Anna set the pace, not pushing for information she's not ready to share. And it's working. Better than working. I can't remember ever feeling this way about someone. This connected, this … happy.

My phone buzzes on my desk, showing an unknown number. I almost ignore it, but something makes me answer.

"Matt Roberts."

"Mr. Roberts, this is Detective Worthington with the SFPD. We spoke a couple of years ago regarding the Ezra Martin case."

My blood runs cold. CJ must see something in my face because she straightens, concern replacing her teasing expression.

"I remember," I say carefully.

"I was hoping you could come down to the station this afternoon. There are some follow-up questions we need to ask."

"About what?"

"I'd prefer to discuss it in person. Are you available?"

Every instinct screams that this is bad. "I can be there in an hour."

"Perfect. Just ask for me at the front desk."

I hang up and meet CJ's worried gaze.

"What was that about?" she asks.

"The police. About the case from two years ago." I'm already standing, grabbing my jacket. "I need to go."

"To meet the police? Right now?"

I grimace. "Apparently."

"Matt, wait. Maybe you should call a lawyer first."

"And tell them what?" I ask pointedly. CJ presses her lips together but doesn't respond, clearly having gotten my point. I wave a hand. "I've done nothing wrong. I'm sure it'll be fine." But even as I say it, I wonder. What could they need after all this time?

The police station smells exactly like I remember — terrible coffee, industrial cleaner, and something indefinably bureaucratic. Detective Worthington meets me in the lobby, looking older and more tired than he did two years ago. He's accompanied by a younger detective, who eyes me with barely concealed suspicion.

"Mr. Roberts, thank you for coming. This is Detective Liu. If you'll follow us?"

They lead me to a small interview room, and alarm bells start ringing in my head. This isn't a casual follow-up. This is an interrogation room.

"Have a seat," Detective Worthington says, gesturing to the metal chair across from them.

I sit, keeping my expression neutral. "What's this about?"

Worthington leans forward. "Tell us again how you knew Ezra Martin."

"He showed up for an interview at my company," I respond.

"And were you the one interviewing him?" he presses.

"I was there to support the main interviewer, but yes, I took part in his interview." I pause, anxiety churning in my gut. "Is there a reason you're asking about this now?" I counter. "It's been two years."

Worthington and Detective Liu exchange a look.

"Did Martin ever mention having a partner?" Liu asks. "An accomplice?"

My pulse spikes. "No. Why are you asking?" I repeat.

"We've had some new information come to light," Liu says. "We need to know if there's anything you didn't mention the first time. Anything at all."

"I told you everything I knew," I insist. "After the interview he just … told me what he'd done."

"And a serial killer just confessed to you, some guy he'd never met before," Liu says, skepticism dripping from every word.

"This feels an awful lot like an interrogation," I say, sitting back. "Am I under arrest?"

"No," Worthington says quickly. "We're just trying to understand —"

"Then am I free to go?"

Another look between them. Liu's jaw tightens, but Worthington nods. "Yes, you're free to go."

I stand, heading for the door on legs that feel unsteady. I need to get out of here, need to think —

"Mr. Roberts."

I turn to find a different detective standing just outside the room. He's older, with salt-and-pepper hair and bright blue, intelligent eyes.

"That was smart," he says quietly. "Not saying more than necessary."

"I'm sorry?" I hold his gaze, trying to figure out if he's the next wave of interrogation, trying to catch me off guard.

"Detective Ray Sullivan." He extends his hand.

"I'm sorry, but I don't shake hands," I say automatically.

He huffs an amused laugh. "Me neither, kid, I was just going to give you this." He lifts his hand to show me he was holding a business card. After a moment's hesitation, I take it.

"If anyone calls you in again," Sullivan says, "let me know first. My cell's on the back."

My brows bunch together. "Why would they call me in again?"

Sullivan's expression is carefully neutral. "Just in case. Have a good day, Mr. Roberts."

He walks away, leaving me standing in the hallway with his card and a growing sense of confusion … and dread.

Back home, I fire up my laptop and start digging. It doesn't take long to find what I'm looking for, and when I do, my stomach drops.

Ezra Martin is dead. Apparent suicide in prison a few months ago. The article is brief, clinical, but the timing …

I search for recent murders in the Bay Area, and there it is. A woman was found dead last week with multiple stab wounds in her apartment. The details are sparse — though I know the police always withhold information to weed out false confessions — but the sparse details match what I Saw two years ago. The positioning, use of a knife, even the victim profile.

"Fuck." I run my hands through my hair, pieces clicking together.

Someone is picking up where Ezra Martin left off. Which can only mean someone else knew what he was doing, and was likely in on it.

The killer had an accomplice. That's why they called me in, why they asked that specific question. With Martin dead, someone else is carrying on his work, and the police ...

Holy shit.

They think it might be me.

Of course they do.

I would too, but ... fuck.

My phone rings, Anna's name lighting up the screen. For a second, I consider not answering. But that would only worry her.

"Hey, beautiful." It's a struggle to keep my tone normal. Thankfully, I've had plenty of practice at pretending the shit hasn't completely hit the fan, thanks to my job. And my ability.

"Hey yourself. I just got off work. Want to grab dinner?" Her voice is bright and soothing, and all I want to do is say yes.

But I can't. It's one thing to pretend over the phone. I know I wouldn't be able to in person.

"I ..." I close my eyes. Should I just tell her? *How* would I tell her? How would I explain that the man who tried to kill her might have had a partner? That the police think I might be involved? That I was even ever involved in the first place? "Rain check? I'm not feeling great."

"Oh no, are you sick? I can bring you soup."

I sigh. Of course, she would offer that. My chest aches. "No, no. Just tired. Long day at work."

"Okay." She sounds disappointed but not suspicious. "Feel better. Text me later?"

"I will," I promise.

I hang up and stare at the articles on my screen. If there's another killer out there, someone who knew Martin's methods, his preferences, his victims ...

That also means that Anna could be in danger again.

Unfortunately, this time I can't go to the police. They clearly already suspect me, so anything I say will only make it worse. Especially that I'm now dating his last intended victim. And I sure as hell can't explain how I really knew about Martin without exposing what CJ and I can do.

I'm trapped. And somewhere out there, a killer is hunting again.

My phone buzzes with a text from CJ.

I'm dying to hear what happened with the police today.

I stare at the message for a long moment before typing back.

Not over text. I'll come over before work tomorrow.

Matt, you're scaring me.

Tomorrow, CJ.

It's tempting to go over tonight, but I still feel like there's something missing.

I set the phone aside and go back to the articles, reading

everything I can find. The new victim was early twenties, blonde, small build. Just like the women in my vision two years ago.

Just like Anna.

And she wasn't the only one. I find two other similar articles, with similar murders, over the last few months. The killer had a type, and now his partner is following the same pattern. Which means it's possible that he plans to finish what Martin couldn't. Possibly including Anna.

I think about Anna's laugh, her smile, the way she feels in my arms. The way she makes *me* feel … and how I'm already a better man because of her. I can't lose her now. I can't stand the idea that she might be in danger. That someone might be after her … again, after all she's already been through.

But how do I protect her from a threat she doesn't even know exists? How do I keep her safe without telling her the truth about what I can do?

I remember when CJ was in this position with Drew. How little sympathy I had for her, or him. God, I was such an asshole.

I close my laptop and head to bed. Not to sleep. I know that won't happen tonight. But I need to lie down and think all this through. And then I need to get up tomorrow morning, apologize to my sister for not understanding how tough a decision this is, and figure out what we're going to do about it. Because I'm not giving Anna up without a fight.

Not that stopping a killer is going to be easy … especially not when the police think I might be one.

CHAPTER THIRTEEN

CJ

Matt shows up at our apartment at six-thirty Wednesday morning, looking like he hasn't slept at all. Drew's still asleep, which is probably for the best given the state my brother's in.

"Coffee?" I offer, already knowing the answer.

"Please." He slumps onto our couch while I pour two mugs. When I hand him his, he wraps both hands around it like he's trying to absorb its warmth. "CJ, I'm sorry."

"For what?"

"For not understanding. When you had that vision about Drew, when you were trying to decide whether to tell him about your vision ... I was such an ass about it."

I sink into the chair across from him. "Matt, what's going on?"

He takes a shuddering breath and tells me everything — the police interrogation, Martin's suicide, the multiple new murders that fit the same pattern. By the time he finishes, my coffee's gone cold.

"They think you're involved," I say, the pieces clicking together. "That's why they called you in."

"And there's another killer out there. Martin's partner." His eyes meet mine, haunted. "Anna could be in danger."

"We don't know that," I point out, even as my stomach twists. "Just because there's another victim doesn't mean they'll go after Anna specifically."

"Same victim profile. Same MO. What if they're trying to finish what Martin started?"

I set down my mug, knowing what he's going to ask before he says it. "Matt ..."

"I need to know if she's in danger. There's only one way to find out for sure."

I sigh heavily. I should've seen this coming. Oh, the irony. "You want me to read her."

"I know it's not ideal, doing it without her permission, but —"

I hold up a hand. "I'll do it." The words come out before I can second-guess them. Because he's right. If Anna's life is at stake, my discomfort about invading her privacy doesn't matter. I let out another sigh. "I'll text her, see if she wants to have dinner tonight."

Relief washes over his face. "Thank you. I know this isn't easy."

"It's Anna. Of course I'll help." I pull out my phone. "You should probably work late. Give us a reason to meet without you."

He nods, understanding immediately. "I'll text her later about having to stay at the office. Which I probably should do anyway, given that I was out all yesterday afternoon."

I send Anna a quick message asking if she's free for dinner. Her response comes fifteen minutes later, when Matt's already gone.

I'd love to see you! Let me check with Matt and get back to you.

I smile vaguely at the fact that they're already so coupley.

An hour passes before she texts again, when I've just gotten to work.

Matt has to work late :(So yes, I'm free! Where do you want to meet?

We settle on a Thai restaurant in the Mission, and I spend the rest of the day trying not to think about what I might See.

Anna's already at the restaurant when I arrive, nervously shredding a napkin.

"Hey," I say, sliding into the booth across from her. "Everything okay?"

"Yeah, just ..." She forces a cheery expression. "It's nothing."

"Anna."

She sighs. "I've just been overthinking while I waited for you."

I huff a laugh. "Boy, do I know how that goes. About what?"

She rolls her eyes at herself and shakes her head. "Maybe

I'm just being silly, but I can't help worrying. Is Matt pulling away? I mean, last night he canceled with some vague excuse about not feeling well, and now he's suddenly working late ..."

"Oh, honey, no." I reach across the table but stop short of taking her hand. Not yet. "Matt is absolutely crazy about you. Trust me, I've never seen him like this with anyone."

"Really?" The relief on her face is clear. Boy, she's really got it bad. Then again, so does Matt. My heart lurches for them both. For what they're about to face. Hopefully together, unlike how things went down with Drew and me.

"Really. Work has been insane lately. If you don't already know, this is how he gets — total tunnel vision when there's a crisis."

She relaxes slightly. "I can see that. He's obviously very into his job."

"Yes, he is; that's it exactly. It has nothing to do with you."

Anna is noticeably relieved and we order a bunch of dishes to share — Crispy Rolls, Pad Thai, Pork Larb, and Pa-Naeng — then fall into easier conversation. But I notice her studying me as we dive on the rolls that came out first.

"Is everything okay with you and Drew?" she asks suddenly.

I swallow a bite of crunchy, steamy, vegetably goodness. "Yeah, of course. Why?"

"I don't know. Your energy just seems ... off. And the last-minute dinner invitation ..."

I force a laugh. "Honestly? Drew's working tonight, and I

was bored. Figured, why not catch up with my friend?" I polish off the rest of my roll while she picks at hers.

"Oh." She looks embarrassed. "Sorry, I'm being weird. I guess Matt's mood has made me paranoid about everything."

"Don't apologize. I get it. I'm shacking up with someone whose moods, as you know, change with the wind. Or with however dinner service is going." I grimace, and Anna laughs, and suddenly the tension evaporates. Well, hers anyway.

The rest of the food arrives, and it finally entices Anna into eating, which continues to boost her mood. We talk through dinner — about her family, about work, about everything except what I really need to know. I decide to wait until we're saying goodbye to read her. If it's bad news, I don't want to sit through the rest of dinner knowing. Anna is way too observant to hide from.

Finally, we're standing outside the restaurant, full and each sporting a bag with half of the leftovers.

"This was nice," Anna says. "Thanks for talking me off the ledge about Matt."

"Anytime." This is it. I need to do this. "Anna, can I ask you something?"

"Sure."

"Do you see a future with Matt? I mean, I know it's only been a few weeks, but ..."

Her face softens. "Yeah. I really do. Is that crazy?"

"Not at all." I reach out and squeeze her hand. "I think you two are perfect —"

The vision hits like a sledgehammer.

Complete darkness, like the world has disappeared. Again.

An empty void I've seen twice before. Unlike the premonition of Auntie Betty's accident, this one feels just like Drew's; murder. Death. *Nothing*.

My blood turns to ice.

"CJ? You okay?"

I force myself to focus, to not let the horror show on my face. "Yeah, sorry. Just got dizzy for a second. Carb coma probably."

"We can take a walk. That always helps me," she offers.

I smile as warmly as I can considering the ice in my veins. "No, I'm … I'm good. I should get home." I pull her into a quick hug, fighting to keep my voice steady. "Text me if you need to talk about Matt stuff, okay?"

"I will." She promises, giving me a last squeeze before letting me go. "Feel better!"

I make it to my car before my hands start shaking. I drive straight to Matt's, using every technique I know to keep from completely falling apart.

He opens the door before I can knock, taking one look at my face and pulling me inside.

"What did you See?"

"Nothing." My voice cracks. "Matt, I Saw nothing."

His face drains of color. "You mean …"

I nod. "The kind of nothing that means she's going to die." The words taste like ash. Despite my horror, I let the feelings from the vision marinate the entire way here. So I add, "Soon."

"No." He sinks onto the couch, head in his hands. "No, there has to be something we can do."

I sit beside him, my own tears finally falling. I've lived this before, with Drew, but to see Anna's future go from marrying my brother to this? Devastated doesn't even cover what I'm feeling. What Matt must be feeling.

"I'm so sorry. I wanted to be wrong. I wanted to See her future with you, but there was just ... nothing."

"There has to be a way to change it. There has to be." The desperation in his voice cuts me deeply. Even though I know there's nothing I can do, I wish there were. The only thing I have to offer is encouragement.

"You're right. I changed Drew's fate, didn't I? Maybe ..." I wipe my eyes, trying to think clearly. "Maybe if you read her? You said you get fragments when you touch her. Maybe you could See something about the killer, some detail that could help identify whoever they might have been doing this with?"

He looks up, a spark of hope in his eyes. "It's worth trying. Though it's strange — you can read her easily but I can't. It's always choppy, incomplete."

"Maybe it's because of your connection to her, or how traumatic it was. Sometimes powerful emotions can interfere. And I'm pretty sure she has fears around romantic relationships that I don't think apply to our friendship," I offer.

"Maybe." He straightens, determination replacing despair. "I'll try tomorrow. I'll find a way to read her properly. There has to be something there, some clue about who's coming after her."

"What if she notices? What if she realizes something's wrong?"

"I'll be careful. But CJ ..." His voice breaks slightly. "I can't lose her. Not now. Not when I just ..." He chokes back a tortured noise.

I pull him into a hug, and we sit there in shared grief for a future that might never be. My best friend, his soulmate, the woman who survived once only to face death again.

"We'll figure this out," I whisper, even though I don't know how. "We'll save her."

Because the alternative — letting Anna die when we know it's coming — is unthinkable.

But as I hold my brother while he tries not to fall apart, one thought keeps circling through my mind: can you really cheat death twice?

CHAPTER FOURTEEN

ANNA

I'm just about to head into work on Thursday when my phone rings. The number looks vaguely familiar, but I can't place it. I let it go to voicemail. I haven't even made it a few blocks when my voicemail chimes. I look at the transcript and see the words "Detective Worthington" and "SFPD" and my stomach heaves. My anxiety goes from zero to a hundred in half a second flat, and I don't even bother listening to the fourteen-second voicemail that's probably just asking me to call him back. Which I do immediately, halting at a bus stop bench and taking a seat.

"Detective Worthington."

"This is Anna Martella. You called?"

"Ms. Martella. Thanks for returning my call so quickly. I'm not sure if you remember me, but I was the detective in charge of Ezra Martin's case."

Like I could forget him, or any of what happened. Just

hearing Ezra's name makes me break out in a cold sweat. "I remember."

"I was hoping you could come down to the station this afternoon. There's been a development we need to discuss."

"A development?" My voice comes out higher than intended. "What kind of development?"

"I'd prefer to discuss it in person. Can you be here within the hour?"

I blow out a breath. "I'm headed into work. Can it wait until tomorrow?"

"This is important, Ms. Martella. It concerns your safety."

That gets my attention, in the worst way possible. Could he have said anything that would've made my anxiety worse than that? Yes, I realize. He probably could. And will. Shit.

"Um. Okay. Yes, of course. I'll be there," I say, swallowing against the emotion choking me.

When I hang up, I have to take a few moments to compose myself before calling out of work for the day. Because I know even if this doesn't take long, I won't be in any shape to go in.

I make my excuses to Mallory, Drew's sous chef, and make the fifteen-minute walk to the police station like a zombie.

I'm only waiting a few minutes when Detective Worthington appears. He's aged a lot in the short couple of years since I saw him. Gray streaks his black hair, and he looks as grim as I feel. I can't imagine it's a profession that leads to a long life. Stress lines his face in the tense set of his jaw and the hardness of his dark eyes.

"I'm sorry to have to call you in, Ms. Martella. Please, follow me."

I nod, not sure how to respond, and let him lead me into his office. It's the same drab, depressing oak-paneled room with an industrial steel desk, littered with empty takeaway coffee cups and stacks of papers.

He gestures to the barely padded metal chair across the desk from his own.

I sit nervously on the edge as he takes his seat.

"Thank you for coming," he says. "I'll get right to the point. The killings have started again."

My heart drops into my stomach. He's still as blunt as ever. And now I feel like vomiting.

"What?"

"Three women in the past few months. Same MO as Martin's victims."

"But ..." I lean forward and grip the edge of the table. "He's dead. I read he died in prison."

"He did. Which means someone else is continuing his work." Worthington leans forward. "I need you to think carefully. During your interactions with Martin, was there anyone else? Anyone he mentioned he was close to? A friend? A family member?"

"No." I shake my head, trying to push down the rising panic. "I told you everything back then. He was a regular at the restaurant where I worked, always alone. He asked me out for drinks. We met once, and ... you know what happened."

Worthington nods, but there's something else in his expression. Something he's not saying.

"What is it?" I ask. "What aren't you telling me?"

He shifts uncomfortably. "It's clear now that he must have had an accomplice, or someone who at least knew what he'd been doing, and how he was doing it. We … have a potential suspect. In looking into this person, we discovered something you need to know."

My head spins. This is too much. First, there are more murders. Then they think they're connected. Now there's a suspect … one that apparently I need to know something about?

"What?" I ask, confused and terrified beyond belief.

"You're dating him."

His words don't compute at first. In his usual fashion, with the subtlety of an anvil, I can barely wrap my head around the first thing he said, much less this. "I'm ... what?"

"Matthew Roberts. You're in a relationship with him, correct?"

Matt is their suspect? How in the … I shake my head. What world am I living in? How is this even possible?

"Yes, but ..." My mind races, trying to make sense of everything he's so unceremoniously dumped on me. "You think *Matt* is involved? That's … that's insane. It makes no sense. What does he have to do with Ezra Martin?"

"We have our reasons for suspicion, Ms. Martella. Reasons I can't share with you."

I narrow my eyes as I study him. Do they suspect Matt simply because he's dating me? That maybe I'm the common thread here? I blink hard. No, that doesn't make sense either.

But then again, none of this does.

"Did Martin even say he had an accomplice?"

Worthington shakes his head. "Martin insisted he had acted alone. There was no evidence to suggest otherwise. But now, with these new murders ..."

"You're looking at all the angles," I finish numbly. And I guess I can see why they think the person I'm dating now might have something to do with it.

"Exactly. Ms. Martella, I'm not saying Mr. Roberts is guilty. But given the circumstances, I felt you had a right to know about our suspicions. Be cautious. With everyone." He slides a business card across the table. "That has my current cell phone number on it. Call me if you need anything. Or if you remember anything that might help."

I take the card with shaking hands. "Is that all?"

"For now. Be careful, Ms. Martella."

I walk home in a daze, my mind spinning. Matt? Connected to Ezra Martin? It doesn't make sense. But then again, neither did Martin being a killer until he tried to murder me. It has to be me. I have to be the connection that's making them suspicious of Matt. Or ... am I? This feels like a puzzle that's missing a lot of pieces.

I need answers. And maybe Matt can give them to me.

So I text him.

I need to see you as soon as possible.

His response is immediate.

Is everything okay? I can leave work.

I breathe a sigh of relief. I contemplate going to his office, but this probably isn't a conversation he'd want to have there. And apparently I shouldn't trust being alone with anyone right now.

No. I'll meet you at Tempest in 20?

Thirty seconds later I get a terse *OK,* and I head his way.

I walk into the dark pub near Matt's work twenty-two minutes later and spot Matt at a table for two beside one of the few slender windows. There's a good lunch crowd enjoying beers and greasy food, but Matt only has a soda in front of him.

He rises to greet me as I approach. The very sight of him makes my heart ache, and I let him pull me into his embrace.

"Anna, what's wrong?" he murmurs into my hair.

I pull back and look up into his face. "Maybe we should sit down."

His brows pull together, but he obliges, and we sit, leaning toward each other across the small table.

"I don't even know how to start …" I blow out a breath, still numb with shock.

Matt shakes his head. "Just say it. You're killing me here."

I chew my lip for a moment, trying to hold back the tide of questions. My brain still can't make sense of these two parts of my life suddenly colliding.

"Is it true? The police think you're connected to the Martin case?" The words spill out, and I immediately wonder if he'll even know what I'm talking about.

His face goes pale. "How did you —"

Shit. Clearly he does. I breathe slowly. "You know about

Ezra Martin," I whisper. A pained look crosses his face, but he nods. "You know … about me?"

Matt looks down into his hands, then up again. Now, there are tears in his eyes. He nods again. "I can explain —"

"Is it true that the police suspect you're … picking up where he left off?" I repeat.

He takes a deep breath. "Yes, they questioned me. And yes, I know it looks bad. But I swear to you, I had nothing to do with any of it, then or now."

"Then why do they suspect you? And don't give me a vague answer. If you want me to trust you, I need the truth."

Matt looks around the bar, then back at me. "Not here. Can we … take a walk or something? There's a park across the street."

I consider that. It's still public. And I guess I get why he wouldn't want to be overheard. So, against my better judgment, I follow him outside. We walk outside, and I lead him across the street to the small park on the corner. We take a seat on a stretch of unoccupied concrete seating surrounding the small bits of greenery under the artsy Bluemetal Trees. And I look at Matt expectantly.

He lets out a long breath. "The police questioned me because I was the one who turned Martin in two years ago."

I blink. Not that I'd been able to think much about any of this, but that's … *very* unexpected. "You ... what?"

"I interviewed him for a job back then. During the interview, he ... said things. Made comments that set off alarm bells. So I told the police."

"What are you saying? Did he tell you he liked to murder

women for fun? During a job interview?" I can hear the skepticism in my voice.

Matt runs a hand through his hair. "I was going to do this differently, but ... fuck. I know I need to put all my cards on the table, Anna. I *want* to. The thing is, not all the cards are just mine."

I'm so overwhelmed by everything I want to cry. But I close my eyes and ask, "What does that mean?"

"I need to make a call. Just ... can you give me a minute?"

I reopen my eyes to him waiting for me to acknowledge what he said. I give an exasperated wave of agreement. He pulls out his phone and steps away. I can't hear the conversation, but when he comes back, his jaw is set with determination.

"Okay. Yeah. Okay ... we're doing this," he says, clearly psyching himself up. He shakes his head, then looks up, holding my gaze. "Anna, what I'm about to tell you is going to sound crazy. But I need you to listen."

I let out a wry laugh. What the hell, why not add some more crazy to this day?

"I'm listening," I reply wearily.

Matt's chest rises and falls. "I'm ... I can ... Shit, this is harder than I thought." He clenches his hands into fists and then releases them as if he's pumping himself up to get out whatever he's trying to tell me. "I can see people's memories through touch, Anna. At the beginning of Martin's interview, I shook his hand and saw what he'd done. What he was planning to do. So I went to the police and told them he'd confessed."

And here I thought this couldn't get more … well, *more*. I stare at him, trying to wrap my brain around this, on top of everything else. "You're … psychic?"

"In a way. It's called retrocognition. I See the past."

"I … you …" I blink several times. "Why is that 'not just your cards'? Who did you just call?" The questions barely makes sense to me, but hopefully they do to him.

"I called CJ."

"CJ."

He nods but says nothing.

I pinch the bridge of my nose. "Look. On a normal day, I might be able to figure out what that means, but I'm a little overwhelmed right now, so you're going to have to tell me why CJ has …" I trail off as the pieces click. That box she gave me to give Drew last Thanksgiving that contained the rare, expensive mushrooms we didn't have enough of for dinner service. Holy. Shit. I always thought that was weird. And if Matt can see the past …

"Yes," Matt says softly, clearly seeing the wheels turning. "CJ can see the future."

"She … how … what …" I can barely form a sentence. This is getting more unbelievable by the second. Maybe I'm dead. Maybe Martin's accomplice already killed me and I'm in some whackadoo after-death fugue state.

"Look, I know how this sounds. But it's the truth. The police suspect me because I knew things only the killer should know, because I Saw them in his memories, and my story about him confessing is flimsy at best. I can't tell them the truth without sounding insane. Or becoming a permanent lab rat while dragging my sister down with me."

I look up at the glistening metal above us. This can't be real. Can it?

"You sound insane *now*," I point out. And yet, some part of me has always known that there's more to this world than what you can see. Even so, what he's talking about is … it's impossible, right?

"I can prove it." He scoots closer. "I can read you if you'll let me. But you'd have to cooperate, really focus on a specific memory."

My mouth opens and shuts several times trying to figure out what to do with this.

I should leave. I should go home and process all of this before I try to make sense of Matt's claim that he's psychic. But something in his eyes stops me. Vulnerability. Complete rawness that I've *never* seen from him. And it sways me.

"Will it hurt?" I ask.

He shakes his head, concern written all over his face. "Not at all. And we can stop anytime you want."

I take a deep breath. "Okay, let's do this." I offer my hands, palms up.

He wraps his large hands around mine and holds them between us. "Close your eyes. Think about Martin. About what happened that night."

Of all the memories to ask me to relive … but given what's unfolding, I guess I can see why he'd pick that. And while I don't want to, I do as he asks.

I think about his visits to the restaurant, always sitting in my section. The way he'd smile, seemingly harmless. Our date at that wine bar, how uneasy I felt but ignored it. And then ...

The sharper memories flood back. Ezra forcing me into his car. The warehouse. Running because he let me, because he liked the chase. Being tied up, gagged. The knife he showed me, telling me exactly what he planned to do. How he liked to watch the light leave their eyes ...

Tears stream down my face as I relive it all. The terror. The certainty that I was going to die.

"Anna." Matt's voice pulls me back. "Open your eyes."

When I do, he's looking at me with such pain. He reaches up and wipes the tears from my cheeks while one skitters down his own.

"The warehouse smelled like gasoline," he says quietly. "He used zip ties and duct tape. Told you he'd start with small cuts, make it last. The knife had a wooden handle. You bit him when he removed the gag to ... to hear you scream." He chokes on the word. "That's when the police sirens started."

I'm shaking now. "How could you possibly know all that?"

"Because I just Saw it. Through you." He pulls me into his arms ... and I let him. Completely broken by this abrupt new reality. "I'm so sorry. God, Anna, I'm so sorry you went through that."

I cling to him, my mind reeling. It's impossible. But he knows things he couldn't know any other way.

"You really can see memories," I whisper against his chest.

"Yes."

"And you turned him in."

"Yes."

I pull back to see tears pouring down his face, as they are again down mine. "You saved me. You're the reason the police got there in time."

"Yes." It comes out choked, and his chin trembles.

I blink hard, trying to stem my own tears. "I believe you."

He lets out a heavy sigh of relief. "Thank you. For the record, CJ said you would."

I blanch. "Did she See that?" I ask, the possibility that CJ has been looking into my future without me knowing finally occurring to me.

He shakes his head. "No, CJ tries very hard not to read people. She just knows you. She reminded me you're different. That you have a touch of your own magic, too."

My chest tightens, for a different reason this time. At CJ's faith in me. I nod. "I guess I never thought about it that way. But I've always believed there's more to the world than what we see. That there are no coincidences." I take a shuddering breath. "And now ..."

"Now there's another killer. And I don't know who it is." His hands frame my face. "But I swear to you, Anna, I'll figure it out. I won't let anyone hurt you."

"We'll figure it out," I correct. "Together. Because we can't go to the police with this, and I really don't want to die."

"Anna —" he starts, a warning in his voice.

"No. I'm not sitting on the sidelines waiting for some psycho who may or may not come after me."

Matt looks like he wants to argue, but finally nods. "Okay. Together."

He pulls me into his embrace, and I hold him tight, trying to process everything. My boyfriend can see memories. His sister can see the future. And this killer is connected to the man who tried to murder me.

But I survived once. Thanks to Matt. Now we're together, and with both his and CJ's abilities, we have an advantage that the killer doesn't know about. So I'll survive again.

Even thinking that, I feel its truth deep in my bones. Given all that I've learned, clearly Matt and I were meant to be in each other's lives. What sense would that make if it was all for nothing?

CHAPTER FIFTEEN

MATT

Once again, I'm at CJ's door before seven in the morning. This time, Drew answers fully dressed.

"Let me guess," he says, stepping aside. "Early morning crisis meeting?"

"Something like that."

"She's in the kitchen. I'm heading out — try not to give her any more anxiety before eight a.m., yeah?"

"I'll do my best."

He huffs out a disbelieving breath. Not that I can blame him because this conversation is going to be anything but anxiety-free.

I find CJ at the dining room table with her coffee and what looks like Drew's homemade scones. She takes one look at me and pushes the plate my way.

"Eat. You look like shit."

"Thanks, but I'm not hungry." But I take a scone anyway. "Where's lover boy off to so early?"

CJ snorts. "He's going to look at some spaces for a new restaurant."

My brows rise. "Is his restaurant moving?"

She shakes her head. "First, it's not his restaurant; he's just the head chef. But the spaces he's looking at *would* be for *his* restaurant. As in he'd own and operate it. He's wanted to do this for a while."

"That's … huge. I hope it works out for him."

CJ tips her head and gives me a look. "Thanks, but that's not what you came here for, right?"

Exhaling slowly, I admit, "No, it's not." I pause, unsure where to begin. "I told Anna everything." Sitting down across from her, I pull the scone apart absentmindedly. It smells amazing, its steaming insides dotted with blueberries. I take a bite despite my complete lack of appetite. That's how good it smells.

"How'd that go?" CJ asks carefully.

I fill her in on yesterday and what led me to the call where I abruptly asked if I could tell Anna about us — the police calling her in, her confronting me, my confession about what I can do, and everything that came after. CJ listens without interrupting until I finish.

"You showed her you could read memories by having her relive the attack?" She sets down her mug carefully. "Matt, that's …" She trails off, but the disapproving look on her face says it all. As if I didn't already feel like a big enough asshole for it.

"I know. But I needed her to believe me, and I thought maybe I'd See something useful. Some detail about Martin that might point to who his partner is." I take another mindless bite of scone.

CJ raises a brow. "And?" She takes a sip of her coffee, waiting expectantly.

I shake my head. "Nothing. Just what Anna already knew." I rub my eyes. "She took it better than I expected, actually. Apparently, she's always believed in this kind of thing."

"I'm not surprised," she murmurs. "But … you didn't tell her about my vision."

It's not a question. I shake my head.

"Matt —"

I know that tone of reproach, so I hold up a hand to stave off the coming lecture.

"She was already processing so much. Finding out the police suspect me, that I can see memories, that you can see the future ... I didn't want to pile on that she's going to die, too."

"Well, *going to* is a little strong. Because the plan is that we won't let that happen," she replies forcefully. Then her expression softens slightly. "You need to tell her."

I sigh heavily. "I know. And I will. We have plans tonight. I'll tell her then." But god, do I wish I didn't have to. I hate seeing her upset.

"So, the detective told Anna you're a suspect," CJ muses. "Are you pissed they gave up your name? Wasn't your tip supposed to be anonymous?"

I shrug. "Under normal circumstances? Yeah, I'd be furious. But given what's at stake, I understand why he told her. And honestly, I'm glad she knows now. We can face this together instead of me trying to protect her from the shadows."

"That's very mature of you." Her facial expression is insultingly shocked.

"Don't sound so surprised." I down the last piece of scone. "Besides, what good would it do to complain? They already suspect me. Drawing more attention to myself won't help. And I always knew making that report was a risk."

"True." She's quiet for a moment. "So what's the plan?"

"I don't know yet. After I proved I could read her, I took her home. She needed time to process everything. We're supposed to talk tonight."

"No family dinner?"

"We're skipping it, given everything that's happened. I think we both need a night to just ... deal with all this."

CJ nods. "Probably smart. Her family seems lovely but intense."

"That's one way to put it."

"So when are you going to bring her to meet Aunt Meg and Uncle Chuck?" CJ asks, smiling from behind her mug.

I give her a look. "Let's just ... get through this first." I stand, exhaustion weighing on me despite the early hour. "Thanks for listening. And for letting me tell her about your ability."

"Of course. We're family. And Anna ... she's becoming family too."

The weight of what she's not saying — that Anna might not live long enough for her to officially become family —

hangs between us. And says a lot about what she Saw. I scrub my hands over my eyes to wipe away the tears forming.

"I'm going to save her, CJ."

"I know you're going to try. And I'll help however I can."

It's not the reassurance I want, but it's honest. That's CJ — supportive but realistic.

"I'll let you know how tonight goes," I promise.

"Matt?" she calls as I reach the door. "Be honest with her. About everything. She deserves that."

I nod and leave, knowing she's right. Anna deserves the truth, even the terrifying parts.

I show up at Anna's after ten, since she didn't get off work until late. She opens the door looking tired but composed. She's changed from work clothes into jeans and an oversized sweater that makes her look younger, more vulnerable.

"Hi," she says, stepping aside to let me in.

I note the physical distance she's leaving and do my best to respect it, walking in but keeping my hands to myself.

"Hi. How are you doing?"

"Honestly? I don't know." She leads me to her garishly dark pink couch. "I've been thinking about everything all day. My boyfriend has superpowers. It sounds like something out of a comic book."

"I prefer 'enhanced abilities,'" I say, trying for levity. But there's no mistaking the twinge in my heart at her calling me her boyfriend. I like it. A lot.

She manages a small smile. "Of course you do."

We sit facing each other, and I can see the questions in her eyes.

"So," she says, "what do we do now?"

"We figure out who Martin's partner is before they can hurt you."

Anna's face pinches. "I meant like … order takeout and watch a movie or go out?" She shakes her head. "Can we just … not talk about all that? For a little while? I'm still processing the fact that psychic abilities are real and my boyfriend has one."

"Anna …" I take her hand carefully, making sure not to read her. "I understand you need time to process. But if there's even a chance you're in danger, we need to act."

"The police only called me in because they think I'm in danger from you," she points out. "Which I'm clearly not. And there's no evidence that this new killer cares about me at all. Martin's dead. Maybe his partner, or whoever it is, is just … doing their own thing now."

"Actually …" I take a breath. Here goes. "There is reason to be concerned."

Her eyes narrow. "What do you mean?"

"CJ had a vision. About you." The silence that greets my declaration is deafening.

The color drains from her face. "What kind of vision?"

"The kind that means you're in danger. The kind where … you don't have a future." I swallow hard.

I see the moment Anna realizes my meaning when her eyes widen with fright.

"And you didn't think to mention this yesterday?" Her

voice rises. "When you were telling me all about your psychic abilities and how you used them to turn in the guy who tried to kill me?"

"You were already dealing with so much —"

"That's not your call to make!" She stands up and starts pacing the small living room. "God, Matt. You can't just decide what I can and can't handle."

"You're right. I'm sorry." I rise to block her path, grabbing her gently by the shoulders and looking her in the eye. "I should have told you immediately. I was trying to protect you, but that wasn't fair."

She's quiet for a long moment, then sighs. "I guess I understand why you did it. Yesterday was ... a lot. But no more holding back, okay? If we're doing this together, I need to know everything."

"Agreed. No more secrets," I promise.

She sinks back onto the couch, and I follow her lead, sitting at the other end.

"So CJ saw ... what exactly?"

I choose my words carefully. "She saw nothing. A void where your future should be. It's what she sees when someone is going to —"

"Die," Anna finishes quietly. "She saw that I'm going to die."

"We won't let that happen."

"How can you be so sure?"

"Because CJ's visions aren't set in stone. She's changed them before. Well, once before. When it really mattered ...

she saved Drew's life by warning him, by helping him change the outcome."

Anna absorbs that. "Well … that explains a lot, actually," she says contemplatively. And I know she's going to be after CJ to give her the full story there. "Okay. So we need to figure out who the killer is. But how? You already looked at my memories of Martin. And obviously you didn't get anything else that would help. Where do we even start?"

"Maybe you could go back to the police? See if they'll tell you about other suspects?"

"Worth a shot, I guess." She pulls her knees up to her chest. "Though I don't know why they'd tell me anything."

"You're a potential victim. They might share information if they think it'll keep you safe."

"Maybe." She looks at me. "Will you come with me to the police station?"

"I don't think that's a good idea, given that they suspect me," I hedge. But I want to go with her, especially if she really wants me there.

She nods, then surprises me by sliding closer and resting her head on my shoulder. "You're probably right." She sighs heavily. "This is insane. All of it."

"I know," I murmur in agreement.

"But I'm glad I'm not facing it alone." She looks up at me with gratitude.

I wrap my arm around her carefully. "You're not alone. You have me, CJ, your family — even if they don't know what's happening. We're going to get through this."

"Promise?" she asks in a small, anxious voice.

I press a kiss to the top of her head. "I promise."

It's a promise I have no right to make, but I mean it with every fiber of my being. Whatever it takes, whoever this killer is, I'm going to make sure Anna survives.

Because the alternative — losing her now, when we're just beginning — is unthinkable.

"How about we do something normal to take our minds off of all of this. I'm down for takeout and a movie," I murmur into her hair.

She looks up into my eyes and nods. There's tension between us. Some of which I can feel is based on all the revelations of the last couple of days … but some of which is the good kind. The kind that has me aching to kiss her. Take her to bed. Reassure her physically in whatever way I can that I'm here for her, in every way. But I resist. I can tell she still needs space.

So we order greasy Chinese food and watch a comedy, snuggling on the couch but going no farther than that. And yet, it's everything.

ANNA

Somehow the police station feels even more oppressive on a Saturday morning. Detective Worthington keeps me waiting for twenty minutes before finally appearing, looking harried.

"Ms. Martella. I wasn't expecting to see you so soon."

"I need to know who else you're looking at," I say without preamble as he leads me back to his office. "The other suspects."

He settles behind his desk, already shaking his head. "I can't share that information."

"You told me about Matt," I protest, sitting across from him.

"That was different." He leans back in his chair, folding his arms over his chest.

"How?" I lean forward, frustration building. "You said it was because of potential imminent danger. Well, if this killer is picking up where Martin left off, then every suspect is potentially an imminent danger to me."

Worthington's jaw tightens. "Ms. Martella —"

"I'm not asking for their addresses. Just names."

"I'm sorry. I've already shared more than I should have."

Huh. Well, that's interesting. It occurred to me that sharing the name of a suspect was odd, but with that admission … maybe if I threatened to report him, he'd cooperate.

But then again, that could blow up in my — and Matt's — face all too easily. Guess I'll have to try a different tactic.

"What if I know them? Wouldn't that help your case?"

He pauses. "You don't know them."

I slap the desk and he flinches with surprise. "So you'll warn me about my boyfriend but not about anyone else who might want to kill me?"

"My concern is that you are involved with a suspect. We don't know that anyone wants to target you specifically."

"But you don't know that for sure," I push.

"No," he admits. "But I can't compromise this investigation based on speculation."

I snort and stand abruptly. "This is ridiculous. You call me in, tell me there's a killer copying the man who tried to murder me, drop the bomb that you suspect my boyfriend, and then tell me I'm on my own? I see how it is. You can compromise the investigation just fine for your own speculation, just not mine."

Worthington's eyes flash and a muscle in his jaw ticks. "We're doing everything we can." His tone is so rote it's completely unconvincing. I got to him. Good.

"Clearly." I don't bother hiding my sarcasm. "Thanks for nothing, Detective."

I storm out, nearly colliding with an older detective in the hallway. He sidesteps smoothly, offering a brief nod before continuing past. With my path clear, I storm out of the station.

I spent my entire shift trying not to lose my shit with customers over my frustration with Detective Worthless. Instead, I take them out on the stairs up to Matt's door. Unsurprisingly, having likely heard the racket, Matt opens the door before I can knock.

"No luck with Detective Worthington?" he guesses, reading my expression.

I shake my head violently as I follow Matt inside. "He wouldn't tell me anything. He said he'd already shared too much by naming you. The hypocritical bastard." I follow him inside, still fuming. "It's like he wants me to be a sitting duck."

"He's probably worried about vigilante justice or compromising their investigation," Matt says reasonably.

I put my hands on my hips at Matt's use of the same defense Worthington gave. "Whose side are you on?"

He suppresses a smile. "Yours. Always yours." He pulls me into a hug. "But getting angry at Worthington won't help us."

I deflate against his chest. "I know. But he deserves it for being such an asshole. And I just ... I hate feeling helpless."

"You're not helpless. We'll figure this out another way." He pulls back to look at me. "But maybe we can take a break from it tonight? I was planning to cook dinner."

My stomach rumbles at the thought. Apparently being pissed off and anxious as hell makes me hungry. "What are you making?"

"Beef enchiladas with Mexican rice. Nothing fancy."

"Your 'nothing fancy' is better than most restaurants. Can I help?"

"You've been on your feet all day, so you can help by keeping me company. I even got you some sparkling cider."

I sigh. That sounds pretty good right now. "I can do company and sparkling cider," I agree. He's trying so hard to make this normal, to give me some peace in the chaos. I go on my toes and kiss him gently. "Thank you."

He palms my cheek and kisses me again. "Anything for you."

I melt into him and allow him to kiss me again. This was exactly what I didn't know I needed. Unfortunately, he breaks it off too soon, but leads me into the kitchen where he feeds me bits of food as he cooks it. The beef that's been braising in spices all day melts in my mouth, and the smell of chilis cooking mellows me right out. As he works, Matt encourages me to distract myself by letting me ask him questions about his job, his childhood, and so much more. I feel like I have to revisit everything now, knowing that he can read memories. In all the upset, I hadn't had time to consider how freaking cool it must have been for him to be able to do that his whole life.

Dinner is delicious, as always. Matt tells me stories about disastrous cooking attempts when he and CJ first lived alone, and I counter with tales of my mother's failed attempts to teach me even basic recipes. We migrate to the couch for a movie, but I can't focus. My mind keeps circling back to Worthington's refusal, to the three women who've died, to CJ's vision of my non-future.

"Anna?"

I realize Matt's paused the movie and is watching me with concern.

"Sorry. I'm not very good company."

"Are you okay being here? With me?"

The vulnerability in his voice breaks my heart. "Of course I am. Why would you think I'm not?"

He looks down at his hands. "I still can't believe you just ... accepted it. What I can do. I've never told anyone outside of family before — well, except Drew, because I was basically forced to, what with everything that went down — but if the tables were turned, I'm not sure I'd be as understanding as you've been."

I choose to ignore the part where Drew already knows about Matt's ability. It's vastly more important for me to set Matt straight.

"Matt." I shift to face him fully. "Look at me."

When he does, I see all his fear laid bare — fear of rejection, of being seen as a freak, of losing me.

"You're wrong," I tell him firmly. "You would accept it because you're an amazing man. You've accepted me and all the baggage that comes with that. My paranoia, my walls, my crazy family."

He looks confused. "Your family isn't crazy. They're wonderful."

"See? You even defend them." I cup his face. "I trust you, Matt. With my life, apparently, since we're hunting a killer together. But more than that, I trust you with my heart. Do you understand?"

His eyes soften and darken all at once. "Anna ..."

"I love you," I say, the words coming easier than expected. "I know it's fast. I know we've only been dating for barely a month. And I know the timing is insane, but —"

He kisses me, deep and desperate, and I melt into him. When we break apart, we're both breathing hard.

"I love you too," he says roughly. "God, Anna, I've never fallen this fast. This hard."

This time when we kiss, it's different. There's an urgency born not of passion but of mortality — the knowledge that we might not have forever makes right now even more precious.

"Bedroom?" I whisper against his lips.

His eyes widen, and in answer he stands and pulls me with him. We barely make it down the hall before we're kissing again, hands fumbling with buttons and zippers. When we fall onto his bed, it's with a desperation we've both been holding back.

"I need you," I gasp as he trails kisses down my neck. "Please, Matt. Make me forget anything but right now."

"Anything for you." He sheds the last of his clothes and pulls off mine before sliding over me.

He looks down at me with a tenderness that both breaks and warms my heart. He knows I haven't been with anyone in a long while, and he's assured me he's safe.

"I want to feel you inside of me," I breathe.

He buries his face in my neck and groans. "God, Anna, you're perfect." He leans back up and kisses me passionately. I wrap my arms around him and nudge my core up against his hard length. He reaches down without breaking the kiss and seats himself, entering me in a slow, smooth thrust.

I gasp into his mouth as he fills me. Jolts zing over my skin where we touch at my core, where our hands explore each other's skin, where our lips meet.

He rocks slowly into me, and I meet his thrusts with my own. Every inch of my skin touching his is on fire for him. For this.

Every touch, every kiss, every part where our bodies join feels like a promise — that we'll survive this, that we'll have more nights like this, that our love is stronger than whatever darkness is hunting us.

"God, Anna," Matt moans.

The sound of his pleasure has me tightening around him. "Yes, Matt," I reply in encouragement. "I'm —" I gasp as my orgasm crashes over me, as all of my muscles bunch together before release explodes through me. Matt's orgasm follows mine … and the waves of emotion that radiate from him as he comes bring tears to my eyes. I can feel each thread: protective, possessive, and passionate love woven together.

Afterwards, we lie tangled together, my head on his chest listening to his heartbeat slow.

"I won't let anything happen to you," he murmurs into my hair.

"I know." And I do. Whatever else happens, I know Matt

will do everything in his power to protect me. And I'll do the same.

I just hope it's enough.

———

"This one's hideous," Francesca declares, wrinkling her nose at the puffy monstrosity she's just emerged wearing.

"They can't all be winners," I reply with a shrug. She sighs, lets me unhook the complicated back, and retreats to the dressing room of the third bridal shop we've visited today. "What about the halter one?"

"Better, but I want to see the one with the sweetheart neckline again." She sounds muffled, which probably means her head is buried in tulle trying to get that beast off.

"Do you need help?" I offer.

"No, thanks," she replies tersely.

I let out a breath and allow myself a moment to be as distracted as I am without having to pretend. Trying to muster excitement for my sister's wedding dress shopping has taken what little energy I had right out of me. Plus, my mind keeps drifting to last night with Matt. It was … amazing. It had been so long, but nobody has ever made me feel like Matt did last night. Safe. Loved. Blissful.

But unfortunately it hasn't been enough to distract me completely from Worthington's refusal to help, or the constant fear that's taken up residence in my chest.

"Francesca?" I call through the curtain, realizing it's gone eerily quiet in there. "You okay?"

"Fine! Just ... zipper issues." I hear a zipper closing and a yelp of triumph before Francesca steps out. "Ta-da."

"That's not the sweetheart neckline," I breathe, putting a hand to my mouth in shock.

"You think?" She smirks.

I shake my head in disbelief at how amazing she looks as she steps up onto the stool in front of the three-way mirror. The straight, low neckline connects to cap sleeves, and the heavy material of the skirt hugs the curve of her hips before flaring out. I step forward to settle the skirt and straighten the crinoline underneath. It's stunning. Simple but elegant, it makes Francesca look like a princess without overwhelming her petite frame.

I'm happy for her. So happy. And yet ... seeing her as a beautiful bride makes me realize I may never get to be one. Still, I give my best impression of a smile.

"This might be the one," she says, then catches my expression in the mirror. "What's wrong?"

"Nothing," I protest, shaking my head and trying harder to show how happy I am for her. "You look amazing."

"Anna." She turns to face me directly. "Something's been off all day. Are you and Matt okay?"

"We're fine. Better than fine, actually." I blush, and she gives me a knowing look.

"Then what is it?"

I force a nonchalant expression. "Just work stuff. Drew's been extra grumpy lately." The excuse sounds feeble, even to me.

She doesn't look convinced but lets it drop as she goes

back to admiring the dress, which she says is *the* dress. As she works with the shop assistant to accessorize, I realize this is just the beginning. Mom will definitely notice something's wrong. And Sophia, who also knows about my past with Martin, will probably put the pieces together too if I'm not careful.

But what can I tell them? Certainly not that my new boyfriend has a psychic ability and was somehow the person who turned in the guy who tried to kill me. And definitely not that said killer apparently had an accomplice who is also going to try to kill me — unless there's a totally unrelated person out there planning to off me, which is obviously highly unlikely — but in any case, my psychic boyfriend and I are working on that.

They'd think I'd lost my mind.

Hell, *I* frequently think I've lost my mind these days.

No, until there's something concrete I can share — something that doesn't involve revealing Matt's abilities — I know I have to keep this to myself. The last thing I need is my family's well-meaning interference when we're trying to stay under the radar.

"This is it. This is definitely it," Francesca announces, beaming at her reflection. "Dress decision made ... now only a million other decisions to go."

"Can't wait," I say, injecting enthusiasm I don't feel into my voice. She laughs, so she must be distracted enough to buy it. Thank god.

As she changes back into her regular clothes, I catch my reflection in the mirror. I look tired, stressed, and older somehow than I did just a week ago. But beneath that, there's something else — determination.

I survived Ezra Martin. I'll survive this too.

I have to.

Because if nothing else, Francesca will kill me if I don't help her wedding go off without a hitch.

CHAPTER SEVENTEEN

MATT

My phone buzzes Monday afternoon, showing Worthington's number. I let it go to voicemail, already knowing I don't want to deal with whatever he has to say. When the voicemail notification comes through, I listen to the message. His voice is clipped and professional.

Mr. Roberts, this is Detective Worthington. I need you to come in for some follow-up questions. Please call me back as soon as you can.

I set my phone down next to my keyboard and stare at it, unease crawling up my spine. This has to be about Anna's visit on Saturday. What else could it be? Either way, I'm not walking back into that interrogation room without backup.

I scroll through my contacts and call James Cartwright, the lawyer who helped me buy the townhouse. His secretary answers on the second ring.

"Cartwright and Associates."

"Hi, this is Matt Roberts. I need to speak with James. It's urgent."

"I'm sorry, Mr. Roberts, but Mr. Cartwright is in depositions all day. Can I have him return your call?"

"Please. As soon as possible."

"Of course. He should be free by five."

Five comes and goes. Then six. By seven, I'm pacing my living room like a caged animal. I pull out Detective Sullivan's card, turning it over in my fingers. The guy seemed to know more than he should, but maybe that's exactly what I need right now.

Before I can talk myself out of it, I dial his number.

"Sullivan."

"This is Matt Roberts. We met last week at the station."

"I remember you, Mr. Roberts. What can I do for you?"

"Detective Worthington wants me to come in for more questions. You said I should call you if that happened. So I thought ... maybe you'd have some insight."

There's a pause. "I might. Would you be comfortable with me coming by? I have some information that might be relevant."

Every instinct screams that this is a bad idea. But Anna's life is on the line, and I'm running out of options.

"Fine. I'll text you my address."

Sullivan shows up thirty minutes later, looking more like someone's grandfather than a detective in his worn cardigan and khakis, even though he's probably Uncle Chuck's age, mid-fifties. He accepts my offer of coffee and settles onto my couch like we're old friends.

"So," I say, sitting across from him. "How can you help with Detective Worthington's investigation?"

"First, I'd like to hear your version of events. Not just what's in the reports, but your own words. Start with your original tip about Martin."

I hesitate, but figure I've already told this lie enough times that one more won't hurt. "I interviewed Martin for a position at my company. After the interview, he made some comments that concerned me. So I reported it." I rehash the things Martin "said" just as I had for Worthington back then. Words that, even though they were lies, I'll never forget. Because they were true to the vision that still haunts me.

"And your recent meeting with Worthington?"

"He asked if Martin had mentioned an accomplice. I told him no. Then he asked me to explain again how I knew Martin. When I repeated the same story, both he and his partner, Detective Liu, seemed unsatisfied ... suspicious, even. That's when I asked if I was free to go and left."

Sullivan nods slowly. "And Ms. Martella? How does she factor in?"

"Technically we met last October. I organized a dinner for our department, and scheduled it at the restaurant where she works. But I didn't really remember her until we met again at a housewarming party a few months ago. We started dating not long after that. I didn't know of her connection to Martin until recently."

"I see." He sets down his coffee mug, completely stone-faced. Man, this guy is hard to read. "Matt, I'm going to give you some advice: lawyer up. Don't meet with Worthington again without representation."

"Already working on it."

"Good. Especially given that you have something to hide."

My whole body tenses. "As I've said from the beginning, I have nothing to hide and *nothing* to do with these murders."

"I know you're not involved." Sullivan's eyes are steady on mine. "That's not what I'm talking about. I'm talking about your ability."

My throat goes dry. "I don't know what you mean."

He smiles, but it's sad rather than mocking. "I think you do. And I don't think Martin said any of those things to you, but I believe that you Saw them. In his memories." I'm so shocked that I can't school my expression, and he notes it. "You have nothing to fear from me, Matt. I'm like you. Well … not *exactly* like you. You're the first I've met with your particular gift. But my gift is sensing the abilities in others. It's how I found your parents all those years ago."

My world tilts, and my heart races. "My parents?"

He nods solemnly. "They were part of an organization that searched for people like us, trained them, helped them understand they weren't alone. Your father could See the history of objects — psychometry, it's called. Your mother was clairvoyant. She could See things happening in the present, anywhere in the world. It was she who found the lost ones. The ones that needed guidance."

I can't breathe. Can't process. All these years of wondering if our abilities came from them, and now ...

"Show me," I whisper.

Sullivan extends his hand. After a moment's hesitation, I take it. The memories flood in — not mine, but his. My parents, younger than I remember them, sitting in a circle with others. My father touching an antique watch and describing its history in perfect detail. My mother, with her eyes closed, narrating events happening across the city. Their wedding, where half the guests had abilities of their own. The pride in their eyes when they talked about their twins on the way.

I pull back, tears burning my eyes at the avalanche of memories. I've rarely Seen so much so fast, and my head is spinning. I breathe deeply for a minute as I try to make sense of them all. But it's his last words, about what my mother could do that stick out.

"How did she not See the accident coming?" I ask, looking up to meet his patient gaze.

"People with abilities often can't use them on themselves. It's a blind spot, a cosmic balance perhaps. She may have Seen it and been unable to prevent it, or she may not have Seen it at all."

That tracks. I've never been able to read my own memories, to See my past the way I can with others, relive details and feelings as if I were there. And CJ can't see her future directly, only others' futures. Those close to her, whose futures may affect her, but never exactly as it involves her.

All the questions I've ever had about my abilities, CJ's

abilities, flood back. Are there really people out there who can answer them? Is Ray Sullivan really one of them?

"This organization," I say roughly. "Does it still exist?"

Sullivan sighs heavily and leans forward, eyes on his hands. "It fell apart after your parents died. They were ... central to its functioning. Without them, people drifted away." He looks up at me, and I can see the disappointment all over his face.

"And you? Is this ... are you trying to restart it?"

"No. Others of our kind fear me too much, I think. I'm just a cop who has a gift. But when I sensed your ability at the station, I knew I had to reach out. You're in trouble, Matt. Worthington's building a case against you, and your story about Martin confessing is tissue-thin."

I let out a sigh of my own. "I know." I shake my head, not sure where to even start. Why he's even telling me all of this. "So what do you want from me?"

He purses his lips as he contemplates me. As if he's still deciding what and how much he wants to tell me. Finally, he says, "To work together. To find the *actual* killer, since Worthington's convinced it's you. Preferably *before* Worthington railroads you for it."

Shit. Shit, shit, shit. I knew I was on Worthington's list. But I didn't think I was his *prime* suspect. That changes things. But not the fact that there's literally nothing I can do about it.

I stand abruptly. "I need time. To process all of this."

Sullivan rises as well. "Of course. But Matt? Don't wait

too long. The killer's still out there, and Worthington's closing in."

I close my eyes and rub them hard. When I reopen them, I nod. "I won't. I'll be in touch."

He dips his chin and leaves without preamble.

The silence that falls in his wake is ominous.

I pick up my phone and call CJ.

"Can you come over? Now?" I ask before she can even say hello.

"Matt? What's wrong?"

"Everything."

CJ arrives twenty minutes later, and I tell her all of it — Worthington's call, Sullivan's visit, the memories of our parents.

"He can *sense* abilities?" She sinks onto the couch, looking as shell-shocked as I feel. "And Mom and Dad were like us … and part of some organization?"

"According to his memories, yeah."

"Matt, this is … wow. Well, it's a lot of things. I don't even know how to wrap my head around it," she murmurs, drawing her legs up and wrapping her arms around them.

I lean against her, rubbing my temples, hoping to work out the headache forming there. "Yeah, that's about where I'm at."

She furrows her brow. "I don't know. Doesn't this just seem a little odd? I mean … it's actually super suspicious.

How do we know he is who he says he is? What if he had something to do with their deaths?"

"I thought about that. But the memories felt real, Cee. And he knew things — specific things about their abilities."

"Maybe we should ask Aunt Meg and Uncle Chuck?"

I shake my head. "They were shocked when we told them about our abilities. They had no idea we were different, much less anything like that about Mom and Dad. I mean, I don't think Dad and Uncle Chuck had much in common besides being brothers. They weren't that close. And I don't want to worry them with all this. Especially the part where the police think I'm a serial killer."

CJ's expression softens. "I get it. But, we need more information. What if they know something that could help?"

"Like what?" I scoff.

She shrugs.

I shake my head. "Not yet. Maybe never. I just ... I can't handle them looking at me like I might be capable of murder."

She squeezes my hand. "They would never think that."

"Worthington does. And he's got evidence — twisted evidence, but evidence."

We sit in silence for a moment before CJ asks, "Are you going to tell Anna?"

"She's working tonight. We're not supposed to see each other until Thursday." I rub my face. "This is too heavy to drop in a text."

"Agreed. And I hate to do this, but I should get home. I didn't even stop to let Drew know where I'd be after you called, and I don't want him to worry when he gets home and

I'm not there." She stands to leave, then pauses. "Matt? Be careful. With Worthington, with Sullivan, with all of it."

I nod and wrap her in a hug. "I will. Thanks for coming over, Cee."

"Anytime, buttface."

I let out a halfhearted chuckle and walk her to the door, watching until she's safely in her car and headed down the street.

But later, after she's gone and I'm lying in bed, staring at the ceiling, I wonder if careful is enough. Sullivan claims our parents were part of something bigger, something that died with them. Worthington thinks I'm a killer. And somewhere out there, the actual murderer is still hunting.

I reach into my nightstand and pull out one of the few keepsakes I have from my parents — my father's old watch that hasn't worked since I was a kid. I instantly thought of it when I Saw Sullivan's memory — Dad always had a thing for watches. I close my eyes and try to summon my father's gift — to See the history of objects. But I get nothing. All I have is the past of people I've touched, memories that aren't mine but feel like they are.

But according to Sullivan, there may be more I can do that I just haven't learned yet. That gives me a kernel of hope in a dark situation. Maybe I'll be able to expand my abilities enough to save Anna.

The thought keeps me awake until dawn, tossing and turning over questions I may never get answered and dangers I can't See coming.

CHAPTER EIGHTEEN

ANNA

My feet are screaming by the time I finally clock out Tuesday night. Or Wednesday morning, technically, as it's past midnight and I've been on my feet for nearly twelve hours straight. Two servers called in sick, leaving me and Becky to handle the entire dining room on what turned out to be an unexpectedly busy night. At least I got a piece of the new cheesecake — bananas foster — to make up for the shit show that was my shift. It wasn't as good as the cactus pear cheesecake, but I'll never say no to cheesecake.

Now, as I trudge up the three flights to my apartment, fishing for my keys, I'm only fantasizing about my bed. And Matt. God, I miss him. We've been texting, but between our work schedules and everything else going on, I won't see him until Thursday.

My fingers find my keys just as I reach my door. I go to insert the key, but the door moves at my touch.

It's already open.

My blood turns to ice, and heart-pounding adrenaline wipes away my exhaustion. I know I locked it. I always lock it. I triple-checked this morning because of everything that's been happening.

I back away slowly, my heart hammering. Someone's been in my apartment. Someone might still be in there.

I sprint down the hall to 3C and pound on the door, praying Christopher's awake. He's always up playing video games until dawn.

"What the —" He opens the door in boxers and a ratty T-shirt, headset around his neck. "Anna? What's wrong?"

"My door was open. Someone broke in. Can I come in? Please?"

His eyes go wide. "Shit, yeah, of course." He steps aside, and I practically fall into his apartment. "You want me to check it out?"

"No!" The word comes out sharper than intended. "No, please don't. They might still be in there. I need to call the police."

"Yeah, okay. Sit wherever. You want water or something?"

I shake my head, already pulling out my phone. My hands are trembling so badly it takes two tries to dial 911.

"911, what's your emergency?"

"Someone broke into my apartment. I don't know if they're still in there."

The operator takes my information and assures me officers are on the way. As soon as I hang up, I call Matt.

"Anna?" His voice is thick with sleep. "What's wrong?"

"Someone broke into my apartment." The words come out in a rush. "I'm at my neighbor's. The police are coming."

"*Fuck*," he says, sounding much more awake now. "I'm on my way."

Shit. So are the cops. I should've thought this through better, but I'm not exactly in my right mind. "No, wait. I'm sorry. You probably shouldn't be here when the police arrive. Given ... everything." I dart a glance at Christopher, who's politely pretending not to listen while he scrolls through game stats.

There's a pause on Matt's end. "Damn. You're right. But I'm picking you up the second they leave."

"Okay," I agree, relieved.

"Are you safe right now?" The intensity in his voice sends goosebumps over my arms and somehow calms my racing heart.

"Yeah. I'm with Christopher, my neighbor."

"Stay there. Don't go back to your apartment alone." His concern wraps around me like a warm blanket.

"I won't," I assure him, my voice thick with emotion.

"I love you," he says fiercely. "Let me know as soon as the police leave."

"I love you too," I murmur, my cheeks heating.

I hang up and realize Christopher's given up pretending not to listen and is watching me from the couch.

"Boyfriend?" he asks.

"Yeah," I reply sheepishly.

"Good that you have somewhere to go." He shifts

awkwardly. "Did you ... um, see anyone? When you got home?"

"No. Just that the door was unlocked. But I know I locked it this morning."

He lifts one shoulder helplessly. "I haven't heard anything. But I've had my headset on, playing Call of Duty with my squad. Sorry."

I wave him off. "Gosh, it's not your fault. Thanks for letting me in."

"No problem. Scary shit." He pauses. "You think it's connected to those murders? The ones in the news?"

My stomach drops. "What?" I hadn't realized the killings had made the news. And I'm also shocked that he somehow made that connection, even if they are.

"There's a serial killer. They say he's targeting blond women in their twenties. They found another body yesterday. My girlfriend's been texting me articles about it non-stop."

I force myself to breathe normally. Another murder. Another body. Just yesterday. Surely the killer can't already be looking for another victim?

"I don't know. Maybe it was just a regular break-in." It's wishful thinking, because I know Christopher probably just hit the nail right on the head.

Because why would someone be breaking in at a time I might be home? Christopher's face tells me he's having similar thoughts. That regular break-ins usually happen during the day, when they know nobody will be home. I swallow hard against the knot in my throat.

"Yeah, uh, maybe," he says self-consciously, clearly

realizing that probably wasn't the best thing to say to his freaked out, twenty-something-year-old blond female neighbor. "Probably had nothing to do with it. Sorry …"

I'm saved having to respond by a knock at the door — a uniformed officer who looks barely older than me who tells me his partner is clearing my apartment.

The partner joins us almost immediately — my one-bedroom unit being that tiny — saying he's cleared it. No one was inside. So they walk me over to check for anything missing.

But my apartment looks normal. Nothing's gone or even out of place that I can see. But I can *feel* that someone was in here. It feels like eyes on the back of my neck, shadows creeping out of the corners. The idea of them being in my space, touching my things, makes my skin crawl.

"The lock was definitely picked," one officer says, examining my door. "Professional job, too. No scratches or obvious damage."

"So someone with experience," I say numbly.

"Most likely. Have you noticed anyone following you? Any strange encounters recently?"

Just a serial killer who might want to finish what their predecessor started. "No, nothing like that."

They take my statement, have someone dust the door for prints they probably won't find, and give me a case number. I know Worthington will probably hear about this too, but the thought of talking to him again makes me nauseous.

"You should stay somewhere else for a few nights," the

younger officer suggests. "And maybe invest in a better lock. A deadbolt, security chain, that kind of thing."

I nod weakly. "I will."

"We'll have patrol cars do extra drive-bys of this area," the older one adds. "But if you see or hear anything suspicious, call 911."

They leave me with sympathetic looks that do nothing to make me feel safer.

I text Matt from my doorway, not wanting to be inside alone.

They're gone.

Already here. Out front.

Coming down now.

Matt is standing next to his car when I burst out of the main door to the building. I practically run into his arms. His warmth seeps into me as the sob I'd felt coming dies in my chest. His presence and his embrace soothe the ragged edges of my nerves in a way I didn't expect.

He presses me into his side and turns to open the passenger door for me. I practically collapse into Matt's car, the adrenaline finally wearing off and leaving me shaky and exhausted.

He climbs into the driver's seat beside me. "I can take you to your parent's house if you want, or you can come stay at my place."

I melt at his words. That he's not assuming I'll come to his place and is offering options to make me feel at ease. "Yours. Please."

He gives me a small, sad smile and takes my hand as he drives, thumb rubbing soothing circles on my palm. Neither of us speaks until we're safely inside his townhouse.

"Tell me everything," he says, guiding me to the couch.

I relay the full story — finding the door unlocked, running to Christopher's, what the police said. Matt's jaw gets tighter with every word.

"It was him," I finish quietly. "The killer. It had to be."

"We don't know that for sure."

"My lock was professionally picked. Nothing was taken. What else could it be?"

Matt pulls me against him and I burrow into his warmth. "I should have been there."

"You couldn't have known."

"I should move in with you. Or you with me. You shouldn't be alone."

"Matt ..." I close my eyes, a million emotions flooding me at the suggestion.

"I'm serious. This changes things."

I shake my head. I'm too tired and scared to argue. "Can we ... can we not talk about it anymore tonight? I just want to forget for a little while."

"Of course." He presses a kiss on my temple. "What do you want to talk about?"

"You. What have you been up to?"

He sighs. "It's heavy."

My brows bunch, given that our last texts were from lunchtime yesterday. If something big happened, why didn't he tell me? I chew my lip, deciding not to push it. Tonight already sucks anyway. But I am curious enough to want to know what he means.

"Tell me anyway. I need the distraction."

Matt sighs, lacing his fingers with mine and kissing the back of my hand. "Okay. But only because I told myself I'd tell you the next time I saw you, and you need to know." He pauses as if bracing himself. "Worthington called yesterday. He wanted me to come in for more questioning."

"Shit," I curse, then remember what Christopher said. "Though apparently they found another body yesterday, so that's not surprising. Did you call him back?"

Matt's eyes widen. "Well, that would explain it," he says drily. "No, I didn't. I called my lawyer, who says he's handling it. But before that, I called the detective who had approached me at the station. Sullivan."

I pull away and sit up to look at him. "And?"

"He came by. He ... told me some things about my parents. About others like us — people with abilities." Matt's voice is carefully neutral, but I can feel the tension in his body. "He says he can sense abilities in others. That he knew my parents through some organization for people like us."

"Wow ... I did not see that coming." I examine Matt's carefully blank expression. "Do you believe him?"

He frowns and shrugs, and the slight gestures speak to his inner conflict. "I saw his memories. They felt real. But CJ thinks it's suspicious, the timing of it all."

"What do you think?"

He takes a deep breath. "I don't know. Part of me wants to believe him. To have someone who knew my parents, who might have answers. But ..."

"But trusting him could be dangerous," I finish.

"Yeah."

I consider what he's told me. "What if ... what if he's telling the truth? Having a detective on our side, especially one who knows about abilities, could be helpful. We don't exactly have a lot of options. And what's the risk if he's not?"

"That's what I keep coming back to. We're running out of time and leads."

"So maybe we take the risk. Carefully."

Matt nods slowly. "Maybe you're right. Maybe I just don't tell him anything I don't absolutely have to. See how he can help."

We fall into silence. Despite everything — the break-in, the fear, the uncertainty — I feel safe here in Matt's arms. His heartbeat under my ear is steady, grounding.

"I woke you up," I remember, startling upright and noticing for the first time that he's been in pajamas this whole time. "Oh my god, Matt, I'm so sorry. You have to get up for work in a few hours. You should go to bed."

Matt's eyes are tired as he cups my face. "I'm glad you did," he says, leaning in to kiss me. "And *we* should go to bed."

"Shit, I forgot to bring any clothes with me." I smack my forehead.

Matt grabs my wrist, stopping me. "Hey, it's okay. You had a lot going on. Don't worry. CJ left some here. I'm sure she wouldn't mind if you borrowed some until I can take you back to your apartment for yours."

I lean in and kiss him gently. Not just for the offer of clothes, but for thinking ahead enough to go with me when I go back to my place. I didn't realize until he just mentioned it that I don't think I could stomach doing it alone.

"Thanks. But I can just wear one of your shirts to bed. I'll worry about the rest tomorrow."

Matt raises an eyebrow and stands. "Come on," he says, scooping me up. I gasp as he holds me against his chest and carries me up the stairs.

He sets me down gently on the low bed, the blue flannel comforter soft and inviting, and fishes out an old, large navy UC San Francisco shirt, then directs me to the bathroom between his and CJ's old bedroom. I get changed quickly and return to Matt, who is now lying under the covers. He lifts the other side, and I slide in next to him. It's already nice and toasty, and I snuggle into him.

"Thank you," I mumble against his chest as exhaustion catches up with me.

"You never have to thank me for taking care of you."

I sigh happily against his shirt as he kisses my forehead. "Stay here," he murmurs. "Not just tonight. Until this is over."

"Okay," I whisper, too tired to overthink it.

As sleep finally takes me, one thought echoes through my mind: someone was in my home. They know where I live, how to get to me.

But they didn't take me tonight. Was it luck or just timing? Or are they waiting for something?

An icy chill spider-walks down my back. It's a feeling I've had before when I know I've guessed right.

The killer is toying with me. It's all part of their plan.

I just hope we figure out what that is before it's too late.

CHAPTER NINETEEN

MATT

I wake up just before five and shut off my alarm before it can go off and wake Anna. Even though I didn't get much sleep, having Anna here, in my arms, I slept deeply and feel wide awake. But there's no way I can go into work today. So, for the first time in … well, years, I text Dani to let her know I'm taking the day off. She doesn't even question it, letting me know she'll take care of everything. She probably figures I'm overdue for a mental health day. If only she knew.

Anna's still asleep when I slip out of bed, but she stirs when I return with coffee after I've checked my work email to issue a few instructions and make sure I'm not missing out on anything major. Thankfully, I'm not.

"Morning," she murmurs, accepting a mug gratefully. "What time is it?"

"Eight-thirty. I called out of work. Figured we should get your things from your apartment today."

Her face clouds. "Right. That."

I settle on the bed next to her, tugging at a blond lock. Her hair is a wild, tangled mess, and she's never looked more beautiful. "We don't have to go right now. Whenever you're ready."

"No, let's get it over with." She takes a long sip of coffee. "The sooner I have my own clothes, the better. Not that CJ's style isn't great, but ..."

"But you're not a skirts and blazers kind of girl?"

"Exactly." She gives me a wary look. I take the cue not to talk about last night, and we get up and get ready to leave.

An hour later, we're standing outside her apartment door. She hesitates with the key in her hand.

"I can go in first," I offer.

"No. I need to do this." She unlocks the door, though it seems more finicky now that it's been picked, so it takes longer than usual before she's able to push it open.

"I can take care of getting that fixed," I offer.

She grimaces. "Thanks, but the super will do it. I just have to send him an email."

I nod as we walk in. The apartment looks exactly as she described — nothing out of place, nothing missing. But I can feel her tension as she moves through the space, grabbing clothes and toiletries with quick, efficient movements.

"That's everything?" I ask when she emerges from her bedroom with a small pink suitcase.

"For now." She takes one last look around. "Let's go."

Back at my place, I help her carry her things upstairs.

She's quiet, lost in thought, and I don't push. After she's settled, I kiss her forehead.

"I have to run an errand. Will you be okay here for a bit?"

"Yeah. I might take a nap before I have to go into work. I didn't exactly sleep my best last night."

"Sounds like a good idea," I agree. "Text me if you need anything."

Once I'm sure she's comfortable, I go downstairs and call Sullivan.

"Ray Sullivan," he answers.

"Hi. It's Matt Roberts. Can we meet? There have been some developments."

"Of course. How about lunch? Pinecrest Diner on Geary?"

"I know it. Noon?"

"See you there."

Sullivan's already in a window booth when I arrive, coffee in hand and the remnants of a Danish on his plate.

"Matt. Thanks for calling."

I slide in across from him. "Thanks for meeting me."

"I assume this is about more than just processing what we discussed?"

"Things have escalated." I accept coffee from the server before continuing. "Someone broke into Anna's apartment last night. They picked the lock, but didn't take anything."

Sullivan's expression darkens. "She's okay?"

"She's scared, but safe. She's staying with me now."

"Good. That's good." He pauses. "What can I do to help?"

I consider that. Before we go any further, I need to see if I can trust him. "First, I need to ask you something." I clear my throat.

"Shoot."

I meet his eyes. "What do you know about my parents' death?"

He doesn't flinch at the implication. "You want to know if I had anything to do with it."

"Did you?" I ask bluntly.

"No," he replies instantly, leaning forward. "There was no foul play. I had it investigated thoroughly — by people like us who would have Seen if something was wrong. It was an accident. A terrible, tragic accident."

"Why should I believe you?"

Instead of answering with words, he extends his hand. I hesitate, then take it.

The memories flow — Sullivan on his beat, learning about the crash over his walkie talkie. His genuine grief when he arrived at the scene to find out who it had involved. Sullivan reviewing every piece of evidence, consulting with other gifted individuals. A woman who could see the last moments of the deceased confirming it was just rain, just a moment's distraction. Sullivan visiting their graves year after year, wondering if he could have done more to protect them.

More memories follow — Sullivan being trained by my parents, learning to hone his gift. His abilities growing and changing over time. His gratitude to my parents. His desire to train others the way they trained him. A telepath learning to filter thoughts. A precog developing control over their visions. A —

I pull back, overwhelmed.

"It was your parents who showed me that our abilities can expand," he says. "With practice, you could learn to control what you See, to dig deeper or pull back as needed. With full control, you could've pulled all those memories, and any others you wanted, faster and without me pushing them to you. Hell, your father could read objects, so you might be able to as well."

"But I'm not there yet."

"No. Which is why I'm going to give you information as a token of good faith." He signals for more coffee. "I know Ms. Martella went back to Worthington asking about other suspects."

I stiffen. I never told him that.

"I saw her come in and hung around in case I needed to step in," he says, reading my expression. "Which I didn't, because she handled herself beautifully. Firecracker, that one. Anyway, the point is, you both deserve to know who else is being investigated. Especially now that someone's actively targeting her."

Something about his phrasing catches my attention, but I file it away. "What can you tell us?"

"There are currently three other suspects. Martin's siblings — a brother and sister — and his former fiancée. My money's on one of the siblings."

"Why?"

"I worked the original case, mostly on the evidence side,

so I had to sign off on the final report. Martin's family history is … dark. His parents died in a murder-suicide when the kids were young. The father killed the mother after discovering an affair, then himself."

"Jesus."

"When we caught Martin, he insisted his victims deserved it. When pressed, he just kept saying, 'Cheaters never prosper.' The same phrase his father supposedly said before killing himself. It was also in the suicide note Martin left in prison."

My stomach lurches. "He was targeting women who cheated?"

"That's the working theory. That he was repeating his parents' pattern — murders like his mother's death, then suicide like his father." Sullivan's voice is clinical, detached. "Of course, we don't know if that's how the current killer is choosing victims. They could just be emulating Martin without the same psychological motivation."

"Right." My voice sounds strange to my own ears as my stomach hollows out. "The trauma of being connected to a serial killer." Except that doesn't change the fact that the original killer targeted *cheaters*. My hands shake as I process the implications of that. I'm so dazed that I have to set my coffee cup down before I spill it all over the place.

"Exactly. Any of them could have snapped after his death, and carried on his work."

We discuss a few more details — the siblings' names, last known locations, the fiancée's new married name. I memorize everything, even as one thought pounds through my head like a drum.

He targeted Anna because she cheated on someone.

"Matt? You still with me?"

I blink, focusing on Sullivan. "Yeah. Sorry. Just processing."

"It's a lot. But now you have leads. Actual information to work with."

"Thank you. This helps."

"Be careful how you use it. Worthington can't know it came from me."

"Understood."

I leave cash for my barely touched coffee and head home, my mind — and stomach — still churning.

Anna's gone when I get back. A glance at the clock tells me she's at work. I stand in my bedroom doorway, staring at the empty bed, where we'd been curled up together only hours ago, and try to reconcile what I'm feeling with what I've just learned.

Martin targeted her because she cheated on someone. Just like Alyssa cheated on me.

Am I repeating the same mistake? Falling too fast for the wrong person?

I think about CJ's vision of Anna and me having a future together. But what if that's not what fate intended? What if I was just meant to save her, not be with her?

The questions torture me all afternoon. I throw myself into

work emails from my home office, trying to distract myself, but it's useless. Every time I think about Anna, I see two versions — the woman I've fallen for, and a stranger who betrayed someone the way I was betrayed.

I stew all day. I'm in bed doing more of that when Anna gets home. I stiffen at the sound of the door closing, wondering how I'll feel when I see her. Will my feelings have changed?

"Hey," she says, appearing in the bedroom doorway. "How was your day?"

"Fine." The lie tastes bitter. But the sight of her … well, I still feel that pull to her. She's gorgeous. Inside and out, or so I'd thought.

"You okay? You seem tense."

I clear my throat. "Just work stuff."

She doesn't push, but I can feel her concern. "Okay, well … I'm going to shower."

"Sounds good."

As soon as I hear the water running, I drop my head into my hands. I'm being an idiot. Whatever happened in Anna's past doesn't change who she is now. And it shouldn't have to change how I feel about her.

Except it does. Because now I'm wondering what else I don't know. What else she hasn't told me.

I still want to protect her. Still want to find whoever's hunting her and stop them.

I just don't know what it means for *us* anymore.

When she emerges from the shower, smiling and reaching

for me, I kiss her and pretend everything's fine. Because she needs me to be strong right now. She needs to feel safe.

But inside, doubt has taken root, and I don't know how to dig it out.

Maybe Sullivan was right about one thing — I need to learn to control what I See. Because right now, all I can see is the possibility that I've fallen for another beautiful liar.

And this time, I'd have no one to blame but myself.

CHAPTER TWENTY

ANNA

The super shows up Thursday morning with enough hardware to fortify a bank vault. I watch from my doorway as he installs a metal plate around the lock mechanism, a heavy-duty deadbolt, and something he calls a "deep-set security lock."

"This baby goes three inches into the frame," he explains, demonstrating. "Can't be picked, can't be cut, can't be kicked in. You'd need a battering ram to get through this."

"Thanks, Mr. Kowalski, I really appreciate it." I fidget nervously, leaning against the kitchen counter just inside the apartment. I can't bring myself to go in further. The vibes in the apartment are just still too … off.

He gives me a concerned look. "You sure you're okay, Anna? Maybe you should stay with family for a while."

I chew on my thumbnail anxiously and nod. "I'm … considering it."

And I am. Even with Fort Knox-level security, I can't shake the feeling that someone's been in my space. Touched my things. Violated my sanctuary. And their energy is still here, a faint but present threat.

By the time I get back to Matt's that afternoon, I've decided.

"I don't think I can live there anymore," I tell him over dinner. "Even with the new locks, I just ... I don't feel safe."

He nods, pushing pasta around his plate. "That's understandable."

"So maybe ... I should take you up on your offer? About moving in together?" I try to keep my voice light, but my heart's hammering.

Matt's fork stills. He looks up at me, and there's hesitation in his eyes. "Anna ..."

Shit, it's in his voice, too.

"Too fast," I finish, trying to hide my disappointment. "You're right. I know you probably only suggested it in the first place because you were in shock, like I was."

He leans back in his chair with a frown. "You're probably right. But it's not just that. I mean, with everything going on, maybe it's better if you stay somewhere with more people around. Your parents' house would be perfect. You'd be the safest there. Don't you think?"

Something's still off about his tone, his body language, but I can't put my finger on what. Even though his logic is valid, I sense that's not why he's suggesting it. Or maybe I'm just reading too much into it, as usual.

"Yeah. You're probably right," I agree with a placating smile. "I'll let my mom know I'll be coming home tomorrow. She'll be thrilled."

Matt lets out a relieved breath. "I'm glad. You'll be safe there," he adds, finally meeting my eyes. "Especially this weekend. I've got a work emergency, and I'll probably be pulling all-nighters through Monday. In fact, I have to work in my office tonight."

"Oh. Okay." I look back down at my empty plate, then abruptly stand to take it into the kitchen. Not knowing how to fix whatever's gone wrong here. Or if anything even has. Everything is just … off lately. It's probably just the danger that's making me question everything.

So as Matt heads into his office and the weird vibe intensifies, I chalk it up to stress. We're both under pressure. A serial killer wants me dead. Of course things feel strange.

———

Friday night dinner is an interrogation from the moment I walk through my parents' door with my suitcase.

"What happened to your apartment?" Mom demands before I've even put my bag down.

"Why aren't you staying with Matt?" Lucia adds.

"Where is Matt? Is everything okay?" Dad's voice carries a note of paternal concern that makes me want to cry.

"I'm fine," I lie, plastering on a fake cheerful face. "Just some maintenance issues at my building. Figured I'd crash here for a bit. And Matt has to work this weekend."

I can tell that nobody buys it. By the time we're clearing dishes, the questions have become relentless. Sophia corners me in the kitchen while Mom's serving panna cotta.

"Okay, spill," she says quietly. "What's really going on?"

I look at my older sister — the only one of my sisters who knows about Martin, who held me through nightmares two years ago — and suddenly I'm exhausted from carrying this alone.

"Someone broke into my apartment Tuesday night," I whisper, my eyes darting to the kitchen door.

Her face pales. "Anna —"

I shake my head for her to stop. I can't stand the horror and pity in her voice. Not when I'm just getting started. "I was at work, and nothing was taken. But with everything that's happened lately ..." I trail off, losing my nerve.

Sophia leans in and catches my eye. "What *everything*?" she pushes in that older sister tone that promises a knuckle sandwich if I don't answer.

My chest warms at her protectiveness. And then I take a shaky breath. "The police think Martin had an accomplice. The killings have started again."

"Oh my god," she gasps. "That's … how … what?!"

I nod. "Yeah, that's about as far as I've gotten with all this."

She tilts her head, and her face pinches. "God, Anna, I'm so sorry," she murmurs, pulling me into a fierce hug. "When are you gonna tell Mom and Dad?"

I pull back, shaking my head. "I'm not. I *can't*. They'll totally freak out."

Sophia makes a noise of dissent. "They'll freak out more if something happens and they didn't know." She pulls back, studying my face. "Maybe it's time you told everyone, sweets.

You kept it so quiet the first time … and I think that made it harder for you to heal." She closes her eyes and sighs. "And you were finally coming back out of your shell."

I snort. "And if I tell the whole family, I'll have to go right back in!" I protest. "They'll be relentless. And the last thing I want to do is think about this more than I have to."

Sophia scoffs. "Sweets, you've *moved back into our parents' house*. Newsflash: you're already back in your shell. You don't think everyone out there —" she points emphatically at the kitchen door "— wouldn't go to bat for you?"

My eyes fill with tears. Because I know she's right.

"But that's exactly why I can't," I explain. "I don't want to bring this to everyone's doorstep. It's not fair. Francesa's planning a wedding, for fuck's sake! She shouldn't have to worry about her baby sister getting murdered."

Sophia looks at me like I'm nuts. "Do you hear yourself?" she asks incredulously. "She's gonna be pissed if she finds out that you didn't tell her. That you'd rather pretend everything is fine instead of letting her be there for you. You think she cares more about a wedding than her sister?"

I deflate. "No, I don't think that."

Sophia's expression softens. "Then tell her. Let her be there for you. Let all of us be there for you."

My heart lurches. I want to. But I'm just too scared. "She'll make me step down as maid of honor," I point out.

"Damn right, and you should. You've got enough on your plate."

My nostrils flare. "I don't, though. It's not like there's anything I can *do*. It's not like I ever do *anything*."

"Is that what you think? That you're useless? That you should just roll over and let this guy kill you?" Sophia's eyes flash. "Where's your fire, Anna? Because I know it's in there. You're letting life live you, not the other way around."

"Just stop," I say, throwing my hands over my ears. "This. This is exactly why I don't want to tell everyone else. I don't need your judgment or your criticism. And I don't need any of you to stop living *your* lives because mine is falling apart again. So stop telling me what I should be doing. I'm not telling anyone I don't have to, and I'm sure as hell not backing out of my sister's wedding." I slam my hand on the counter beside us, my chest heaving with anger.

"There's that fire," she says softly with an approving smirk. "Don't let it go. You're gonna need it, sweets." She leans in and kisses me on the cheek before heading back into the dining room.

I let out a slow breath and collect myself. Sophia may be pushy, and she may be prone to picking fights, but I know she only does it because she loves me. Like Nonna always says, Italians only yell at you because they love you.

I huff out a laugh. She must love me a *lot*.

But she's also right about one thing. I've been acting like a victim. And that needs to stop now.

When I wake up on Saturday morning, I decide I won't let Matt get off so easily either. I know something is up, and I'm finished with all the walking on eggshells I've done since Tuesday, not just around him. I refuse to be afraid anymore. Of anything. Including his likely bogus "work emergency." So I text him: *How's the work emergency going? Do you have time to talk today?*

No response.

By Saturday afternoon, I'm antsy.

By Saturday night, I've gone from resolute to concerned.

Maybe something big really is happening if he's not even responding. That's *very* unlike him.

Thankfully, on Sunday morning, I meet CJ for brunch at our usual spot, so I can at least ask her if he's still alive.

CJ looks tired but happy, and I let her chatter about Drew's restaurant plans, as apparently he got an accepted offer this past week for a restaurant space. I make a mental note to ask Drew if he's hiring. A change of job location would probably be a good idea during this whole serial killer mess. Or just in general. I need something to shake me out of the rut I've let my life fall into. You know, something besides a serial killer. Something good.

"How's work been?" I ask casually when she finishes, sipping my mimosa. Booze in the morning is definitely called for given the circumstances.

"Good! Busy, but nothing crazy. Why?"

My stomach drops. "Just wondering. Matt mentioned some emergency project. I texted him yesterday, and he never responded, so I figured it must be pretty bad ..."

CJ's brow furrows. "Not that I know of. And I'd know —
I'm his assistant, after all."

I clench my jaw. Well, that confirms my suspicions about
Matt's weird behavior, the sudden "work emergency," and his
lack of response.

He's avoiding me.

I don't say anything to CJ, swiftly moving the
conversation along to Francesca's wedding planning, having
moved back in with my folks, and pretty much anything
besides mentioning the cloud hanging over all our heads,
mine particularly. I'm grateful for CJ's ability to keep to
normal, non-serial-killer-y topics. I'm also concerned for what
kind of awful crap she must have gone through in her life to
have developed that skill.

Still, as usual, we part ways both feeling better about our
day. A surge of gratitude flows through me as I head into
work. Even if things go south with Matt, I know CJ and I will
always be friends. We pinky swore and everything.

I get back to my parents' house that evening and collapse in
bed after a hot shower. Still no texts or calls from Matt. I
decide to try one more time. To my surprise, he answers on
the third ring.

"Hey," he says, sounding tired. "How's your parents'
place?"

"Cut the bullshit, Matt."

Silence. So I press on.

"CJ says there's no work emergency. So what's really going on?"

He sighs. "Anna —"

"Just tell me," I plead.

Rustling, then silence. I almost cave when he finally says, "Sullivan told me something. About Martin's victims. About why he chose them."

I freeze, even my breath halting in my throat. "And?"

A heavy sigh. "He targeted women who were cheaters. His whole psychosis was about punishing infidelity."

The words hit like a physical blow as I put the pieces together. "So you think *I'm* a cheater?"

"I don't know what to think." His voice is strained. "I know it shouldn't matter. I know that even if you had cheated on someone in the past, it doesn't mean you'd cheat on me. But after Alyssa —"

He's comparing me to *that* bitch? "Are you fucking kidding me right now?" Rage floods through me, hot and clean. "I'm not a cheater, Matt. How could you believe that about me?"

"I didn't want to believe it, but the killer's entire motive —"

"Was based on the delusions of a psychopath!" I'm practically shouting now. "Martin was insane! He thought women deserved to die because, what, he had some grudge with cheaters?"

"His father killed his mother over an affair," Matt offers.

I snort in disbelief. "And you're going to believe his assessment of my character over me?"

"Anna —"

I can't. I can't listen to him defend this insanity. "No. You know what? Fuck off, Matt. I'm dealing with someone who wants to murder me, and instead of being there for me, you're judging me based on a serial killer's fantasies?"

"I'm not … it doesn't matter. I'm still trying to protect you —"

"By abandoning me when I need you most? Great job." I'm crying now, angry tears streaming down my face. "I thought you loved me. I thought you knew me. But apparently, you think so little of me you'll believe a murderer over your own girlfriend."

"That's not —"

I hang up.

I sob as quietly as I can as Matt's words loop through my mind, shattering the miracle I thought our relationship was, and the progress it helped me make, leaving me cold and empty.

I cry myself to sleep in my childhood bedroom, surrounded by old posters and stuffed animals that can't protect me from the terror crushing my chest.

Someone wants to kill me. The man I love thinks I'm a cheater. I let him in, trusted him … and he just showed me exactly what he thinks of me.

Maybe we only fell so hard so fast because of the circumstances. Trauma bonds people quickly, but that doesn't mean it's real. I should've realized that didn't mean we'd go the distance. I should have been thinking with my head instead of my heart.

And Sophia's right about one thing — how can I be there for Francesca when I can barely hold myself together? How can I pretend to be happy and plan centerpieces and flower arrangements when I'm waiting for a killer to find me? As much as I want to, as much as I don't want to let this ruin what sense of normalcy I've regained, as much as I don't want it to affect the people I love … how can it not?

I pull a pillow over my head, trying to muffle my sobs so my parents won't hear. Tomorrow I'll have to face their questions, Francesca's wedding planning, the reality that Matt and I might be over before we really began.

But tonight, I just let myself break.

CHAPTER TWENTY-ONE

MATT

Monday morning finds me once again at CJ's door at an ungodly hour. This time Drew answers in nothing but boxers, looking murderous.

"Seriously?" he growls. "This is becoming a thing now?"

"Sorry, man, but I need to talk to CJ."

"At six-thirty in the morning. Again. Before work. Where you see her every day." He steps aside with exaggerated reluctance. "She's in the kitchen. And Matt? Maybe consider dealing with this shit when I'm at work."

CJ's at the table with her coffee, but she doesn't push food my way this time. Just gives me a look that could peel paint.

"I fucked up," I say without preamble.

"You think?" She sets down her mug with enough force to slosh coffee. "I had brunch with Anna yesterday. She thought she was being sly asking me questions about your 'work emergency' but it didn't take much to put together that you've been avoiding her. On purpose. After a serial killer broke into her apartment."

And I'm a complete asshole because, despite her angry rant, I'm just relieved she doesn't know I accused Anna of being a cheater because a serial killer said so.

Instead, I say, "I know. I just … I'm having trouble dealing with all of this, but I know I need to fix this. How do I fix this?"

"You apologize. Grovel. Beg. Whatever it takes." She pauses. "And by the way, Uncle Chuck and Aunt Meg want to know why you weren't at Sunday dinner."

I groan. "You told them?"

"I didn't tell them everything. Just that you were seeing someone who was in danger, kind of like what happened with me and Drew." I give her an incredulous look and she throws up her hands. "Well, *someone* had to stop keeping them in the dark. They knew something was up with you, and they were *worried*, asshole! They've been there for us our whole lives, Matt. They deserve to know what's going on."

I know she's not wrong, but the fact that she told them without asking me first has me from zero to pissed off in half a second flat. Even though I know it's not fair.

"CJ —"

"No," she interrupts, slamming a hand down so abruptly it makes me jump back. "I'm done with the secrets. They're the only people in the entire world that we don't have to hide from and they want to meet Anna, so you'd better get your shit together and make things right."

I slump in my chair, the weight of this burden finally too much. "You're right. I'm sorry."

"I'm not the one you need to apologize to," she says crossly, clearly not mollified by my apology in the least.

Drew appears in the doorway, still looking grumpy. "And I'm here to say it again: no more stopping by at the ass crack of dawn. It's really disrupting my sleep schedule."

"Sorry," I mutter. "I'll ... work on my timing."

"You do that." But his expression softens slightly. "Good luck with Anna. You're gonna need it."

After the longest day of work of my life, endlessly churning over what I'll say to Anna, I stand on the Martellas' porch, flowers in hand, trying to work up the courage to knock. Before I can, the door flies open and I'm face-to-face with Sophia.

"You," she says, voice dripping venom. "You have some fucking nerve showing up here."

"I know. But I need to talk to Anna —"

"After what you did? After you abandoned her when she needed you most?" She steps onto the porch, closing the door behind her. "Give me one good reason I shouldn't kick your ass right now."

Shit. Well, I guess I'm glad Anna is at least talking to her family about what she's going through. Someone should be there for her, especially since Sophia is right — I sure as hell wasn't.

"Because I deserve it, and that would be letting me off too easy?"

She blinks, apparently not expecting that. "You hurt my sister."

I sigh, lowering the flowers. "I know. I'm an idiot. A complete asshole. I let my own issues cloud my judgment, and I hurt the woman I love."

"Love?" She scoffs. "You don't accuse someone you love of being a cheater based on a psychopath's fantasies."

I grimace. "You're right. I don't deserve her. But I need to try to make this right."

Sophia studies me for a long moment. "If you hurt her again, I'll end you. Sister's boyfriend or not. We clear?"

"Crystal." I let out a relieved sigh.

She narrows her eyes but turns back, opens the door, and yells, "Anna! Someone's here for you!"

Anna appears in the hallway a few moments later and freezes when she sees me. Even from here, I can see her eyes are red-rimmed. And she's still in her pajamas. How can she look so tired when she's still in her pajamas at six p.m.? My heart clenches.

"Can we talk?" I ask. "Please?"

She crosses her arms, looking decidedly less forlorn and more pissed off. "You have five minutes."

She joins me on the porch, keeping a significant distance between us.

"I'm sorry," I start. "I'm so fucking sorry, Anna. I let my past with Alyssa poison my thinking. I was scared and stupid, and I hurt you."

"You believed a serial killer over me," she says quietly but forcefully. "Do you have any idea how that feels?"

I shake my head in supplication. "No. But I know I betrayed your trust when you needed me most. There's no excuse for that."

"Then why are you here?"

"Because I love you. Because I was wrong. Because there's more about my conversation with Sullivan that you need to know." I take a breath. "He told me about the other suspects. Martin's siblings and his ex-fiancée. I'm working on a plan to investigate them safely."

Her expression shifts slightly. "Other suspects?"

I nod, encouraged that she's listening. "Three of them. I've been researching, trying to figure out how to approach this without putting anyone at risk." I meet her eyes. I see sorrow and wariness there. Wariness I know I earned. "I know I don't deserve it, but I'm asking if you want in on this. We're stronger together."

She's quiet for so long I think she's going to send me away. She finally says, "I'm not sure I can forgive you, Matt. You broke something between us."

I look down at the flowers still in my hand, tears swimming in my eyes. "I know."

"But I also know I need help to find whoever's after me." She wraps her arms around herself. "So yes. When you have a plan, let me know. That's all I can offer right now."

"That's more than I deserve. Thank you."

"Don't thank me yet. This doesn't mean we're okay."

"I understand." I hold the flowers out lamely. "These were

for you. Though it doesn't begin to show you how sorry I am. But I will. I promise."

Anna stiffens. "I don't want flowers and promises." She sighs. "I want you to *show* me I can trust you again."

I swallow hard, a tear spilling down my cheek. "I will."

She stares at me for a long moment before going back inside without another word, leaving me alone on the porch with my regrets.

Back home, I make a late dinner for CJ and me, who I texted to come over, enticing her with an apology meal of her favorite stir-fry. Benefits of Drew being at work, because I know she's pissed off enough that she wouldn't have come unless there was food.

"How'd it go?" she asks, digging in.

"I apologized. She's not ready to forgive me, but she wants to help investigate the suspects."

"That's something."

"Yeah." I push rice around my plate. "Sullivan said something else. About expanding my abilities. He thinks I could learn to control what I See better."

CJ perks up. "Like, you might be able to do what Dad could? See the history of objects, not just people?"

"Maybe. He showed me memories of people training, developing their gifts. It didn't seem like you could make your abilities do things unless it was already within their scope."

"Well, either way, we should practice," she says immediately. "See what you *are* capable of."

I suppress a self-satisfied grin. I mentioned it because I knew she'd go for the idea. And as soon as I Saw it in Sullivan's memories, I knew it would come in handy. Especially now that I'm going after the other suspects.

So after dinner, we sit cross-legged on the living room floor. Using techniques I glimpsed in Sullivan's memories, I focus on pulling specific memories from CJ without her actively sharing them.

"Holy shit," she gasps as I rifle through her morning with Drew. "That's invasive."

"Sorry." But I'm not, not really. This could be useful. "You can feel it?"

She shrugs. "Only because I know what to look for. I don't think most people would notice."

I nod and try pushing harder, searching for memories she's actively trying to hide. It's like hitting a wall, but I can feel cracks, places where I might break through with practice. But after an hour, the effort leaves me with a splitting headache.

"Enough," CJ says, pressing a cool hand to my forehead. "You're burning up. You're pushing too hard."

I sigh. "But I need to get better before I approach the suspects."

She studies me with a look that says she realizes what I was up to all along. "No. You need to not give yourself an aneurysm."

I roll my eyes. "Don't be dramatic. I'll be fine. Can we do this every night that Drew's at work?" I ask.

She smirks. "So long as you keep feeding me, I'll keep being your guinea pig, padawan."

I give her a dry look. "Okay, Yoda."

She snorts. "If you're going to make me a Star Wars character, I'm more of a Leia, don't you think?" she teases.

I blanch. "Ugh. I know we're twins, but I am *not* going to be the Luke in this equation."

CJ tips her head back and laughs. "I didn't even think about the twin thing, but it's *perfect.* You are *so* Luke." She pats me on the shoulder. "See you tomorrow, *Luke.*"

With a wink, she's gone. And I can't help grumbling after her, "Fuck that. I'm totally the Mando in this equation."

Tuesday after work, I decide to go see Sullivan before making CJ dinner. He agrees to meet at a coffee shop near the station. When he sees me, he takes one look at me and sighs.

"You told her about the cheating connection."

I blanch as I take a seat across from him. "How did you —" I shake my head. The man has an ability that I don't know the limits of. It was a stupid question. "Never mind. Yes. I fucked up."

"You think?" He leans back, studying me. "Let me guess. You have trust issues from a past relationship and projected them onto her."

Geez, this guy's good. Or he's capable of far more than I expected. "Something like that," I reply vaguely, unwilling to give him more information than is necessary. He may be helping me, but I still don't know for sure what he's after. So I only trust him so far.

Sullivan huffs a sarcastic laugh. "Matt, serial killers don't need reality to match their fantasies. The women don't actually have to be cheaters. They just have to trigger something in the killer's mind. Could be she smiled at him wrong. Could be she reminded him of someone who *was* a cheater. Hell, could be he assaulted her and decided that made her 'impure.'"

While I knew Martin was unreliable, it didn't even occur to me that his fundamental motive could be so flawed in its execution. I suddenly feel sick. "So Anna might not have —"

"Probably didn't," he cuts in. "But the point is, it doesn't matter. The killer's perception is what matters, not reality. And you just accused an innocent woman — a *victim* that barely escaped with her life — based on a madman's delusions."

"I know. I mean ... I didn't know just how badly I'd gotten it wrong, but ... God, I know." Nausea roils through me.

"Focus on the danger," Sullivan says firmly, tapping the table to get my attention. "Everything else can wait. If you're going to investigate these suspects, you need to be careful. The brother especially. Clean records often hide the darkest secrets."

"I know, I've been researching them. The brother's in Redwood City. The sister's harder to pin down — it looks like she's been in and out of rehab, but I can't find a current address. The fiancée remarried quickly after getting a big payout for a tell-all interview about Martin."

"Interesting." Sullivan sips his coffee. "You'll want to approach cautiously. Use your ability, but don't push too hard. And Matt? Don't go alone."

"I won't."

He gives me a knowing look. "I assume your twin will go with you?"

My eyes meet his. In all our talks, CJ has never come up. I purposely haven't mentioned her. But then, I Saw in his memories that he was there when our mother was pregnant.

When I don't respond, Sullivan smirks. "I'm no threat to your sister, Matt. I don't care what her ability is, if she has one at all. But the Roberts twins, working together?" A new light enters his eyes. "Your parents would be proud."

The mention of my parents hits unexpectedly hard. And my trust in him shifts just a little, for the better. "Would they?"

He nods. "They believed in using gifts to help others. To protect the innocent." He stands, and if I didn't know better, it was to hide the sorrow he couldn't keep out of his eyes. "That's what you're doing now. Just ... try not to destroy your relationship in the process."

After he leaves, I head home and dive back into research before CJ comes over. The brother — Ezekiel Martin — has a LinkedIn profile, a Facebook page full of hiking photos, a spotless record. But Ted Bundy had a clean record too.

The sister — Esther Martin — is a ghost online. Last

known address was a halfway house that closed six months ago. She could be anywhere.

The fiancée — now Leah Walsh — lives large in the wealthy Pacific Heights. Her new husband is a tech executive, but my bet is the tell-all interview money clearly also went to good use.

I stop my research to make dinner — since I was basically done or at dead ends anyway — and split the seafood pasta with CJ. Afterward, I practice on CJ again, pushing my ability until my nose bleeds. She forces me to stop, but I can feel progress. I'm getting better at directing what I See, at pulling memories she doesn't want to share.

Though I could've lived without knowing that she keeps a diary where she rates all of my girlfriends on a scale of one to ten for "sister-in-law potential" with detailed pros and cons lists. Fittingly, Alyssa was a three because "Matt deserves better plus too fake and laughs like a hyena." Whereas Anna is an eleven, for obvious reasons, but I definitely tease her hard about the high score. What are we, thirteen?

I'd say I need to retaliate by keeping my own journal, but she and Drew … well, fate and all. No point now. Besides, it's sweet that CJ is so invested in making sure I end up with someone worthy of me.

Sibling bickering aside, the session not only helps me push my abilities but also makes me too exhausted to do anything remotely physical afterward. So, I think a lot about how to approach the suspects.

By the time I collapse in bed, I have the beginnings of a plan. Approach Ezekiel first — he's the most accessible. See what I can pull from him. Then track down Esther. Leave Leah for last — she seems like the most protected, the most suspicious, with that interview payout and how quickly she moved on.

And as much as it goes against my instincts, I text Anna because I told her I'd tell her what I was up to. *Working on the plan. Should have something solid by Thursday. Still willing to help?*

Her response comes almost an hour later. *Yes. But this is just about finding the killer. Nothing more.*

My heart sinks. *Understood.*

I stare at her message until my eyes blur. I've lost her trust, maybe lost her entirely. But if I can keep her alive, maybe that's enough.

Maybe it has to be.

CHAPTER TWENTY-TWO

ANNA

Wednesday night's service is brutal. Not because we're slammed — we're not — but because I can't stop replaying Matt's apology in my head. By the time we're tearing down the kitchen, I'm moving on autopilot.

"Okay, what's wrong?" Drew asks, appearing at my elbow as I'm wrapping the leftover mise en place that can be stored overnight. "You've been moping all night."

"I'm not moping," I protest … in what I realize is a very mopey voice. God, I'm totally moping.

"You accidentally served table twelve's dessert to table eight," he points out gently.

I wince. Drew has ripped into servers for less. "Did they complain?"

"No, they were too polite. But I noticed." He leans against the prep counter, studying me with those sharp eyes that miss nothing in his kitchen. "Is this about Matt?"

I shouldn't be surprised that he knows. CJ probably told

him everything. Still, I'm reluctant to dump my relationship drama on my boss.

"Anna." Uncharacteristically, his voice softens slightly. "Did he hurt you? Use his ability on you without permission?"

"No, nothing like that." I abandon the button mushrooms I'd been wrapping and turn to face him. "It's just ..." I search for how to put this simply "... he doesn't trust me. How can I be with someone who doesn't trust me?"

"What makes you think he doesn't trust you?" Drew asks, brows bunching together.

"He accused me of being a cheater. Based on what ... someone unreliable thought." The words come out bitter. "I can't be with someone who thinks so little of me."

Drew surprises me by laughing. Actually *laughing*.

"What's so funny?" I ask crossly.

"Sorry, it's just ... CJ and I went through this dance when I found out about her ability. The doubting, the accusations, the drama." He shakes his head. "Roberts twins, man. They can be exhausting."

"This is different. His ex cheated on him, and he immediately assumed I was a cheater too without even talking to me first," I protest.

"Can you blame him?" I scoff, but he holds up a hand as his expression turns serious. "Think about it. He found out she cheated while having an ability that lets him see people's memories. That probably made him question everything — every moment, every memory, wondering what else he missed or misread."

I open my mouth to object, then close it. I hadn't thought about it that way.

"Living with abilities like theirs ..." Drew continues. "Knowing things others don't, seeing things that can't be unseen. It would make anyone paranoid. Add heartbreak to that? I'm surprised he's willing to date at all."

The words sink in slowly. Matt, discovering Alyssa's betrayal. Probably seeing it in her memories, unable to avoid the brutal truth. Then meeting me, falling fast, and suddenly being told I was targeted as a "cheater" by a killer whose whole MO was punishing infidelity.

"Shit," I mutter, realizing he's right.

"Yeah." Drew tosses his towel into the hamper. "Look, I'm not saying he didn't do anything wrong. But maybe cut him some slack? The Roberts twins don't do anything halfway, including fucking up."

I lean against the counter, seeing everything differently. I was so busy being hurt by Matt's assumptions that I didn't realize I'd made plenty of my own. Assuming his past with Alyssa was just typical relationship drama. Assuming he should just trust me because I said so. Assuming his ability made things easier for him when maybe sometimes it makes everything harder.

"I need to go," I say suddenly.

Drew smirks. "Finally. Go fix things with your boyfriend. But Anna? Next time you two have drama, maybe keep it from affecting your table service?"

"Yes, chef," I say with a mock salute, already untying my apron. I lean up and kiss him on the cheek. "And thanks."

He winks at me. "Anytime."

I snort. A year ago, Drew would've publicly dressed me down for the mistakes I made tonight. CJ really has changed him for the better.

As I leave, I realize that a year ago, a copycat killer would've sent me into hysterics. I would've been a mess. And while I'm anxious, I'm managing, mostly anyway. Maybe Matt has changed me for the better, too.

———

I texted Matt first thing this morning, and he agreed to meet me at his place this evening. So here I stand, at Matt's door, heart pounding.

When he answers, the hope and wariness on his face nearly break me.

"Hi. Can I come in?" I ask when he says nothing.

He shakes himself out of his stupor. "Of course." He steps aside, and I follow him to the living room.

"I owe you an apology," I start before I can lose my nerve.

His eyebrows shoot up. "You? Anna, no —"

"Let me finish." I take a breath. "I was so focused on being hurt that you didn't trust me, I didn't think about what you've been through. Finding out about Alyssa with your ability ... that must have been horrible."

Matt sinks onto the couch. "It was. I hadn't read her throughout our entire relationship ... until I found something that made me realize that was a mistake." His vibe turns desperately sad, and my heart squeezes. "So when I did ...

well, I Saw everything. Every lie, every time she was with him when she said she was somewhere else. It was like watching my entire relationship reveal itself as a fraud."

"And then I came along." I sit beside him, careful to leave space between us. "And suddenly you hear I was targeted as a 'cheater' by a killer. Of course you spiraled." I want to kick myself for not realizing how deep this pain went for him.

"That doesn't excuse what I did," he says quietly. Apologetically.

I can't help it; I reach out and touch his knee. He meets my eyes, and I see so much pain in his. "No, but it explains it," I offer. "And I should have tried to understand instead of just being angry." I look away, ashamed. "I made assumptions too. About you, about what you should or shouldn't feel. That wasn't fair."

"Anna —"

My phone rings, interrupting whatever he was going to say. It's Detective Worthington.

"I should take this," I say apologetically, showing him Worthington's name on the screen.

Matt nods, and I answer. "Detective?"

"Ms. Martella. I need to inform you of a development. There's been another victim."

My stomach sinks. I'll never get used to his abruptness. Especially when he says things like that. "When?"

"Early this morning. Ms. Martella ... her name was Anna."

I'm so shocked that the phone nearly slips from my hand. Matt must see something in my face because he moves closer, not touching me, but present.

"They're sending a message," Worthington continues. "You're in danger."

"I see." My voice sounds surprisingly steady.

"You don't sound surprised," he says skeptically.

"I'm not. I ... had a feeling something like this might happen," I offer feebly. Though it's true. Even though I already knew they'd come after me, since they started their campaign of terror, some part of me has been waiting for an escalation.

Worthington pauses. "I'm giving you a number. Whichever officer who is physically closest to you will always answer, day or night. If anything happens — anything at all — you call."

I take down the number with shaking hands. "Thank you."

"Be careful, Ms. Martella."

After I hang up, Matt immediately asks, "What happened?"

"Another victim. This one was named Anna." I set the phone down carefully, like it might explode. "The killer's sending a message."

"Fuck." Matt runs his hands through his hair, a wild look in his eyes. "That's it. We're getting you somewhere safe. Out of the city, maybe out of state —"

"No," I say firmly.

"Anna —" he starts to protest.

"I said no." I stand, needing to move. "I'm not running. I'm not letting fear control my life again."

"This isn't about fear; it's about survival," he snaps. His energy is frantic, panicked.

"It's about both." I turn to face him. "After Martin, I hid for two years. I stopped dating, stopped living. I won't do that again." I sigh. "And this also might mean Worthington comes after you harder now. Uses this as evidence that you're involved. If I leave, that won't help you."

"Are you kidding me? Anna, someone just killed a woman with your name to send a message. I'm not worried about me. I'm worried about *you*." He stands too, reaching for me and then stopping. "Please. Let me protect you."

My heart aches. He must really love me. If the tables were turned … well, I'd be saying the same thing. Still, it doesn't change my mind.

"I'll be careful," I promise. "I'll never be alone. I'll check in constantly." I step closer to him. "But I'm not running. I learned a lot after the last time. I know how to keep myself safe."

"I know you think you can, but this person is *dangerous*. And unpredictable. If they really want to get at you …" He shakes his head wildly like it could dislodge the idea of what would happen next.

I sigh. "This is my choice, Matt. You can help me or not, but I'm staying."

He looks like he wants to argue more, staring at me for a long minute before dipping his chin in strained agreement. "Fine. Then we stick to the plan. Investigate the suspects. Find this bastard before he finds you."

"Together?"

A muscle in Matt's jaw ticks. "I'll keep you in the loop," he says. Something about the phrasing tells me he's got ideas about doing it on his own. And the look on his face definitely says he hates the idea of me being anywhere near the other suspects. "I promise," he breathes, likely in response to the look of disbelief on my face. This time he reaches for me, pulling me into his arms. "I'm sorry. For everything."

"I'm sorry too." I breathe in his familiar scent, feeling safer than I have in days. "We're going to get through this."

"We are," he agrees, but I can feel the tension in his body.

"Matt …" I breathe, looking up into his eyes.

The intensity of his gaze strips me bare. And I realize how much I missed him. Missed being in his arms. Looking into his eyes. Seeing his love for me there. Because it shines through, radiating from him as his eyes drink in my face. How could I have ever doubted it? The distance did us no favors. But now that I'm here, my concerns melt away.

So I kiss him. His surprise quickly melts into ardor, our bodies colliding with need. He takes me upstairs and we're just as quickly undressed.

I push him to the bed and climb on him, sliding him into me. He sits up, pulling me into him, tilting his hips frenetically. I slam down to meet his rhythm.

"God, Anna," he gasps. I can feel the possessive fire that's consuming him in every slide into my body.

I lean in, dipping my tongue into his mouth, wrapping myself around him as I ride him, needing him inside of me everywhere all at once.

"I need more," I groan. "I need you."

He flips us, continuing his punishing assault, his body

melded to mine as his cock slams home over and over. "Fuck, Anna, I need you."

"You have me," I gasp, scratching at his back.

It spurs him on to a bed-shaking pace. His love and angst and heartache melt into my skin, joining my own. Our climb is one, our bodies one, as our hearts and minds join and we both tip over the edge together, reuniting our very souls. I feel it so deeply that I can't help the tears that escape.

He slows and stops, and makes to pull away. But I hold him tighter, despite our sweat-slicked bodies. Because of it. Our heaving chests, his receding manhood, the mind-numbing pleasure still tingling in my limbs … it's all so real. Tangible proof of our deep connection.

And yet, as he holds me, as the feeling of oneness seeps through every pore, I can't help the dread that pulls at my heart.

Another Anna is dead. The killer is escalating, getting bolder. And we're running out of time.

But I meant what I said. I'm done running. Done hiding.

This time, I'm going to fight for my life. For this love. This time, I'm going to fight back.

CHAPTER TWENTY-THREE

MATT

I may have promised Anna I'd keep her in the loop, but as I lie awake with her sleeping peacefully beside me, I know I can't. Not after last night. Not after we made up. Not after the kind of love we made. Not when another woman named Anna is dead. Not when the killer is escalating.

By morning, I've made my decision. I'll investigate the suspects while she's at work this weekend. Fast, efficient, and most importantly — without putting her in danger. She's … everything to me, more deeply, more completely than ever. And risking her … I can't stomach it. No matter what I promised.

So, as soon as I get to work, I pull CJ into my office.

"Well, Drew was impressed you didn't show up at our place this morning," she says, taking a seat across from my desk.

I sink down into my chair, already tired and it's not even nine a.m. "Cute. Look. Anna and I made up last night, but she got a call from Worthington. There was another murder. The victim's name was Anna."

CJ's eyes widen. "Holy shit," she gasps.

I nod. "It's an obvious message that she's in danger, but she doesn't seem deterred by it. If anything, she's more determined than ever not to let this person stop her from living her life."

"That's … good?" CJ hazards, clearly confused.

I frown. "Yeah, except for the part where she still wants to help me investigate the suspects."

"Ah," CJ says, finally getting why I'm in a mood. "Yeah, that wouldn't be good."

"No, it wouldn't. So here's the plan. I want to do this quickly, but I may need your help. Can you come with me to question the suspects tomorrow while Anna's at work?"

"Matt ..." Her tone is wary as she pulls at a curl. A sure tell that she's anxious about this. Which I get. But I still need her. "That could be dangerous. I mean, one of them is likely a serial killer."

"Which is exactly why I need you. Your ability could give us a warning if something's about to go wrong."

CJ's nose scrunches up. "I take it Anna doesn't know about this new plan?"

I snort. "Of course not. She's safer not knowing."

"Matt —" Now her tone is chastising, so I decide to stop her right there. I know it's not the best thing to do after promising Anna I'd let her help. But I've already decided.

"Please, CJ. I can't lose her. You said it yourself — you've Seen our future together."

A long pause. "That was before I Saw *nothing*. Before her future disappeared."

"Which is why we have to do this. Before it's too late."

She sighs. "Drew will kill me. Then he'll kill you."

I grimace. "He doesn't have to know."

"Right. Because I'm so good at hiding things from him." Another sigh. "Fine. But we're telling someone where we're going. I'm not disappearing without a trace."

"I'll call Sullivan. He'll be our backup."

"You trust him?" she asks skeptically.

I nod. "I do. I can't say I fully know his motives, but he was loyal to our parents. He …" I think back to his memories, tinged with sadness "… he misses them. And he wants to help us."

She raises a brow. "Us? He knows about me?"

"He was there when Mom was pregnant," I explain. "I don't know if he met us as kids, but yes, he knows about you. I mean, that you exist, not about your ability."

She twists that curl for another minute before slowly nodding. "Okay. But we've got to be careful."

"I know. We will be."

CJ leaves, and I take a deep breath before calling Sullivan.

He answers almost as soon as I hear it ring.

"Matt. What's happening?"

"CJ and I are going to approach the suspects tomorrow. Can you be on standby in case something goes wrong?"

I hear him take a deep breath. "You're sure about this?"

"Did you hear about the last murder?" I ask pointedly.

"I did," he responds grimly. "That's why I asked."

"Then you know why I can't wait any longer."

There's a long silence before he says, "All right. Be smart. Be safe. And keep your phone in hand. I'll be ready."

The next day I drop Anna at the restaurant, kissing her goodbye and promising to pick her up after her shift. Not telling her what I'm about to do sits heavy in my stomach, but not as heavy as the thought of losing her.

When I get to CJ's apartment, Drew is still there. And he looks pissed.

"So I hear you're going somewhere today?" he asks, arms crossed.

CJ appears behind him, looking guilty. "He knew something was up. He asked me directly if I was doing something dangerous."

"And we don't lie to each other." Drew's glare could melt steel. "So. You're dragging my girlfriend into your serial killer hunt?"

"Listen —"

"No, you listen." He steps forward. "I know you two have this weird twin bond I try to ignore, but this is too fucking far."

"We've had only each other most of our lives," I snap back. "You're going to have to accept that CJ and I are close. That there are things you won't understand."

"Close is one thing. Getting her killed is another."

"You think I'd let anything happen to her?" My voice rises. "She's my sister."

He takes a menacing step forward. "And now she's my girlfriend. And I'm not letting her —"

"Stop." CJ pushes between us. "Both of you. Drew, I'm going. This is my choice. Matt won't let anything happen to me, and we have backup."

"CJ —"

"Remember when I asked Matt to help find out who was after you? He said no at first. He didn't want to get involved." She looks at me. "Tell him why you changed your mind."

I meet Drew's eyes. "Because I realized it was what was best for CJ. Because I love her, and I knew it was fate that brought you two together."

Drew blinks, apparently not expecting that.

"Just like fate brought me and Anna together," I continue. "And doesn't Anna mean something to you too? You're friends. You've been there for her."

"Of course she means something to me. She's —" He stops, frustrated.

"Family," CJ finishes. "She's family. Which is why we're doing this."

Drew looks between us, then focuses on CJ. "You said something about backup?"

He prompted CJ, but I answer. "A detective. Ray Sullivan. He knows what we're doing, where we're going. First sign of trouble, I get CJ out."

Drew's steely gaze flicks back to me. "You promise?"

"I promise," I respond resolutely. And mean it with everything I have.

Drew's shoulders drop slightly. "If she gets hurt —"

"You'll kick my ass. I know. And I'd deserve it. Hell, I'd kick my own ass."

"Damn right." But his anger has shifted to concern. "Be careful. Both of you."

CJ kisses him goodbye, and I'm surprised when Drew turns to me with a resigned expression and says, "Go figure this shit out for Anna's sake. Good luck."

Ezekiel Martin's apartment is in a rundown complex in Redwood City. But when we knock, no one answers. Well, that was a lot of anticipation for nothing.

"Maybe he's at work?" CJ suggests.

"On a Saturday? I guess he could be." I try peering through the window, but the blinds are closed. "Well, I still don't have an address for the sister, so let's try the fiancée. We can come back here later if she's a dead end."

As we drive back through the city and into Pacific Heights, our surroundings change drastically. Leah Walsh lives in a different world — a veritable mansion with security gates, perfect landscaping, and a stunning view of the bay. She answers the door herself, looking exactly like her Facebook photos. Long dark hair, bright blue eyes, alabaster skin, and a designer dress that probably cost more than my car. Polished, pretty … and wary.

"Can I help you?" she asks, a slender eyebrow raised haughtily.

"Mrs. Walsh? I'm Matt Roberts. This is my sister CJ. We're friends of Anna Martella."

Her face shifts oddly ... and I realize it's likely because she's confused, but her Botox injections aren't allowing her eyebrows to move.

"I don't know who that is," she says, swinging the door closed.

I lift a hand, asking her to wait, and miraculously she does. "She was Ezra Martin's last victim ... the one the police saved. But I'm sure you've heard the killings have started again, and she might be in danger. We just have a few questions."

Her face pales, and her already haunting eyes widen. "I don't ... I can't talk about him." But she doesn't close the door.

"Please," CJ says gently. "We're trying to stop whoever's continuing his work."

Leah's hand flies to her throat. "Why would I know anything about it?"

"You were involved with the original killer. Maybe you know something that could help Anna," I say, including her name again to drive home that this is a real person, in real danger. "Please, can we come in and talk? I promise we won't take up much of your time."

She hesitates, then eventually steps aside.

The inside of the house is as magazine-perfect as the outside, with lavish furniture, ornate window dressings, and stylish décor. But I notice her hands shake as she leads us to a sitting room.

"I didn't know," she says, settling onto a high-backed chair that's stunning but not terribly comfortable looking. "About what Ezra was doing. I loved him. I thought we were going to have a life together."

CJ and I settle on the similarly uncomfortable divan beside her that looks like one of those old fainting couches. Leah angles herself toward me, our knees almost touching, as if beseeching me to understand.

"It must have been horrible," CJ offers from my other side. "Finding out."

"It destroyed everything. My job, my family, my friends — everyone looked at me differently. Like I should have known. Like I was complicit." Tears well in her eyes. "The interview ... people think I'm some gold digger who profited from tragedy. But I had nothing, and no one, and unfortunately ... well, I needed money. It may have been no better than blood money, but it was money. I had to take it if I wanted to survive."

I extend my hand in an offer of comfort. "I'm so sorry for what you've been through."

She takes it automatically ... and the memories flood in. Horror at discovering her fiancé's crimes. Months of intensive therapy. Sleepless nights wondering if she'd missed signs, thinking of the victims that could've been saved if she hadn't. Meeting her current husband at a support group for crime victims. The relief of being believed, being loved despite her past.

She's clean. Traumatized for sure, but clean.

"Do you know anything that could help us stop whoever is doing this?" CJ asks.

Leah shakes her head, a tear slipping down her cheek. "I don't think so. I never knew any of his friends or family. And he kept me isolated from mine. He was secretive, but I never imagined …" She trails off, shaking her head again.

I give her hand a reassuring squeeze. "I understand. Thank you for talking with us," I say, releasing her. "We won't take any more of your time."

Leah rises. "I'm sorry I couldn't be of more help."

CJ reaches out and squeezes her hand too. "Don't be. We knew it was a long shot. I'm sorry for everything you've gone through."

Leah smiles sadly and shows us out, wishing us well.

Outside, CJ looks at me. "She's not our killer."

"No. Which leaves the siblings."

I call Sullivan as we drive. "Leah Walsh is clear. We're going back to check on the brother, but I can't find anything on the sister."

"I might have something. Esther Martin. Recently checked into a halfway house in Oakland. Sending you the details now."

"Thanks."

"Matt? Be careful with this one. Addicts can be unpredictable."

The Bay Bridge is at a crawl, as usual, so it takes us a long time to get there. CJ and I are quiet on the drive, save filling her in on Leah's memories and CJ letting me See her future. A child, though she didn't look pregnant yet. Beneath my concern for Anna, I'm … happy for Leah. That she's healed and is building a life, despite what happened. I can only hope Anna gets to do the same.

We arrive at the address Sullivan texted me to find that the halfway house is a converted Victorian in a rough part of Oakland. The manager, a tired-looking woman named Carol, eyes us suspiciously.

"You cops?"

"No," CJ says. "We're looking for Esther Martin. Is she here?"

"Might be. Might not. Residents got privacy rights."

"It's important," I say. "Related to her brother's case."

Carol's expression shifts. "That bastard? Yeah, Essie's here. Been clean two months, don't need you stirring up trouble."

"We just want to talk."

She stares at us warily for another moment before gesturing for us to follow her. She leads us to a common room where a woman sits alone, staring at a TV that's not on. She's thin, gaunt, with the hollow look of someone who's been through hell.

"Essie? Some people are here to see you."

Esther Martin looks up, and I see Ezra in her features. Same eyes, same sharp cheekbones. But where his eyes held cold calculation, hers show damage.

"Who are you?" Her voice is raspy, suspicious.

"Friends of one of your brother's victims," I say carefully. "We're trying to understand —"

"No." She stands abruptly. "No, I don't talk about him. I don't —"

"Someone's copying his murders," CJ says. "We think you might —"

Esther's eyes go wild. "You think I'm killing people? Like him?" She backs toward the door. "I'm not him! I'm nothing like him!"

I reach out instinctively to calm her. "We're not accusing —"

"Don't touch me!"

But my hand brushes the skin on her wrist for just a second before she pulls away. And in that second, I See.

Blood. So much blood. A woman's face, frozen in death. Hands — Esther's hands — covered in red.

"Oh god," I breathe without thinking.

Esther must see something on my face because she bolts. I chase after her, but she knows the building better. By the time I get outside, she's vanished into the Oakland streets.

"Matt!" CJ catches up, breathing hard. "What did you See?"

"Murder. She's killed someone."

And I'm glad I took Sullivan's advice, because all I have to do with the phone in my hand is press a button and I'm calling him.

"Matt. What's happening?"

"We lost her," I say immediately. "But she's our killer. I Saw it."

"I'll get units out looking. Get somewhere safe. And

Matt? Call Anna. Now. I'll send a unit her way too, just in case."

My blood turns to ice. "She's at work. You don't think Esther will go straight there, do you?"

"Even if she did, we'll get to her first, but better safe than sorry."

"Okay," I say and hang up, directing CJ back to the car.

I'm already dialing as we climb in. The phone rings once, twice, three times.

"Please," I whisper. "Please answer."

Four rings. Five.

Then, finally: "Matt?"

The relief nearly drops me to my knees. "Anna. Thank god. Are you okay?"

"I'm fine. Why? What's wrong?"

"Stay at the restaurant. Don't leave. I'm coming to get you."

"Matt, what —"

I hear Anna's muffled scream, a thud, and the line goes dead.

CHAPTER TWENTY-FOUR

ANNA

The lunch rush is finally winding down, and I'm grateful for the break. My feet are killing me, and I keep checking my phone, hoping for an update from Matt about whatever he's doing today. He was cagey this morning when he dropped me off, and I have a feeling he's up to something he doesn't want me to know about.

"Anna, trash is overflowing," Becky calls from the kitchen.

"On it."

I grab the massive bag and haul it out the back door to the dumpster. The alley is quiet, just the usual sounds of the city filtering through. I'm wrestling the bag up and over when my phone rings.

It takes me a few moments to get the bag to successfully tip into the dumpster before I can answer. When I see Matt's name lighting up the screen, despite everything, I smile.

"Matt?"

"Anna. Thank god. Are you okay?"

His voice is pure panic, and my stomach drops. "I'm fine. Why? What's wrong?"

"Stay at the restaurant. Don't leave. I'm coming to get you."

"Matt, what —"

A hand clamps over my mouth from behind, cutting off my words. The phone tumbles from my grip as I try to scream, but the sound comes out muffled against rough skin that smells like dirt and cigarettes. I thrash, trying to break free, but an arm locks around my waist, lifting me off my feet.

No, no, no —

Something hard connects with the side of my head, and the world explodes into stars before everything goes black.

I come to in darkness so complete I wonder if I'm blind. My head throbs with each heartbeat, and when I try to move, I realize my hands are bound behind my back, rough rope cutting into my wrists. A gag fills my mouth, tied so tight my jaw aches.

Don't panic. Don't panic.

But it's hard not to when every direction I turn, I hit metal. Cold, unforgiving steel that tells me I'm in some kind of small room or box. The air is thick with the smell of damp earth and rust, and I have to fight not to gag against the cloth in my mouth.

I kick out, hoping to find a weak spot, a latch, anything. But my feet just meet more metal with dull thuds that echo in the confined space, which seems to be somewhere between six and eight feet, roughly square. The rope around my wrists is tight, but I work at it anyway, twisting and pulling until I feel warm wetness — blood from where I've torn the skin.

Think, Anna. Think.

But all I can think about is Martin. The warehouse. The knife. The certainty that I was going to die.

Except this time, Matt doesn't know where I am. This time, there might not be sirens coming.

I twist harder, feeling my nails catch and tear on the rope. The pain is sharp, clarifying, better than the panic clawing at my chest. I need to get free. I need to get *out*.

But the rope won't budge, and the metal won't give, and the air feels thinner with each panicked breath through my nose.

Finally, exhausted and bleeding, I collapse into a corner. Tears stream down my face, soaking into the gag. I'm alive. I'm still alive.

For now.

But for how long? And who has me?

I think about Matt's panicked voice on the phone. He knew something was wrong. He was coming for me. He has to find me.

Please find me.

Because I don't know how long I have before whoever took me comes back. Before they finish what Martin started.

I close my eyes, even though in the darkness it makes no

difference, and try to slow my breathing. Try to conserve air. Try not to think about what comes next.

Unfortunately, all I can feel is terror, cold and absolute, settling into my bones.

But I survived before. I can survive again.

I have to.

CHAPTER TWENTY-FIVE

MATT

"Anna!" I'm screaming into the phone, but there's nothing. Just dead air and the sound of my own terror echoing back.

"Matt, what —" CJ starts, but I'm already dialing 911 with shaking hands.

"911, what's your emergency?"

"My girlfriend's been taken. Just now." I give her the name of the restaurant and the address. "Her name is Anna Martella."

"Sir, are you at that address?"

"No, I'm in Oakland, please —"

"Then how do you know she's been 'taken', sir?" The skepticism in her voice pisses me off.

"We were talking on the phone. She screamed, and the line went dead," I reply aggressively.

"Sir, I need you to calm —"

"Don't tell me to calm down! Send units now! There's a

serial killer after her. Detective Worthington knows the case. Just send help!"

I hang up and floor it toward the bridge, CJ gripping the door handle as I weave through traffic.

"It was Esther," I say, taking a turn too fast. "But she couldn't have gotten there that quickly. We just left Oakland."

"The brother," CJ breathes. "They must be working together."

"Fuck!" I slam my hand on the steering wheel. "I should have seen this coming. Should have —"

CJ grips my arm, either to get my attention or in fear of my erratic driving. "Matt, focus. We need to get there. Preferably alive."

But too soon, traffic is crawling. Saturday shoppers and tourists clogging every lane. I lay on the horn, cut into the shoulder, anything to move faster.

"Come on, come on!"

Twenty minutes feels like twenty hours. By the time we screech into the alley behind the restaurant where I usually drop Anna off, it's swarming with cops. But no ambulance. No Anna.

I'm out of the car as soon as it stops, pushing through the crowd of gawkers.

"Where is she?" I approach the nearest officer. "Anna Martella. Where is she?"

"Sir, I need you to step back —"

"I'm the one who called it in!"

Through the door that leads into the kitchen, I can see officers interviewing staff. Becky's crying. The others — line cooks, servers, and bussers — look shell-shocked. And in the middle of it all, Drew is screaming at a man in an expensive suit — the restaurant's owner, presumably.

"I don't give a shit about dinner service!" Drew's face is red with rage. "One of your employees was just kidnapped!"

"And that's unfortunate," the owner says coldly. "But we have paying customers. The police can do their job while we do ours. Back to work. Now."

"Are you fucking kidding me?" Drew gets right in his face. "Anna could be dying right now and you're worried about table turns?"

"If you have a problem with how I run my business —"

"I do. I quit." Drew rips off his apron and throws it at the owner's feet. "I just closed on my own fucking restaurant anyway, so fuck you, and fuck this place."

He storms toward the door and sees me. Some of his anger shifts to relief. "Matt. Thank god. Have they found her?"

"Mr. Roberts," a voice says from behind me.

I turn to find Detective Worthington approaching, two uniforms flanking him. My blood runs cold at his ferocious expression.

"Detective," I reply coldly.

"We received a tip that someone might try to take Ms. Martella from her workplace today. And here you are, minutes after it happens."

My eyebrows slam together. Is this guy for real? "Because I called it in! I knew she was in danger —"

"Exactly. You knew." He nods to the uniforms. "Matt Roberts, you're under arrest on suspicion of kidnapping."

"What? No!" CJ pushes forward. "He didn't take Anna. He's been with me since he dropped her off at work!"

"Save it for the station." Worthington's eyes are cold. "Cuff him."

"This is insane!" I struggle as they grab my arms. "Anna's out there! The actual killers have her!"

"Convenient story." Worthington watches impassively as they cuff me. "How did you know to call it in, Roberts? How did you know she was being taken?" he asks in a mocking tone.

"We were talking on the phone and I heard her scream!"

"Through the phone. Right," he drawls, making it obvious he thinks I heard that scream up close and personal. That *I* caused that scream. Anger and terror twist in my gut as he turns to the uniforms and instructs, "Get him out of here."

"CJ!" I call as they drag me away. "Find Sullivan! Tell him what happened!"

"I will," she promises, tears streaming down her face. "We'll find her, Matt."

But as they shove me into the back of the patrol car, I know every second counts. Anna's out there, terrified, hurt, maybe dying. And I'm helpless.

The ride to the station is a blur. They book me, take my phone, my belt, my shoelaces. The holding cell smells like piss and desperation.

"I get a phone call," I yell at the guard's retreating back.

"You'll get your chance," he says mockingly.

"You don't understand. She's in danger. If you'd just let me explain —"

But he's already gone.

I sink onto the metal bench, head in my hands. This is a nightmare. Worthington thinks I'm guilty. The actual killers have Anna. And I'm locked in a cage while the woman I love is out there, alone and afraid.

I think about her laugh. Her smile. The way she feels in my arms. The future CJ Saw for us. God, I want that future. I didn't think our last kiss goodbye would be our last kiss. If I had I never would've let her go. If I get her back — *when*, when I get her back — I won't let her go. I'm going to marry Anna. She's my destiny. And I will not let these motherfuckers take her from me.

"Please," I whisper to whatever cosmic force might be listening. "Please let me save her."

But the universe doesn't answer. Just the sound of my breathing and the distant voices of other inmates echoing off concrete walls.

Somewhere out there, Anna is fighting for her life.

And I'm trapped, unable to do anything but wait and pray that someone — CJ, Sullivan, anyone — can find her before it's too late.

Because I can feel it in my bones, that terrible certainty: we're running out of time.

CHAPTER TWENTY-SIX

ANNA

Time has lost all meaning in the darkness. Could be hours, could be days. My throat is parched, my wrists raw and bleeding, muscles cramping from being bound so long.

Then suddenly, the darkness lifts.

The ceiling above me opens — a hatch, I realize — and a dimming early night sky appears like a rectangle of hope. Fresh air floods in, cold and sweet after the stale metal box. I blink against even this faint light, eyes watering after so long in absolute darkness, scrambling to my feet.

But then a shadow blocks out the stars. A man lowers himself into my prison, and as he drops the last few feet, moonlight catches on something in his hand.

A knife. A *big* fucking knife. Nearly identical to the one Ezra Martin held to my throat two years ago.

"Hello, Anna." His voice is soft, almost gentle, but there's something wrong underneath. Something that makes my skin crawl. I can make out brown hair. The glint of light-colored eyes. Blue, maybe? He's about Matt's height, but stockier. And he reeks of cigarettes and the promise of awful things. "I'm Ezekiel. Ezra's brother. It's so nice to finally meet you." His mouth splits in a wide, mocking smile.

I try to speak through the gag, but only muffled sounds emerge.

"You weren't supposed to be his last, you know." He steps up to me, turning the knife so it catches the light. "He had plans. Beautiful plans. But you ruined them when you survived."

My heart hammers against my ribs. This is it. This is how I die.

"You'll suffer for that," he continues conversationally. "Even more than you would have at my brother's hands. See, Ezra only relished the kill. Quick, efficient. But me?" He trails the flat of the blade along my cheek. "I relish the pain."

Rage floods through me, burning away the fear. I won't die cowering. I won't give him the satisfaction.

I jerk back and drive my knee up with every ounce of strength I have left, connecting hard with his groin.

He howls, doubling over, and the knife clatters across the metal floor. I try to scramble for purchase against the wall. Anything that might get me closer to freedom, but it's useless.

"You fucking bitch!" His hand connects with my face so hard I fly sideways into the wall. Stars explode across my vision, and I taste blood through the gag.

He snatches up the knife, fury twisting his features. "I was going to make it good for you before I made it very, very bad, but now —"

The knife presses against my throat, and terror rips through me at his meaning. I close my eyes, thinking of Matt. Of my family. Of all the things I'll never get to —

Car doors slam somewhere above us.

Ezekiel freezes. Voices carry on the wind — more than one, and they're getting closer.

"Shit." He pulls the knife away, glaring at me. "This isn't over. I'll be back to finish what my brother started. And now, when I do, you'll beg for death long before I give it to you."

He hoists himself up and out of the hatch. The metal clangs shut, plunging me back into darkness.

But this time, the darkness feels different. Because somewhere above me, there are people. Maybe police. Maybe rescuers. Maybe Matt.

I try to scream through the gag, to kick the walls, to make any noise that might carry. But my throat is raw, my strength nearly gone.

Still, I keep trying. Keep fighting.

Because if I don't, Ezekiel will be back. And next time, there might not be an interruption.

Next time, he'll make good on his promise.

All I can hope is that someone finds me first … or if they don't, that I'm somehow able to fight back. To escape, again.

I sit back down to rest. To gather my strength. For my last stand.

CHAPTER TWENTY-SEVEN

MATT

I'm on my third hour in this hellhole when the door to the holding area opens and Sullivan walks in with a uniformed officer.

"Detective Sullivan, SFPD," he says, flashing his badge. "I need Matt Roberts released immediately."

The desk sergeant looks skeptical. "He's being held on suspicion of kidnapping."

"Based on bad intel." Sullivan's voice is steel. "Mr. Roberts was with his sister in Oakland when the victim was taken. I have witnesses. Detective Worthington jumped to conclusions without proper investigation."

"I'll need to verify —"

"Every second you waste, a young woman gets closer to death. Release him now, or I'll have your badge."

Something in Sullivan's tone must convince him because five minutes later, I'm being processed out.

"Thank you," I say as we walk to the parking lot. "But what do we do now? How do we find her?"

"I had someone tracking Ezekiel Martin after you couldn't find him earlier. One of my people, not Worthington's." His expression darkens. "That idiot was so convinced it was you, he barely pursued the other suspects." He shakes his head angrily.

I inhale sharply. "So you found him? The brother?"

"Yep. Different address from what you had. We need to move fast."

"Let's go."

Out in the parking lot, Sullivan stops at a familiar car — mine. "I can't officially take you with me. But I can't stop you from following me either. Your sister dropped these off." He tosses me my keys. "Try to keep up."

It's a fifteen-minute drive. Fifteen minutes of going out of my mind with worry. To pray to whatever deities will listen to save my girl. To think about what I might have to do next.

The house is in a quiet neighborhood in Daly City. It looks normal from the outside — small, well-maintained, nothing that screams, "a serial killer lives here."

Sullivan approaches the door while I hang behind him. When Ezekiel Martin answers, he looks so much like his brother. Average height, brown hair, the kind of face you'd forget five minutes later.

"Ezekiel Martin?" Sullivan shows his badge. "I need to ask you some questions."

"About what?" His voice is calm, confused. Too calm.

"Your sister Esther. When did you last see her?"

"Weeks ago. She's in rehab, isn't she?"

Sullivan's not buying it. "Not anymore. She pulled a runner today when questioned about the murders that have been happening. Has she contacted you, Mr. Martin?"

Ezekiel looks puzzled. I almost buy it.

"Gosh, no, I haven't heard from her in a while."

My hackles rise but Sullivan nudges me as if he knows.

"I hate to say this, but given her response, I think it would be best if you came with us down to the station until we can sort this out. Just as a precaution. It'd be in your best interest if it turns out she had something to do with this."

"This is ridiculous. I haven't done anything," Ezekiel protests. But his hand twitches toward his back. I see Sullivan clock it too. Ezekiel's got a weapon.

"Then you won't mind coming with me, since you'll just be released once everything's been settled." Sullivan reaches for his cuffs … or perhaps his gun.

But that's when Ezekiel breaks. He shoves Sullivan hard and tries to bolt past me toward the street.

Instinct takes over. I grab him, both hands clamping down on his arms, and his memories explode into my mind like a breaking dam.

But this time, something's different. Instead of watching like a movie, I'm *in* it, deeper than ever before.

I'm eight years old, crouched under a kitchen table with my siblings. Mom's screaming. Dad has a knife, and there's so much blood. I feel warm liquid running down my leg —

I've pissed myself in terror. My heart hammers so hard it hurts, and Esther won't stop crying.

"See, children," Dad says calmly as Mommy stops moving, blond hair splayed out, splashed with bright red blood. "Cheaters never prosper."

Then he puts a gun to his head and —

The memory shifts … or I make it shift? I must because I wished not to see the rest. Years blur together in a sickening montage. Three children, broken by trauma, finding catharsis in recreating it. Esther luring women. Or sometimes Ezra. All three taking turns with the knife. Sometimes all three *together*, a family united in horror. So long as they were young blondes and so long as one of the brothers made the final kill, it was all they needed. Their mother's punishment, reinforced. *They deserve it.*

But then … Esther's struggles as she got older with keeping their secret. Ezekiel offering her drugs to dull the pain, to keep her compliant.

My stomach churns as I witness rape after rape, murder after murder. Feel his arousal at their fear and pain, his satisfaction at their deaths. But through it all, one thought persists — it's justice. They're cheaters. *They deserve it.*

My revulsion at that thought, voiced in his head over and over, gives me strength to pull back, to separate myself from his perspective. I become an observer instead of a participant, and suddenly I realize what's happened. My anger, my fear for Anna, have unlocked something.

I can control this now.

I dive through his recent memories with newfound

precision. There — this morning. Esther calling, frantic. "Someone was here. I think they know. You need to move up the timeline."

But he was already there. At the restaurant. So he continued watching. He didn't have to wait long until Anna emerged into the alley to take out the trash.

Jump again. Dragging her unconscious body to his truck. The drive here. Opening a hidden hatch in the backyard that leads to —

A buried shed. She's in a buried shed at the back of the property.

One more jump. An hour ago. Ezekiel dropping into the shed, Anna kicking him, and then —

He hit her. Hard. The memory of her body slamming into the wall makes my vision go red.

Before I pull out, I know what I need to do so that this monster can never hurt anyone again. So I do it. I plant the idea. The natural way he knows this has to play out. Because he's a cheater. He's cheated the law. He's cheated the death that's coming for him. For too long. And cheaters never prosper. *He deserves it.*

I plant the message deep. And I let go.

"The shed," I tell Sullivan. "She's in a buried shed out back."

"Go! I'll handle him!"

I look back at Ezekiel and physically let him go. He makes to bolt again, and I can't help it; I punch him in the face hard right before Sullivan takes him to ground.

I sprint around the side of the house, searching

desperately. I barrel through a partially closed gate, my eyes roving the backyard. There — a patch of disturbed earth near the back fence. I drop to my knees, clawing at the hastily placed dirt until I find metal. A hatch.

"Anna!"

I wrench it open and peer in. It's so dark. "Anna?"

Muffled noises come from below. Like someone trying to talk through … shit, a *gag*.

I drop carefully through the hatch. I can just make her out in the pit's darkness. She's there, bound and gagged, eyes wide with terror that shifts to relief when she sees me.

"It's okay, baby. I've got you."

I cut through her bonds with my pocket knife, and she collapses against me, sobbing through the gag. I remove it gently.

"Matt," she croaks.

"Shh. Let's get you out of here."

I lift her — she weighs nothing, as if drained, body and soul — and boost her up before climbing out myself. Then I'm carrying her toward the front of the house, her arms wrapped around my neck.

"Thank you," she keeps repeating, tears streaming down her cheeks as she clings to me.

I approach the cars, deciding to put her in the front seat of Sullivan's unmarked police car.

As I'm placing her there, a gunshot cracks through the night. Both of our heads whip toward the house.

"Stay here," I tell Anna. "Lock the doors."

I close her in and run back just as Sullivan bursts out of the house, holstering his gun.

"Did you get her?" he asks urgently.

I nod. "She's in your car. What happened?"

Sullivan's eyes are hard. "He shot himself."

My mouth thins as I fight a triumphant smile. Sullivan's expression shifts to understanding.

"You need to leave. Now."

I glance back at his cruiser. "But Anna needs medical attention —"

Sullivan growls. "Backup and ambulance are thirty seconds out. I'll make sure she's taken care of." He grabs my shoulder. "Matt, if you're here when they arrive, it complicates everything. Worthington will use it against you. Go home. I'll handle this."

"I can't leave her —" I protest.

"You can and you will. For her sake. Trust me." Sirens wail in the distance, getting closer. "Go!"

I run back to the car where Anna's waiting. She rolls down the window.

"I have to go," I tell her. "You're safe now. Sullivan will take care of you. The ambulance is coming."

"Matt, no —" she sobs, and it rips a hole in my chest. But it'll hurt everyone if I stay.

"I'm sorry. I'll explain later. I promise. I love you." I kiss her forehead through the open window, afraid to kiss her lips with the blood crusted around them. "I love you so much." Tears fill my eyes at having to leave her like this. But Sullivan is right, and I'll do whatever it takes to take care of Anna.

Even if that means leaving her for a little while. At least now she's safe.

But as I'm driving away, my body betrays me. Having to leave her behind wrecks me, and I can barely manage, tears pouring down my face, and my hands shaking on the wheel.

Though by the time I make it home, it seems like it was more than just the trauma. I'm barely inside before the fever hits. My whole body burns as I stumble to the bathroom and empty my stomach. Every muscle aches like I've run a marathon.

Somehow I manage to text CJ: *Need help. Come over.*

She finds me on the bathroom floor twenty minutes later.

"Jesus, Matt. What happened?"

"Pushed too hard," I manage. "New abilities. Anna's safe."

"*Shit*. I'm going to need more than that later, but for now let's get you to bed."

She helps me to my room, forces water down my throat, places cool washcloths on my forehead. It takes a good half hour for the worst of it to pass, but even then I feel completely wrung out, barely able to move.

CJ sits on the other side of the bed, fanning the washcloth until it's cool again before placing it back on my forehead.

"Better?" she asks gently.

I nod meekly.

"So … these new abilities."

I sigh, the heavy breath out burning along my raw throat.

"I could control it. So much more. I was in the memories,

not just watching. I could see whatever I wanted … or not see what I didn't." I shake my head at recalling the image of their father with a gun to his head. "Complete control."

"That's huge, Matt."

"Yeah." I close my eyes. "But I crossed a line. I didn't just watch. I planted my own thoughts … I made him finish it." I swallow hard. "He's dead."

CJ's quiet for a moment. "Good," she finally says. "After what he did? Good."

I drift in and out of consciousness, dreaming of Anna's terrified face, of children under tables, of gunshots in the night.

But through it all, one thought persists: she's safe. Anna's safe.

Everything else we'll figure out tomorrow. It's my last thought before I lose consciousness.

CHAPTER TWENTY-EIGHT

ANNA

The emergency room is too bright, too loud, too much like two years ago. But this time, I'm not fighting for consciousness. This time, I know the monster is dead. This time, I'm stronger.

Was I terrified in there? Yes. But this time I didn't let fear rule me. I didn't crumble. I stayed strong, kept faith, and made it through. Thanks to Matt. As traumatizing as it was … I feel *grateful*. To be alive. To have someone who loves me so fiercely he'd face a serial killer for me. To know *I* have it in me to fight the things that frighten me. I let out a long breath. As I finish my exhale, the doctor enters.

"How are you feeling?" he asks, smiling reassuringly.

I attempt a small, feeble smile back. "Surprisingly not too bad," I admit. But maybe that's the pain medication currently being pumped into my IV.

He steps up, gently peeling back the bandages and examining the bruises on my face and wrists. "Well, your injuries are relatively minor," he says. "We'll observe you for a few hours, make sure there's no concussion, then you can go home."

I let out a sigh of relief. "Thank you."

As soon as he leaves, I fumble for my phone, grateful that Becky dropped it off when she got word that I'd been rescued and taken to the hospital. I didn't know she cared so much, but I was touched.

My hands are clumsy from the bandages on my wrists, but I manage to call Matt.

CJ answers on the third ring. "Anna? Thank god. Are you okay?"

"I'm fine. Just bruises. Is Matt okay? Why do you have his phone?"

"Matt's ... asleep. He overdid it with his ability." She pauses. "He pushed himself to find you, to stop Ezekiel. It drained him pretty badly."

My heart clenches. "Is he okay?"

"He's been out for the last hour, but I think he'll be fine. I can't wake him, but his breathing is steady."

"Don't try," I plead. "Let him rest. Just ... tell him I'm okay when he wakes up? And tell him I love him." My heart swells with all the emotions I'm feeling right now. Love doesn't seem like a strong enough word. Gratitude. Relief. Bone-weary exhaustion.

"I will. Do you need me to come get you?"

"No, I'm going to call Sophia. I need to tell my family everything anyway."

"Are you sure?"

"Yeah. It's time."

I've barely hung up after calling my sister and telling her the full story when a tall, older man with a police badge hanging off his gray overcoat appears — Sullivan.

"How are you feeling?" he asks, pulling up a chair.

"Like I got hit by a truck. But alive." I study his face. "Thanks to you and Matt."

Sullivan's expression doesn't change. "Detective Worthington will be here soon to take your statement. It would be best if you didn't mention Mr. Roberts was present for your rescue."

I grimace. "Because Worthington still thinks he's involved."

"Among other reasons." Sullivan leans forward and drops his voice. "I got you out of that shed. I called for backup and medical assistance. That's all Worthington needs to know."

"You saved me," I say, and it's accurate enough. Without Sullivan, Matt would still be in a cell. "That's what I'll tell him."

"Good girl." He stands. "Take care of yourself, Anna. You've been through hell twice now. This kind of thing is much more impactful for an empath like you, so don't be afraid to ask for help to deal with it."

My mouth pops open in surprise. "Empath?"

His brows furrow. "You didn't know."

I'm speechless for a moment. But … I guess I always dismissed that I'm able to sense others' emotions. I thought all people could do that, to some degree at least. But then, I've always known I can do it … well, *more* than most people. "No," I finally say. "And yes."

He nods as if he understands. And he, of all people, probably does. "Come see me when you're better. We'll talk about it."

I nod, still totally overwhelmed, but he disappears before I can form a response.

Which is good because minutes later, Worthington arrives looking harried and skeptical.

"Ms. Martella. I'm glad you're safe."

"No thanks to you," I mutter.

His jaw tightens. "Can you tell me what happened?" he presses on, ignoring my comment.

I stick to the story. Someone grabbed me outside work. I woke up in a dark metal box. Ezekiel Martin came down, threatened me, but was interrupted. The next thing I knew, Detective Sullivan got me out.

"And you didn't see anyone else? Hear anything that might suggest who else was involved?"

"Just him." I meet his eyes steadily. "Ezekiel Martin kidnapped me. Detective Sullivan saved me. That's all I know."

He asks more questions, pushing for details that don't exist, clearly trying to implicate Matt, until a familiar voice cuts through his interrogation.

"What the hell do you think you're doing?"

Sophia storms into the room like an avenging angel, and I've never been happier to see her.

"I'm taking a statement —" Worthington starts.

"From my sister, who was just kidnapped and assaulted? Who's still in a hospital bed?" Sophia's voice could strip paint. "I don't think so."

"This is an active investigation —"

"And Anna's been through enough. If you need more, she'll come to the station when she's ready. Maybe Monday. Maybe next week. Maybe when hell freezes over."

Worthington's gaze shifts to me. "Ms. Martella —"

"Which one?" Sophia snaps, stepping between us. "Because I'm about five seconds from calling our lawyer. And trust me, you don't want to meet her."

Worthington stares her down, clearly calculating whether it's worth the fight. Finally, he closes his notebook.

He leans to the side slightly to catch my eye again. "Monday would be acceptable. If you're feeling up to it," he adds grudgingly.

"We'll see," I say sweetly.

After he leaves, I pull Sophia into a fierce hug.

"Thank you."

"Nobody messes with my baby sister." She pulls back, eyes searching mine. "You ready to go home?"

"So ready," I sigh.

The house is quiet when we arrive, which should have been my first warning. The second we walk through the door, the entire family descends … but in a surprisingly orderly fashion.

"Anna!" Mom rushes forward, Dad right behind her.

"We're so glad you're safe," Lucia says, tears streaming down her face.

Even Francesca abandons her usual composure to join the group hug that threatens to suffocate me with love.

"Bella," Nonna murmurs, stroking my hair. "My brave girl."

There's no interrogation. No demands for details. Clearly, Sophia told them everything, just as I asked. But there's no judgment about keeping secrets. Just my family, surrounding me with unconditional love.

"I should have told you," I whisper into the huddle. "From the beginning. I should have —"

"Shh," Mom says. "You're here. You're safe. That's all that matters."

But I need them to understand. "I was scared. Not just of the killer, but of ... of having to face it again. I thought if I didn't talk about it, I could pretend it wasn't happening."

"We get it," Sophia says. "After what happened before, of course you wanted to hide from it."

"But you didn't have to hide from us," Dad says gruffly. "We're your family. We face things together."

"I know that now." Fresh tears spill over. "I've always known. I just ... got lost and forgot for a while."

"Well, I'm glad that you remember now," Francesca says. "And next time — though God forbid there's a next time — you'll tell us immediately."

"There won't be a next time," I say firmly. "It's over."

"Bene," Nonna declares. "Now come. You need food. And rest. And more food."

I chuckle. Such an Italian grandma thing to say.

As she herds us all toward the kitchen, I'm overwhelmed by the simple truth of it: this is my family. They'll pile on with love as easily as they pile on with opinions. They'll defend me against anyone, including my own stubborn pride.

I never should have kept this from them. Not because they could have fixed it or made it go away, but because carrying it alone was never necessary.

They're my strength, my foundation, my home.

And I'm finally done trying to protect them from my pain. Because sharing it — letting them help carry it — doesn't make me weak.

It makes us all stronger.

I need to stop thinking of my pain as a burden to those who love me.

"Anna?" Mom pauses at the kitchen door. "Should we call Matt? Let him know you're home?"

I smile through my tears. "I already called and spoke with his sister, CJ. He's resting. She'll have him call me when he's up."

"Good," she says simply. "You tell him to come here and I'll feed him too." I tear up, knowing that means he's family to her already.

As I follow them into the kitchen, surrounded by the chaos and comfort, I finally feel what I couldn't in that dark metal box: safe. Truly, completely safe.

Because I survived. Again. And this time, I don't have to heal alone.

CHAPTER TWENTY-NINE

MATT

I wake to sunlight streaming through my bedroom window. My head is fuzzy and pounding, and I feel wiped, even though I'm fairly certain I've been asleep a while. I turn to see CJ sitting in the chair beside my bed, scrolling through her phone.

"Morning, Sleeping Beauty," she says when she sees my eyes open. "How are you feeling?"

I take inventory. The fever's gone, and the aches have faded to a dull throb. "Like I went ten rounds with a heavyweight. But alive."

"Good, because you've got messages." She sets a glass of water on my nightstand. "Anna called. She's okay. She's safely at her parents' house."

Relief floods through me so intensely I have to close my eyes. "Thank God."

"Also, Worthington called. Multiple times. I let them all go to voicemail."

I groan and reach for my phone. Worthington's messages are terse, all along the lines of, *Come to the station immediately or else.*

"Shit." I sit up, ignoring the wave of dizziness. "I need to call Cartwright."

"I already did," CJ says. "He's expecting your call. I gave him the basics."

"Have I mentioned you're the best sister ever?" I sling my legs over the side of the bed, every movement stiff and painful.

"Not nearly enough." She stands. "I'll make breakfast while you deal with this."

I snort and mutter as she leaves, "Well, if last night didn't kill me, that might."

She turns, eyes narrowed. "I heard that."

I smirk. "I meant for you to. Don't worry about it. I'll just have a protein bar."

CJ's lips purse. "Okay, fair."

I chuckle and stand up, every muscle protesting at the movement. It's going to be a long walk down those stairs.

An hour later, my body has finally stopped protesting every slight movement, and James Cartwright and I are walking into the police station. My attorney looks like he was born in a three-piece suit, and his expression could freeze hell. He asks me a few terse questions on the way in.

"Let me do the talking," he says as we're escorted to an interview room.

Worthington's already there, looking like he hasn't slept. His face darkens when he sees us.

"Nice of you to bring counsel, Roberts. Guilty conscience?"

"Detective," Cartwright says coolly, "my client is here voluntarily. I suggest you remember that."

"Your client was released improperly yesterday. I could re-arrest him right now."

"On what grounds?" Cartwright demands.

"He was at the scene —"

"After calling 911 to report his girlfriend's kidnapping. Which, if you'd bothered to check with dispatch or Detective Sullivan, you'd know. You'd also know my client was in Oakland with his sister when Ms. Martella was taken. Multiple witnesses can confirm this."

Worthington's jaw works. "He knew where she was being held."

"Correction: He knew he was speaking with her on the phone, then suddenly she screamed and the call dropped. He also knew, by your own statements, that a serial killer was once again pursuing Ms. Martella. So naturally, he called 911 immediately. Are you seriously going to arrest someone for helping save a victim's life?"

"I want to know how he really knew Ezra Martin —"

"Detective Worthington," Cartwright's voice could cut glass, "you arrested my client without cause, without evidence, and without even basic investigation. He has an airtight alibi. He was the one who reported the danger. And while you wasted time harassing him, the actual killer — one of the suspects you barely investigated — nearly murdered Ms. Martella."

"Now wait just a minute —"

"No, you wait. We'll be filing a complaint with your supervisor for discrimination and harassment. None of the other suspects faced a fraction of the scrutiny you've shown Mr. Roberts. And as both Detective Sullivan and Ms. Martella have confirmed, it was Ezekiel Martin who was responsible. Not my client."

Worthington looks like he's swallowed something sour. "Fine. Mr. Roberts is free to go."

"He was always free to go," Cartwright says, standing. "You just ignored that fact. Good day, Detective."

Outside the interview room, Cartwright turns to me. "They won't bother you again. If they do, call me immediately."

"Thank you. Truly, that was impressive. And very much appreciated."

He smiles for the first time. "Don't thank me yet. You haven't seen my weekend rates. I'll send the invoice."

I laugh despite everything. "Fair enough."

"Mr. Roberts," calls a voice from the other end of the hallway we're standing in.

I turn to find Sullivan approaching. "Detective."

"A word? In my office?"

I glance at Cartwright, who nods. "I'll see myself out."

I nod and follow Sullivan to his office. It's small but organized, with commendations on the wall and a photo of what must be his family on the desk.

"Coffee?" he offers.

"I'm good. What's this about?"

He settles behind his desk, studying me. "Before Ezekiel Martin shot himself yesterday, he said something interesting. 'Cheaters never prosper.' Ring any bells?"

I keep my expression neutral.

"It's what his father said before killing himself. After murdering their mother." Sullivan leans back. "What his older brother said in his own suicide note. Based on the fact that Ezekiel had tried to run before that, I didn't take him for the suicidal type."

He gives me a meaningful look. When I don't respond, he continues.

"Did you have anything to do with that, Matt?"

My silence is answer enough.

Sullivan nods slowly. "I have mixed feelings about that. On the one hand, you saved us the cost of a trial. On the other ..."

"On the other, I used my ability in a way I'm not sure I can be forgiven for." I swallow hard. "But I'd do it again in a heartbeat to save Anna."

"I believe you. Lord knows I've had to make tough calls in my years on the force." He pauses. "Just be careful, Matt. Our abilities don't make us gods. That's a dangerous line of thinking."

"I know." And I do. The weight of what I did sits heavy on my chest, and probably will for the rest of my days.

"For what it's worth, Esther Martin was found dead this morning. Also from a self-inflicted gunshot wound. And we've started processing both of Ezekiel's residences. There are already mountains of evidence tying both him and his sister to the recent murders. Worthington conveniently left that out of your chat, I'm sure."

"Of course he did." I lean forward, pushing down my irritation at Worthington's malicious negligence. "Why did you help me yesterday? You risked your career in going over Worthington's head. And don't give me the party line about my parents or people like us sticking together."

Sullivan grins. "How about because now you owe me?"

"I don't like the sound of that," I reply warily.

"Relax. I'm not talking about blackmail or forcing you into anything. But someone with your talent could be invaluable in cases like this. When bad people are hard to pin down through conventional means."

"You want me to read suspects for you." I'm a bit taken aback at the realization, though I probably shouldn't be. I can see why he'd want that.

"Only when necessary. Only with oversight. And only if you choose to." He slides a business card across the desk — different from the one he gave me before. This one just has a phone number. "Think about it. No pressure, no timeline. But when you're ready, if you want to use your abilities to help people ... well, I could use someone like you."

I flip the card over in my fingers a few times before pocketing it. "I'll think about it."

"I'm confident you'll make the right choice." He stands, extending his hand. "Give my regards to Ms. Martella. She's a remarkable young woman."

"She is," I agree, shaking his hand. And I can't help it; I verify his words against his memories. But all I See is professional respect and genuine hope for future collaboration.

Sullivan smiles like he knows what I just did.

"See you around, kid," he offers, sitting back down.

I smile back. "Not if I see you first."

Sullivan's grin widens, and he chuckles to himself as I leave.

Outside the station, I get back in the car and call CJ.

"How'd it go?" she asks.

"I'm free. Worthington's backing off. And Sullivan ... well, he wants to work with me. He wants me to use my ability to help with cases."

There's a beat of silence. "What are you going to do?" Pure curiosity, with no judgment, laces her tone.

"Right now? I'm going to go see Anna." I start the car. "Everything else can wait."

Because after everything we've been through, everything we've survived, there's only one thing that matters.

She's alive. She's safe. And I'm never letting her go again.

CHAPTER THIRTY

ANNA

On Sunday afternoon, I find myself waiting in the foyer, which I've never done. But Matt saved my life and my heart, and I won't feel right again until I see that he's okay. So when I hear a car pull up outside, I leap up and am at the door before Matt can even knock, flinging it open to find him standing there looking exhausted but whole.

"Anna," he breathes, and then I'm in his arms, both of us holding on like we'll never let go.

"You're okay," I sob into his chest. "You're really okay."

"I'm fine. Are you?" He pulls back to examine my face, fingers ghosting over my bruises. "God, Anna, when I heard you scream —"

"I'm okay. Thanks to you." I touch his face, needing to feel that he's real. "You saved me."

"Sullivan saved you."

"You called for help. You came for me. You pulled me out of that hell." I shake my head. "Don't minimize what you did." I lean into him, letting his warmth settle me. "Is it over? Really over?"

"Both siblings are dead," he confirms quietly. "Ezekiel shot himself. Esther too. They can't hurt you anymore."

"Good." The word comes out fiercely. "Wait — they're both dead? How?"

Something flickers in his eyes. "Fucking Worthington. He should have told you all of this already." He shakes his head angrily, though I know it's not directed at me. "It's a long story. But I promise you, Anna, I'll never let anyone hurt you again."

"You can't promise that." I pull him inside, away from potential prying eyes. "And don't think I'm not mad at you for going after the suspects without me."

"Anna —"

I hold up a hand. "I know why you did it. I understand. But we're supposed to be partners."

"You're right. I'm sorry." He looks genuinely contrite. "I just couldn't risk losing you."

"I know." I lean into him again, needing the contact.

He runs a hand through his hair. "Anna, I need to tell you something. The timeline — their coming after you so quickly — it might have been my fault. CJ and I went to question Esther on Saturday after I dropped you off at work. She ran. They must have acted immediately."

Sorrow pulls at my heart that he thinks this is his fault. "You were trying to find the killer. To protect me." I take his hands. "I'm just glad it's over, Matt."

He looks at me with such intensity it takes my breath

away. "I realized something through all of this. I can't live without you, Anna. I know it's fast, I know the timing is insane, but —" He drops to one knee right there in my parents' foyer. "Anna Martella, will you marry me?"

My heart stops. "Matt ..."

"I don't have a ring yet. I don't have anything planned. I just know I want to spend the rest of my life with you."

Tears well in my eyes. Partly because I can feel the love and sincerity radiating from him. Partly because I feel the same way. But there's one thing still hanging over my head. One thing I need to clear up before I know we can truly move forward.

"Can we ..." I bite my lip. "Can CJ read me first? You know, to make sure my future isn't still ... nothing?"

Understanding dawns in his eyes. "Of course." He pulls out his phone, still on one knee, which makes me laugh despite everything.

"CJ? Can Anna and I come over? ... Yeah, now. ... Thanks."

He stands, pocketing his phone. "She's expecting us."

CJ yanks the door open before we can knock, pulling me into a fierce hug. It confirms we're two of a kind, considering I just did the same thing to Matt.

"Thank God you're okay," she says into my hair. "I was so worried."

"Thanks to your brother," I say, hugging her back just as tightly.

Drew appears behind her, and Matt extends his hand. "Thank you for standing up to that asshole owner. I'm just sorry you lost your job."

"I didn't lose it, I gave it up." Drew shakes his hand firmly. "I don't want to work for someone who values profit over people's lives. Besides, perfect timing to focus on my own restaurant."

I stare at him. "You quit? Because of what happened to me?"

Drew's gaze hardens. "The guy wanted us to keep serving while you were missing. What kind of person does that?" Then his face softens. "You're family, Anna. Of course I quit. And hey — now you can come work for me when I open. I'll need good servers who actually know food. I mean, if you want to."

"Yes," I say immediately, grinning. "Absolutely yes."

"Excellent. Now, why are you really here?" Drew asks.

Matt and I exchange glances and he asks, "CJ, could you ... read Anna? Check her future?"

CJ's eyes widen in understanding. "Oh! Oh, gosh, of course. Come here." She gestures for me to come closer, so I do.

She takes my hands, closes her eyes, and then —

"Oh my god!" She screeches, dropping my hands. "Are you *kidding* me?"

"What?" Matt and I say in unison, panic rising.

"You're going to *elope*?" She smacks Matt's arm. "I Saw a beautiful wedding! What happened to that?"

Relief floods through me so hard my knees almost buckle. "So I have a future?"

"Of course you do." CJ's expression softens. "A long, happy one. Even if you're going to rob me of planning the wedding of the century." She shoots a dissatisfied look at Matt.

"CJ," Matt groans. "Spoilers."

"Oh please, like you didn't already know you two are meant to be." She hugs me again. "Welcome to the family. Officially … well, soon anyway. Even if you're doing it at City Hall like boring people."

"Thank you," I whisper, tears streaming down my face. "Thank you."

As we leave, I turn to Matt. "Take me home?"

"Your parents' house?"

"Your home. Where I belong."

His face lights up. "Yes. God, yes."

Back at his townhouse, we curl up on the couch, and Matt tells me everything. Finding Esther, the chase, discovering where I was. He glosses over some parts, and I can tell there's more to how Ezekiel died than he's saying.

"Do I want to know?" I ask quietly.

"Probably not."

I study his face, seeing the weight he's carrying. "Okay. Thank you. For whatever you did to save me. You can tell me when you feel you're up for it."

Matt gives me a soft smile. "Thank you. I know I can, I

think I just need some time to come to terms with it all myself."

We have a light dinner and purposely keep the conversation just as light. Then, we move to his bedroom as evening falls, the need to be close overwhelming everything else.

Lying in his arms, hope blooms anew in my chest. And I realize I didn't answer his question. But I'm also not going to give my answer up so easily.

"You must really love me," I tease him.

He looks down at me with a contented smile. "I do," he says simply.

I lean up and kiss him gently. "How much?"

His smile spreads to a grin, and he kisses me deeply. "That much."

"Mmm," I hum against his mouth. "I think you can do better."

He pulls back and quirks an eyebrow as he gets my meaning. "Are you sure? You were just …" He trails off, grimacing, as if not wanting to give voice to the events of less than a day ago. To even let them back in that much.

"I think it's exactly what we need right now." I push him onto his back and straddle him. He looks up at me with shining eyes.

"You're beautiful," he murmurs, sitting up to kiss me. I pull at his shirt, then fling it off the bed. He laughs softly, then does the same to me, trailing kisses down my chest. "You're beautiful," he repeats against my skin.

I tip my head back and run my hands through his hair as he takes a nipple in his mouth through the fabric of my bra.

Then I let him remove it, along with the rest of our clothes. And I settle back over him, his manhood hot and hard against my backside, my slick, warm center just far enough away to tease him.

"Make love to me, Anna," he begs.

I bite my lip and sigh, sinking onto him. The fullness is everything. A feeling of utter bliss and completeness settles over me as we rock together, touching, filling, panting, loving.

Matt encourages me with soft touches and kisses along my arms. I keep eye contact, watching every bit of pleasure pass over his face. Letting him watch what he does to me.

As I approach my climax, Matt's hands settle on my backside, keeping the pace, tilting me over him just so until I tumble into ecstasy. Then he tumbles with me, crying out his pleasure, filling me. Tears leak out of my eyes as I come down, settling on his chest. Our mouths and tongues tangle languidly, and our combined love and pleasure and peace wrap around me like a living thing.

"According to Sullivan, I'm an empath," I murmur onto his chest.

A rumble echoes through our joined bodies. "Any particular reason you're saying another man's name while I'm still inside you?"

I chuckle and tip my head up to look at him. "Because I think I suspected I was different. But now …" I trace a finger over his nipple. "I know it. Because I feel your love," I place a hand over his heart, "like it's my own. In every fiber of my being."

Matt trembles beneath me. I sit up. "And I feel your sorrow like it's my own." I wipe a tear from his cheek. He looks at me in awe. "And I feel your reverence like it's my own."

He sits up, wrapping me in his arms. "I already knew you were special, so I'm not surprised in the least. Boy, I'm never going to get anything by you, am I?" he murmurs teasingly.

I tip my head back and laugh. "I knew you were up to something when you dropped me off. So no. But I also didn't say anything because I trust you." I pause. "Was CJ right? Are we meant to be?"

"My ability led me to you," he says softly. "I saved you before I even knew you. And then fate brought us together anyway. Just like CJ and Drew found each other despite her trying to change his future."

"So that's a yes?"

"That's a yes. I love you, Anna. Past, present, future — whatever timeline we're in, I'll love you."

"Then yes," I say, staring deeply into his eyes. "I'll marry you. Even though apparently it's a foregone conclusion that I'm going to anyway."

He laughs, pulling me in for a kiss. "Spoilers really run in the family."

"Oh, shit." I pull back. "My family won't be happy that we're eloping."

Matt laughs. "It doesn't have to be a true elopement," he offers. "But what CJ said about the courthouse … I'd be lying if I said I didn't want to make you mine as soon as possible. That doesn't mean our immediate families can't come, though."

"I'd be lying if I said the courthouse idea didn't appeal to me too. I'm over big weddings. I like the idea of inviting our families … though it'll be a battle to keep them from inviting everyone else we know."

"We've fought more difficult battles," he reminds me. "They can give this to us, after all we've been through."

I tilt my head to the side. "That might be a good way to convince them."

Matt nuzzles my neck. "I can't wait … though there's no time pressure, really. Let's just enjoy this moment. We've damn well earned it. And right now I just want to love you."

"I love you too," I whisper against his lips. "And I choose this. Choose us. Not because of visions or fate, but because I can't imagine my life without you."

"You'll never have to," he promises.

And as I let Matt make love to me again, as we lose ourselves in each other, I believe him. We've survived serial killers and skeptical cops, psychic visions and family dinners. We've looked death in the face and chosen life, chosen love, chosen each other.

The future CJ saw — a long, happy life together — starts now.

And I can't wait to live every moment with the man who saved me in every way possible. We saved each other, really. We've earned our happily ever after, and I'm going to feel every beautiful moment of it.

EPILOGUE
ANNA

Two months later

"Stop fidgeting," Sophia says, smoothing down the back of my simple white dress. "You look perfect."

"I'm not fidgeting." But I totally am. My hands won't stop moving — adjusting my hair, touching the pearl earrings Mom lent me, checking that my bouquet of white roses and baby's breath is still intact.

"You're nervous," she observes. "Why? You've known for a while that you're going to marry him."

"That's different from actually doing it." I peek out the door of the small waiting room. The courthouse is bustling with Monday morning business, but our families have claimed a corner near the ceremony room. "Oh God, Nonna brought her entire rosary group."

"Of course she did. You're lucky she agreed to the courthouse at all."

"Matt's aunt looks terrified."

Sophia laughs. "She'll be fine once she realizes we don't actually bite. Much."

A knock on the door makes us both turn. CJ pokes her head in, gorgeous in a deep blue dress that goes well with her coloring.

"Ready? Matt's about to vibrate out of his skin with anticipation."

"Is he okay?"

"He's perfect. Just eager to marry you." She grins. "Also, your mother is trying to keep both your dad and your Uncle Alessio from crying already, so we should probably get this show on the road."

I take a deep breath. Four months. It's only been four months since that housewarming party where Matt and I reconnected. Four months of falling in love, facing death, and choosing each other over and over again.

"I'm ready."

The ceremony room is small but sunlit, and I barely see any of it. All I can see is Matt, standing at the front in a dark suit that makes him look unfairly handsome. His energy when he sees me — the pure joy and love radiating through the small space — makes my eyes well up immediately. Not to mention the emotions of everyone else in the room, my own included. It's overwhelming in the best way.

Dad walks me down the short aisle, kissing my cheek before placing my hand in Matt's.

"You look beautiful," Matt whispers.

"So do you."

The officiant begins, but I barely hear the words. I'm too caught up in Matt's eyes, in the feeling of his hands holding mine, in the emotions radiating from him — love so profound it takes my breath away.

"I understand you've written your own vows?" the officiant prompts.

Matt nods, squeezing my hands. "Anna, two and a half years ago, I saved your life without even knowing you. But the truth is, you saved mine too. You showed me how to trust again, how to love without fear, how to believe in fate even when it seems impossible. You're my past, my present, and my future. I promise to love you, protect you, and cherish you for whatever time we're given."

I'm crying openly now, not caring about my makeup, as are most of the women in the room.

"Matt," I begin, my voice shaky. "You literally saved my life. Twice. But more than that, you saved my heart. You helped me find my strength again and showed me that love doesn't make us weak — it makes us powerful. You've seen me at my worst and somehow still think I'm worthy of this, of us. I promise to love you, trust you, and stand by you through whatever comes next. And to never, ever let you forget that you're not your past — you're the man who chose love over fear, who fought for us when it would have been easier to walk away."

"The rings?" the officiant asks.

Drew steps forward as Matt's best man, while Sophia produces the simple gold bands we'd chosen together.

"Do you, Matthew, take Anna to be your lawfully wedded wife?"

"I do." His voice is strong, certain.

"Do you, Anna, take Matthew to be your lawfully wedded husband?"

"I do." Tears spill over my cheeks.

"By the power vested in me by the state of California, I now pronounce you husband and wife. You may kiss —"

Matt doesn't wait for him to finish, pulling me into a kiss that makes me forget we're in a courthouse surrounded by family — oh, and Ray Sullivan, of course, without whom we wouldn't be here.

" — the bride."

There's whistling — probably Lucia's husband — and applause, and I'm pretty sure I hear both my mother and his aunt crying.

"Ladies and gentlemen," the officiant says with amusement, "I present Mr. and Mrs. Roberts."

The reception is at Drew's soon-to-be restaurant space, which is currently just an empty storefront with folding tables and chairs. But Mom and Matt's Aunt Meg have worked magic with tablecloths and flowers, and Drew somehow cooked a feast in the tiny temporary kitchen.

"This is actually perfect," I tell Matt as we slow dance to music from someone's phone, piped into a small bluetooth speaker in the middle of the table. "No fuss, just family."

"CJ's pouting that the elopement was wrong," he agrees.

"Though I'm sure your mother has already started planning a bigger reception for later."

"Oh, definitely. I heard her and Nonna discussing dates." I rest my head on his shoulder. "I love you, Mr. Roberts."

"I love you too, Mrs. Roberts." Pleasure hums through me at hearing my new title.

Over his shoulder, I can see CJ and Drew dancing, lost in their own world. My parents are attempting to teach Matt's aunt and uncle an Italian dance even I don't know that involves a lot of hand gestures. Nonna is holding court with her rosary group, probably telling them about her plans for our "proper" church blessing.

"No regrets?" Matt asks softly. "About the rushed timeline, the courthouse, any of it?"

I pull back to look at him. "Are you kidding? Did you forget? We faced down serial killers, skeptical cops, and my entire family. A courthouse wedding is nothing."

He laughs. "When you put it that way ..."

"Besides," I continue, "CJ Saw this. It was always going to happen."

"Spoilers," he murmurs, but he's smiling.

"Not spoilers anymore. Just our life."

As he spins me around our makeshift dance floor, surrounded by the people who matter most, I feel it — that certainty that we're exactly where we're meant to be. Not because of visions or fate or psychic abilities, but because we chose this. Because we chose each other.

And I know, with the certainty of an empath who can feel

her husband's emotions as clearly as her own, that this is just the beginning of our story.

The best is yet to come.

————

Thank you so much for reading! Please take a minute to leave a review on any retailer, goodreads, and/or BookBub. Even if it's just a couple of sentences, your opinion is important to potential readers and to me.

————

Want more? Check out *Vegas Baby: A Protector Romantic Suspense Novella* at
https://melanieasmithauthor.com/books-vegas-baby.html

————

Sign up for Melanie A. Smith's newsletter to get a FREE book plus all the latest news and more
https://melanieasmithauthor.com/newsletter.html

ACKNOWLEDGMENTS

The further I've come in my author journey, the tighter my circle has gotten, and I couldn't be more grateful for the small group of people behind me who I know always have my back.

To my husband, who is always at the ready to clear obstacles out of my writing path, whether they be in the form of my eleven-year-old or sticky plot points. I couldn't (and wouldn't want to) do life without you.

To my son, who brags about his author mom and keeps asking when he can read my books (the answer is still "never").

To Erin. Gosh, would there even be a point to this without you? You've been a friend, supporter, book bestie, beta reader, a shoulder to do *anything* on — cry, laugh, commiserate … all the messy beautiful parts of this author gig, and I'm beyond grateful for you.

To Anne, my sister from a Scottish mister, the encourager of exploring my own of spiritual gifts, and sharer of all manner of hilarity to keep my spirits up. Your friendship has been one of the unexpected gifts the universe has brought me through the world of books, and now I don't know how I ever did it without you!

To Jacquie, for not just beta reading this novel or for all of your support, but for the quiet strength and perseverance you demonstrate in all things. You're an inspiration, and I'm honored to have you as part of my writing process, and to be a part of yours.

To Jean, for the most gorgeous cover photo, for your friendship, and for being an amazing human being. You're a rockstar, and I'm honored to know you and put your beautiful work on my books!

And, always, to you, dear reader. Without you it would all be for naught, and I hope you enjoyed escaping with me as much as I enjoyed writing this for you.

ABOUT THE AUTHOR

Melanie A. Smith is an award-winning, international best-selling author of steamy romance with smart, self-sufficient heroines and strong, swoony book boyfriends with hearts of gold. A former engineer turned stay-at-home mom and author, when Melanie is not lost in the world of books you'll find her spending time with her husband and son, crafting, or cross-stitching.

Connect with Melanie on:

MelanieASmithAuthor.com

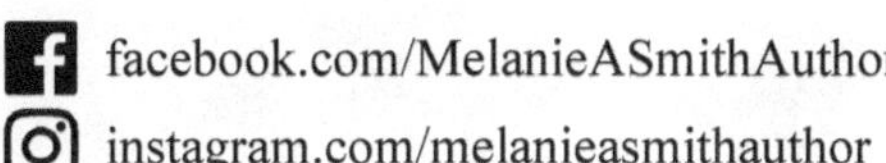

facebook.com/MelanieASmithAuthor

instagram.com/melanieasmithauthor

BOOKS BY MELANIE A. SMITH

The Safeguarded Heart Series

The Safeguarded Heart

All of Me

Never Forget

Her Dirty Secret

Recipes from the Heart: A Companion to the Safeguarded Heart Series

The Safeguarded Heart Complete Series

Life Lessons

Never Date a Doctor

Bad Boys Don't Make Good Boyfriends

You Can't Buy Love

The Heart of Rutherford: The Complete Life Lessons Series

Alpine Ridge

Tough Love

Recklessly in Love

Unscripted Love

Elusive Love

TRUE Love: The Alpine Ridge Complete Series

L.A. Rock Scene

Everybody Lies

Finding His Redemption

Secrets, Lies, and Temptation

L.A. Rock Scene Complete Series

Fate's Gift

Last Kiss Under the Mistletoe

Last Kiss Goodbye

Stand-alones

Vegas Baby

Short Stories

Cruising for Love

Hot for Santa

www.ingramcontent.com/pod-product-compliance
Lightning Source LLC
Chambersburg PA
CBHW020914060726
47591CB00004B/1244